SANTA BARBARA
LIBRARY
a public library system

LIAR, LIAR

WINTER AUSTIN

McIntire County, Book 4

Crimson Romance
New York London Toronto Sydney New Delhi

CRIMSON
ROMANCE
Crimson Romance
An Imprint of Simon & Schuster, Inc.
1230 Avenue of the Americas
New York, NY 10020

First Crimson Romance ebook edition OCTOBER 2017.

Manufactured in the United States of America

ISBN 978-1-5072-0803-8
ISBN 978-1-5072-0692-8 (ebook)

For Julie. No project is complete until your red ink has littered the pages. To make good perfect.

CHAPTER ONE

Sober Saturday night number 836.

Sixteen years dry.

Enough time to move on, to forget what happened that night sixteen years ago. Yet the anniversary would roll around, and he couldn't stop the binge. Sipping on those memories, downing them one after another, drowning in them until he was drunk. Letting her take him to a dark place in his soul he could never purge. By dawn's light, he was left wasted and broken, a shell of a man, lying on the floor. Another piece of his soul lost, buried with her in that cold, dark hole.

Shane Hamilton had lived in this hell for so long, it became a ritual. Every April he prepared for it, taking off the day of and the day after. Even during those bleak six years where he was dodging bullets and bombs, he was swirling in a black abyss. This year, the anniversary fell on a Saturday.

Hands braced on the tile walls, he watched the water snake along his body and pool at his bare feet. No matter what effort he put in to cleansing his body, or mind and soul, the water never baptized him from his sins.

Twinkling under the harsh electric light, the slim, gold circle danced and twirled at the end of the silver chain. She had danced and twirled under the smoky haze of neon lights, laughing and flirting, making promises that never came true.

Shane gripped the diamond ring, ceasing its merry spin, and flattened it to his chest. The emergency room doctor had removed it from her finger and given it to Shane, pity gleaming in the man's eyes. The doctor's fingers were heavy as they pressed the ring into his palm; the memory of the band's slick feel from the blood was branded into his palm. From then on, the ring dangled from a chain around his neck, settling in a place near his heart. A reminder of what he lost in a moment of stupidity.

The jangle of his phone drifted into the bathroom. In the last half hour, he'd heard it go off five times. Lifting his face to the spray of the shower, he commenced with continuing to ignore the persistent caller.

A thrumming ache wove through his muscles and seeped into his bones. Too many years on the rodeo circuit riding some of the rankest broncs and his multiple tours in the Sandbox had left behind a different kind of pain he easily remedied with a few aspirin. Though it was getting difficult to ease the hurt, especially after a night spent on a hardwood floor. Shane turned fifty next month but felt all of seventy.

Finishing his poor man's shower, he shut off the faucet and then stepped out of the stall. Once more the old-fashioned telephone ring of his cell phone reached him. Toweling off, he turned his back to the open door.

Sunday morning rays peeked through the gaping brown, plaid curtains. Before passing away, his mother had decorated her little haven with homey touches only a cowboy like himself would enjoy. She had done it because she missed her husband—who passed two years before she did—and for Shane, who was to inherit the family farm. His mother must have believed in her heart that he'd leave this world as a bachelor, never daring to step into that minefield of love again. In reverence to his saintly mother, Shane hadn't changed a thing.

He wrapped the towel around his waist and then staggered into his bedroom to dress.

Avoiding the bed with its twisted sheets, he pulled on a pair of jeans and skipped his duty shirt. Today was a dark blue plaid shirt kind of day. Finger combing his tightly coiled hair, he stepped into his boots and carefully picked a path down the hall. Each step sent flares of pain up his spine. It might be time to consider taking up Doc Drummond on his offer to make an appointment with an arthritis specialist in Iowa City.

Shane removed the half-full coffee pot from the warmer and slowly poured a cup. Lifting the stout mug to his lips, he inhaled the aroma of dark roast and then sipped the strong brew. During his travels all over the world, Shane had fallen in love with Community coffee in Louisiana. He sniffed, reality punching him in the gut. Louisiana had been his little trick rider's home state; Community had been her favorite coffee. And what she'd loved, he loved, too.

Today was going to be rough. He had to find a way to get past this.

Rummaging through the cabinets, he upended a box of Pop-Tarts and snatched a package. Tearing into the foil with his teeth, he grunted as he bit through both pastries. Almost fifty and still eating like a kid. If she could see him now, she'd probably laugh.

His phone went off like a banshee. Damn it to hell and back! He made a crooked path to the table where the infernal machine continued to squeal. Seven missed calls and eighteen text messages glared at him.

"Shit." He stabbed a blunt finger at the speakerphone icon. "Murdoch, this better be damn important to interrupt me on my sabbatical."

"How damn important is it to you that there's a body in the river, boss?"

• • •

Thumbs hooked in his belt loops, Shane surveyed the scene. Next to him, rising into the spring morning, the bridge rumbled with the sound of passing vehicles. The body drifted facedown in the frigid waters, bobbing and bumping against the tangle of branches and river debris. None of his deputies had disturbed the scene—whip-smart people he had here—until he arrived. Their floater wore dark brown slacks, a white dress shirt, and black socks. His shoes and coat were MIA. Shane couldn't tell the actual color of the man's hair; the water had darkened it.

No suspicious death in his county was good, but this one was giving him a bad case of hives.

"Anything recognizable about him?" he hollered to Deacon Nash.

The normally jovial deputy paused as he picked his way along the shoreline in an attempt to get closer to the body. "Sir, no disrespect, but could you shut the hell up and let me do my thing?"

Shane smothered a smile behind his hand. Most sheriffs wouldn't put up with any lip from their deputies. He had learned long ago—thanks in part to a truly mouthy and tough-as-nails former deputy—that he garnered more respect from his people when he gave them enough rope to hang him with. Though the McIntire County sheriff's department was small, they were a well-oiled machine.

A petite redhead sidled up next to him with her arms crossed at her chest and joined in surveying the mess before them. Deputy Jolie Murdoch was his shiniest and youngest deputy, and also the former sheriff's daughter. She'd proven Shane right last year when he pegged her as his new investigator. What was once an unsure, slightly gun-shy rookie was now a full-fledged cop with enough tart to make your mouth pucker.

"Sabbatical? Really?"

"Hey, if it gets the minions to leave me alone, I'll call it an orgy."

"Not even remotely funny." Murdoch did a poor job of holding back her smile. "Detective O'Hanlon is on his way."

"Slow poke." Shane's best friend's satirical Irish humor was always the pick-me-up he needed in times like these, along with Con's experienced eye as Eider's only investigator. "ETA on DCI?"

"Three hours out. Appears no one wanted to be roused this early on a Sunday morning. Then again, the woman on the line muttered something about 'you've had enough killings down there, you should be damn experts at evidence collection by now.'"

"Be my guest."

She shook her head vehemently. "Way above my pay grade."

Shane checked his watch. "Doc Drummond?"

"Will be here right after he checks on his patients—that was a half hour ago."

Apparently Nash gave up trying to avoid getting wet and waded into the water. "Holy . . . This is cold for a brother!" Carefully picking his way over the rocks, he walked right up to the body. "There's blood on the shirt."

"Maybe he injured himself before falling into the river," Shane muttered. He didn't need nor want another homicide. He just wanted a smooth four years.

"Suicide?" Murdoch asked.

Good God Almighty, he didn't need that, either.

Nash tipped the body, and then with a heave, flipped it. Once it stopped violently rocking, Nash steadied the deceased. His gaze shot up the hill to Shane.

"Sheriff?"

It was a familiar face.

"Oh my God"—Murdoch gasped—"is that…?"

"I'm afraid so. Nash, grab a camera and take pictures. Both of you comb this shoreline and that debris for any evidence. If

DCI wants to take forever to get to the party, then we'll do clean up. Once Doc Drummond gets here, haul our victim out of the water." Shane turned from the body and hiked up the hill.

"Sheriff, what do you think happened?" Murdoch asked.

"It's a damn homicide, Deputy. Someone decided Mr. Gene Avery needed to die." He about-faced and resumed his march up the hill.

"Where are you going?" she called after him.

"To visit the man's widow and give her the bad news." Then lock himself in his office and wish he could drink away this monster of a headache that was about to bring the folks of McIntire County to his front door with their proverbial pitchforks and torches.

CHAPTER TWO

Agent Liza Bartholomew was lost.

Who could blame her, really? The last time she'd been in McIntire County it was winter and snow covered every inch of landscape. She hadn't been focused on driving; since her "partner" at the time was well acquainted with the area, he did all the chauffeuring. With the budding trees, greening grass, and miles of plowed fields, nothing looked familiar. And don't get her started on this damn GPS. Every turn Siri told her to take led to a muddy gravel road and a dead end. Liza was L-O-S-T kind of lost.

Cripes, to get to the sheriff's department—which was where she was headed in the first place—she had no clue which road to take to get there.

"If that asshole gets away from me, again …"

A gas station/convenience store popped into view. Hallelujah! Salvation.

"Thanks, Siri, you've been a real pain in the ass today, but I can get proper directions here." *And a huge cup of jitters to go.* Her mouth salivated at the phantom taste of a peppermint mocha cappuccino. Sweet mercy, that would taste so delicious right now. God, they better have it.

She pulled into the busy lot. It was considerably packed for mid-Sunday morning. She half-expected Eider to be quiet, because all of the residents would be at church. Guess she thought wrong. She parked in the only available spot that happened to block the dumpster—there wouldn't be a dump truck picking up trash today, would there? She cut the engine and relaxed in her seat. The tension in her muscles drained away.

"This is what I get for trying to surprise people."

Gathering her billfold and phone, tucking the unhelpful device in her coat pocket, she vacated the car. As she closed the door, she adjusted her badge and holster to remain concealed under her red leather coat. Iowa had its right to conceal and carry law, but as a law officer, she didn't need to stir up the masses on this bright Sunday morning. Liza learned all too well how fast news of strangers spread through this town—hell, the county. And right now, she didn't need her prey taking off for parts unknown. After a scan of the parking lot, she sauntered to the store.

Liza stilled when she went to pull open the door. Ironic. This was the same convenience store that had brought her here to Eider the first time. Was that more than a year ago? Swinging the glass and metal barrier wide, she strode inside.

Her gaze swept the store's interior to get the layout and plan for emergency exits and possible threats—a habit born out of necessity while growing up and as training with the FBI. To her right were the bathrooms with the other exit point, to her left the rows of display shelves bursting with candy bars, gum, and chips, all the goodies one could want to fuel up for a long road trip. Beyond those evenly spaced shelves was the Employees Only door, which should provide access to the coolers and another exit point. Everything was clear. Yawning, Liza meandered over to the coffee bar.

Yes! They had peppermint mocha.

From her coat pocket the Eagles's "Desperado" sang out from her cell. While pawing out the iPhone, she snagged the largest to-go cup, placed it under the cappuccino dispenser, and punched the peppermint mocha button. Heaven. She tapped the screen with her thumb and pressed Steve Jobs's second greatest invention to her ear.

"This is Liza."

"Where are you?"

She grimaced and hit the cappuccino button again. There wasn't near enough liquid energy in that cup to help deal with the fallout from this conversation. "I'm on the job, Kurt. I can't tell you where I am."

"But you can just up and leave? Without warning? Quinn wanted to see you."

Closing her eyes, Liza took a calming breath and let it out slowly. Dealing with her foster brother was like standing before a falling-down drunk Russian death squad—you never knew which way the bullets were going to fly.

"Look, Kurt, I'm sorry I couldn't be there to see Q. When I get back, I'll give you a call and he can come over."

"And when is that going to happen?"

Liza grated her molars. That man had an infuriating way of "asking." "I don't know. I can't give you a timetable on this. Like I said, I'll call when I get back."

"Liza, that's not good enough. I'm leaving for a new job site in two weeks. You're going to have to stay with Quinn."

Damn it! She slid her cup off the machine and plopped it on the counter. "While I don't mind watching Quinn now and again, I can't be doing this every time you head out for a job. My job isn't stay-at-home mom, Kurt. I work for the freaking federal government, and when they say jump, I jump."

"So, you're telling me it's my fault Steph is dead and I can't handle my own kid?"

Where the hell does he come up with this shit? Strangling the exasperation sinking its ugly claws into her muscles, Liza crossed herself and hailed Mary to give her strength not to throttle her foster brother through the phone. "No, that is *not* what I'm saying. What I'm saying is, I'll call you when I'm on my way back to Cedar Rapids. This shouldn't take too long."

"I still don't get why you're even an FBI agent. Didn't the government do a number on you enough to make you stay away?"

"Says the man who served his country in the military."

Kurt chuckled, easing the taut rope of tension between them. "Hey, everyone was being patriotic after 9/11. If I hadn't, I wouldn't have met Steph."

The second mention of Kurt's deceased wife was a fist of grief punching Liza in the chest. Twenty-one months and counting, and yet neither of them could move on. "I need to get going. Tell Q I love him and sorry I missed him."

"Don't forget to call."

"I promise." She ended the call and slid the phone back in her pocket. This got more complicated with each day, week, hell, even the months that slipped by and Kurt did nothing to change his ways. She couldn't be there to rescue him every time an emergency with Quinn came up. Her supervisor was beginning to pay too much attention to her and the screw-ups, and that woman was not someone to cross.

Behind her, the door dinged the arrival of a new customer. "Hey, Harley, didja hear? Sheriff found the superintendent's body in the river."

Liza froze, pausing as she was sealing the lid on her cup, and then looked over her shoulder. A round man in coveralls and a greasy Case International tractor cap waddled over to the tiny seating area where another man—presumably Harley—sat reading a newspaper and munching on a doughnut.

"Say what?" the cashier asked.

"Yeah," Rotund Man said, "found him floating in the river. Bob was driving by and saw them pulling out the body. Sheriff was giving someone hell on his phone at the top of the hill."

"How'd Avery end up in the river?"

That name burned a path through Liza's brain. *Oh God, please don't let it be him.* She grabbed her beverage and strode over to the register, setting the cup on the counter. Her gaze met the young man's.

"Is that all for you?" he asked.

"I can't believe it. Wonder how bad the sheriff is going to screw this up?" Rotund Man belched.

The muscles along Liza's back tensed, knitting together like chain mail to deflect the verbal barrage. The words weren't about her, but damn it, she was law enforcement and never liked to hear anything bad about a fellow cop. It was especially aggravating when it concerned someone in authority like Sheriff Shane Hamilton.

"Can you point me in the direction of the sheriff's office?"

The hum of the coolers was deafening. The clerk's face flushed red, as his eyes darted from Liza to the two loudmouths behind her.

"Uh, if you … um, take a right out of the lot and head east…"—he gulped—"you'll be in the right direction. The, uh, sheriff's office is outside of town."

Liza pasted on her "be nice to the public" smile. "Thanks."

As fast as the cash register could, the young man rang up her cappuccino. "Three twenty-three."

She passed him a five, shifting to put the two men in her line of sight. As she lifted the coffee to her lips, the edge of her coat rose, exposing the badge and gun. They averted their rapidly blinking eyes, and red fused the men's features.

The cashier handed over her change. Shoving it in her pocket, she gave the young man a curt nod and strolled to the door. "Have a good day, gentlemen."

There were some muttered responses she couldn't make out.

Pushing through, she headed for her car. Tucked inside once more, Liza sat there. She'd jumped the gun when the big one slighted Hamilton, and now she had no idea for certain if her quarry was the same man they claimed was now dead.

Ah hell, I don't need this.

The only way she was going to learn if he was truly the man she'd been after was to pay a visit to Hamilton and crew. That meeting might not go over so well with the small sheriff's department.

• • •

The one thing Shane despised about being the sheriff was telling someone that a loved one had been killed. Roslin Avery damn near tore his heart out—if he'd had a heart left—with her imitation of a banshee. Good God. If he were still a drinking man, that little experience would have called for a double finger of Jack followed by a six-pack of Bud. But that was no longer an option.

Five thousand, eight hundred and forty-four days sober.

Not another drop after Cheyenne.

Shane pulled in behind the sheriff's department; in the past year it had become the sanest place for him to park. Hiding out in the back seemed like the coward's way out of dealing with the public, but what the people of McIntire County refused to understand was, he needed some privacy. In a place where everyone knew everyone's business, he would get a lot of impromptu visitors wanting to "report" suspicious goings-on with other people in town. The end result was he or his deputies following up on these reports and wasting time better suited for other purposes.

Vacating his truck, he headed for the back door. The old brick building was holding up nicely as offices and jail. Fifty-some odd years ago, not long before Shane was born, the county had gutted a former general store and turned it into the sheriff's home-away-from-home. The previous sheriff hadn't bothered with updating the interior, except to add the late twentieth-century technology. After Shane took over, he'd pushed the McIntire County council for newer computers and equipment, which was the equivalent to gelding a bull while riding it. When money was tight, people turned into Scrooge McDuck. But after one of his deputies managed to find signs of some council members playing funny math with the county budget, the whole group suddenly discovered a wad of cash stashed away, even after some of their fellow members lost seats on the county council. That had been a surprise election year.

Shane paused inside the entrance to breathe in the aromatic scent of aged wood, Lysol, and freshly brewed coffee. Snickers and grunts from the front of the building tickled his interest. He crept down the hall like he was approaching a spooked horse, past the holding cells, the interview rooms, and the small "conference" room. The rattle of paper joined the barely restrained glee. Breaching the hallway's end and stepping into the open bullpen area, he stiffened to a halt.

His youngest deputy and her cohort, Shane's resident whiz kid, were throwing wads of yellow legal pad paper at each other.

"Murdoch. Jennings."

Startled to their feet, both whipped around, masks of sheer terror on both of their faces. Shane bit back a grin. Damn, he loved scaring the crap out of his underlings.

"What are you doing?"

Adam Jennings recovered first, the man having dealt with Shane's mercurial moods longer. "Waiting on you, boss."

"Brownnoser," Murdoch snapped. Her gaze swept to Shane. "You've got a visitor, sir." The twinkle in her eyes was probably the reason her fiancé had lost his mind and asked her to marry him.

Shane was immune to his female deputies' wiles. Heading straight for the coffeepot, he removed his Resistol. "Who?"

"It's a surprise."

He peered over his shoulder. "Come again, Deputy Murdoch?"

The twinkling turned into spotlights. Crossing her arms, she tilted up that stubborn chin. Damn it to hell, she was too much like her stiff-necked father. "Like I said, it's a surprise."

Foregoing the tantalizing coffee, Shane strode to his partially opened door and pushed on it. The first thing to come into view was a pair of black knee-high boots, then a lean pair of crossed legs clad in dark blue jeans, a dark-red leather jacket leading up to the sleek, raven-haired woman with a cockeyed mouth and flashing umber eyes sitting on his battered leather couch. She pressed a rounded pen tip to her smooth, brown cheek.

"Hello, Sheriff Hamilton."

"Agent Bartholomew"—he slid an annoyed glare back at Murdoch—"how nice of you to pay us a visit." Sighing, he entered his office. "Murdoch, bring me a cup of coffee."

"Say please."

A snicker from the couch made his shoulders stiffen.

"Please bring me a cup of coffee, *Deputy*."

"Right away, boss."

With a shake of his head, he let the door swing closed as he moved to his desk. "Forgive me for being abrupt, Agent, but why are you here? And in my office?" He sank into his chair, relishing the cushioning on his screaming muscles.

"I have good reasons, but unfortunately, I can't divulge a whole lot. No one is really supposed to know I'm here." She leaned forward, her head canting to the side. "Will your deputies keep it on the hush, hush for now?"

"They can and will. If that's what you want."

Murdoch's knock gave pause to their discussion.

"Bring it in."

The young woman hiked into the office like she owned the whole damn building, carrying his mug and a thick square of something that smelled suspiciously like Mrs. Ginny Murdoch's famous, county fair blue ribbon, lemon-blueberry coffee cake. "Here ya go, bossman, eat this. You're cranky."

Baring his canines, he took the mug from her. "I'm only eating it because your momma made it, not because you told me to. Or because I'm cranky."

"Uh-huh. Jennings and I will just go make our rounds. And when you're finished with Agent Bartholomew, you need to call Detective O'Hanlon," Murdoch threw back at him as she vacated the office, closing the door with a clap.

The agent cleared her throat in a poor attempt to hide her chuckle. "I don't remember her being so fresh with you the last time I was here."

"That is the result of her actually growing into her big-girl pants and falling in love with an ex-marine."

Bartholomew's eyebrows dipped down. "An ex-marine?"

"Do you mean to tell me your former partner hasn't been keeping you up on the gossip?"

She shook her head. "Other than hearing about the birth of Boyce and Cassy's baby girl, he hasn't told me much. Honestly, I haven't had a whole lot of time to keep up. So, what's the four-one-one on the Cliffs Notes version?"

"I don't think there is a Cliffs Notes version with that family. As short as I can, Jolie is engaged to Xavier Hartmann—"

"The Australian bartender from O'Hanlon's Killdeer Pub?"

"Yes. He was a marine, got out when he lost his leg. And here's a kicker for ya—he's actually Nic and Cassy's half brother."

"What?"

"Long story. Have Cassy tell you sometime."

Bartholomew eased back into the lumpy cushion. "Sounds like I need to. Sweet mercy."

Shane took a bite of Ginny's coffee cake, the fluffy, tart, and sweet concoction melting on his tongue. It took a bushel-full of restraint not to moan in pleasure. Ginny's baking skills could make a man wish for things best not imagined.

"What is the top-secret reason for you to be here in McIntire County?" He ate more of the quick bread, and washed down the crumbs with a bracing sip of coffee.

"I need to see the man you fished out of the river."

Had he known she was going to drop that bomb in his lap, he wouldn't have filled his mouth. There was no chance in hell he was going to ever let another FBI agent screw up a murder investigation in his county.

CHAPTER THREE

Liza jolted as Sheriff Hamilton choked on a mouthful of cake and coffee, cringing a bit when a little of the food sprayed from his mouth. Maybe blurting that out when he was eating hadn't been a tactful move.

Once he'd calmed himself by taking great gulps of coffee, he cleared his throat, coughed a few times, and then readjusted his tall, muscular frame in his chair. "Excuse me?"

"First, sorry I dropped that on you. And second, I know about the body. I happened to be taking a pit stop when a few of your more colorful residents were gabbing about it."

"So it's all over town by now."

"If memory serves me right, that was going to happen around here anyway." Time to offer an olive branch; he'd been more than cordial with her, all things considering. Top among them, Sheriff Hamilton was not fond of the FBI in any form or capacity. "I came down here, because a suspect I've been after for a long time was spotted in Eider." From her leather-bound portfolio, she slipped out the last known photo she had of her quarry and passed it to Hamilton. "He's been a slippery SOB, and I'm really hoping he's not the same person you found."

Hamilton studied the photo, his features betraying nothing of what had to be swirling around in that man's head. With his attention on the picture, Liza used the distraction to study him. There was silver dusting his brown-blond hair. Did he always have curls? Of course, when she was around him, she couldn't think of a time when he had removed his hat in her presence, so how would she know? But the dark shadows under his hazel eyes were still there. As was the stern jawline. If she had to take a wild guess at his age, she would put him close to fifty, but the fullness she expected to see in a man of his position and age wasn't showing in his features. Shane Hamilton was lean as a whipcord.

He handed the photo back to her. "Hard to say if that's the same man."

She tucked the photo into her portfolio. "That means I'll have to see him in the morgue."

"Now, I don't see how that's going to be possible."

Liza held up a finger, squashing any further rebuttals. "I'm not here to railroad you or your deputies in a murder investigation. It's not my forte, and given my choice, I'd rather just forgo the whole viewing, but I have to know if this is the guy I'm after. If it's not, I might need to pick that brilliant brain of yours. If he is my guy, I have to go back to my supervisor and explain to her that our suspect has gotten himself killed."

"Which leads to you staying around and attracting the very attention you don't want to draw to yourself, because if your supervisor is anything like Boyce Hunt, she'll dog my ass wanting answers."

Liza didn't bother hiding her smile. Hamilton summed up SAC Ally Montrose in one fell swoop. "That I can't change. I can simply lessen the pain. However, my presence here is only secretive if this guy is still alive."

"And why is that?" Hamilton shifted in his chair as if in discomfort.

She bit her tongue before blurting out some absurdity about him needing to change seats. Shane Hamilton was a man's man, cowboy to the core. And, God forbid, admitting to anything that showed weakness was tantamount to declaring himself impotent.

"You can not utter one word I tell you. If this guy hears that I'm here, he'll vanish. It's happened twice before, and it's driving me batshit crazy. I'm here on a Sunday only because our information was solid, and my super was adamant that we do this on the down low." Liza lowered her voice. "We both suspect this guy has ears in the FBI, and when he gets wind of a move against him, he's gone, like smoke in the wind. And here's the kicker. He never leaves Iowa."

The sheriff's face wrinkled. "What? Why would he not take off for parts unknown?"

"If I finally nab this guy, I'll ask him. He does a really damn good disappearing act. Whole new identity, life, job, everything."

"What are you after him for?"

"Embezzlement, fraud, identity theft, there's a good chance he dabbled in money laundering in real estate, and election fraud. If you can think it, he did it. And this man is brilliant. He can be anything or anyone he wants. He's The Talented Mr. Ripley in the flesh. It's why I've had a hard time catching him."

"And you think he's my dead guy in the morgue?"

"Avery was what the loudmouths said in the store. According to my source, that was the name he was going by down here."

Hamilton's mouth quirked to the side, and he rocked back his chair. As he sat there, his gaze lingering on her, a silence like a warm, soothing blanket draped the office.

"Now, be honest with me, Agent Bartholomew. Did you happen to engage those 'loudmouths,' as you called them, in the store?"

Her face flamed hot. Shit!

Hamilton rocked forward and rested his elbow on the corner of his desk. "If that blush in your cheeks is any indication, I think I just exposed a flaw to your plan. If you came here with the intention of keeping your arrival quiet, you sure blew that out of the water by walking in to that store."

Ire rankling her, she doused that fire. "Despite that, those men don't know my name, who I'm working for, and have nothing to track back to me."

"Don't underestimate the people of this county, Agent. They are more observant than what's good for them. All it takes is one good description of you and any reaction you might have had, and the whole of the county will know there's a stranger in their midst carrying a badge. If your guy is the one laid up in our morgue, then we don't have anything to worry about. If he's not . . ."

Damn him for calling her out like this. Here she couldn't understand how Boyce could be such an ass to the man, and Hamilton went and flew his colors bright and loud, making it perfectly clear why her ex-partner took issue with the sheriff. Pushing to her feet—which stirred the sheriff from his chair, as well—Liza rammed her portfolio under her arm.

"Well, guess I'll just take my leave and pay a visit to the coroner. I tried to do this peaceably, but that doesn't appear to be possible. Afternoon, Sheriff." She about-faced and took one step forward.

Great. She didn't even know how to get the sheriff's department without asking directions. How was she going to find the morgue alone? Where was the morgue, anyway? In small towns like Eider, didn't they use funeral homes? Damn it, this was going to take a ton of phone calls.

"Agent Bartholomew, wait."

She spun back. "What?"

"I wasn't trying to question your process."

"No, you felt the need to embarrass me. And frankly, I can't for the life of me fathom why I bothered to expose myself like that in defense of you, a fellow LEO. But then, perhaps you prefer to be run through the mud by every voting citizen in this county."

Hamilton's handsome features scrunched. "You defended me?"

"In a way. You're surprised?"

"Yeah, I am, and from an FBI agent t' boot."

"We're not all horrible people out to make the average law enforcement officer look like uneducated hacks."

"I'm grateful for that. Truly." He skirted around his desk. And was that a limp in his step? "Why don't we head over to the hospital and have a chat with Doc Drummond, see what he's learned so far, and you can view the body."

The morgue was in the hospital. Of course. Dr. Jasper Drummond was the county coroner, too. Liza hated getting lost, but that was her lot in life. Wait, was he offering to go with her? "Don't you have a phone call to make?"

"I'll call him later." Hamilton's limp seemed to disappear as he strode for the door. "Why don't you ride with me?"

Liza lost all motor skills. "What? Why?"

"It'll be faster that way. And I bet my good hat that you'll be coming back here anyway."

True and true. But ride with him? Couldn't they just take her car? Yet, was she willing to show him how little she knew of his town and county that she couldn't even navigate her way from point A to point B without getting lost? Woo hoo, look at her. The great FBI agent who couldn't find her way out of a cereal box.

She held out a hand. "Lead the way."

So much for not giving Ripley a heads up that she was here. Damn it! Riding around with the sheriff was going to put a huge red arrow sign over her head. If word of a new girl in town hadn't spread already, it was going to burn the place to the ground now. And Ripley would be long gone, again.

CHAPTER FOUR

The drive to the hospital wasn't bad, but it wasn't exactly pleasant, either. Shane took peeks at Agent Bartholomew, who stared out the window, seeming to study the landscape intently. She didn't engage him in conversation or even pay much attention to him at all. By her stiff body posture, he gathered she wasn't in a chatting mood.

He didn't mean to embarrass her. It wasn't like he made a point to chew up FBI agents and spit 'em out. Hell, he'd never had an objection to the agency until Boyce Hunt blew into his town four years ago and made a right big ass of himself. It was Boyce Hunt that Shane had taken issue with, until the day that southern asshole turned his life around and married Cassy Rivers.

Damn it to hell. All Shane had done was point out a huge flaw in Bartholomew's plan. Apparently this woman was a different bolt of fabric type of woman than what he was used to dealing with.

He parked his truck two rows away from the entrance, and before he could utter a word of apology, again, Agent Bartholomew bailed out of the cab like a horde of yellow jackets were on her tail. Speaking of which, that tail was angled just right for him to get an eyeful. Jerking his gaze back to the front, he shook his head. *I'm such a dumbass.*

Easing out of the truck, he winced. Why, oh why, did he sleep on the floor last night? He reached back inside and from the center console, grabbed a bottle of aspirin. Good for his aches and his heart. Dry swallowing the recommended amount plus one, he tossed the bottle onto the seat and then played catch up with the agent.

She still beat him to the doors. “Are you doing okay?”

“It’s called getting old, Agent Bartholomew.”

“Just call me Liza. Agent Bartholomew is a mouthful. And if I want to at least try to keep up my ‘secretive’ status, you can’t call me agent.”

Giving a nod, he gestured for her to enter first. The hospital doors glided open like something out of a *Star Wars* movie. All that was missing on the other side were the droids and marching Storm Troopers. Instead, Gladys Higgins, the friendly “retired” greeter, peered over the top of her reading glasses perched on the tip of her nose.

Shane’s belly quivered at that all-knowing look she gave him, and he removed his Resistol. Mrs. Higgins had been his sixth-grade English teacher, and to this day he couldn’t shake that feeling of her zeroing in on him after she caught him doing God knows what to disrupt her class.

“Good afternoon, Sheriff.” That piercing gaze redirected to the woman at Shane’s side.

“Miz Higgins.” He sidled up to the horseshoe counter and pasted on his “I’ve never done a wrong one day of my life” smile. “How’s Mr. Higgins?”

Her attention returned to him. “Golfing as usual. His addiction to it is why I’m here and not tending to my grandbabies.” Her eyes sparkled, making her statement a bald-face lie.

They both knew she hadn’t taken to retirement. When she wasn’t substituting at the school, she was here at the hospital or helping at the community center with the after-school programs. Gladys Higgins lived to serve people of all ages.

“Well, I’m sure he misses you while he’s out there teeing up.”

Her derisive snort sent a chuckle rumbling in Shane’s chest.

"Who's your lady friend?"

Liza thrust her hand over the counter. "Liza Bartholomew. I work for the state."

Well, not an all-out lie but close enough. Good way to deflect interest off of her.

Mrs. Higgins took the proffered hand with a quirked eyebrow. Shoot, the hospital's gatekeeper was impressed. "I guess you'll be needing one of our special badges?"

"That I would." Liza beamed.

"Now you tell me straight, Sheriff, am I hearing correct, that your department found Gene Avery dead in the water this morning?"

"Miz Higgins, you know I can't tell you anything about an open investigation."

That narrowed gaze was enough to pierce daggers through his soul. "Shane Hamilton, I've known you all your life, and your momma was a close friend of mine. You know good and well that keeping secrets in this town is a losing battle."

"And my job as sheriff is to curtail that kind of talk and pay respect to the next of kin. Now, I'll have none of that gossiping coming from one of my favorite teachers."

Pursing her lips, she eyeballed him, probably hoping he'd crack under the intense pressure of her scrutiny, but he held strong. Gladys Higgins might be a tough old bird, but she couldn't hold a candle to some of the broncs he rode hell-bent to leather to stick it for eight nor any of those piss and vinegar officers who were turning him into a fighting machine.

"Dr. Drummond said to send you on down when you arrived." She handed him a special badge that he and his deputies were to wear when they visited the hospital in an official capacity, something that had become an all-too-often occurrence, which gave demand to have the dang things made. She then gave another badge to Liza.

Shane pinned the laminated card with a generic gold shield to the collar of his jacket. "Give everyone my best regards."

"Keep up your good work. Everyone in the Higgins family will keep on voting for you. We will not stand to lose one of my best behaved students as sheriff."

He rapped his knuckles against the countertop. "Now I know you're lying to me, Miz Higgins. I was your worst behaved student." Holding up his hat in salute, he rounded the counter and headed for the elevator.

"Nice meeting you, Ms. Bartholomew."

"A joy to meet you, too, Mrs. Higgins."

Shane eased his pace for Liza to catch up. The woman moved with the grace of an athlete. Was she a runner?

She chuckled, a low, husky sound at odds with her feminine qualities. "You're surrounded on all sides by dictatorial women, aren't you?"

"I wouldn't say they're dictatorial, just … well, protective."

"And you're not bothered by that? A man?"

At the elevator bay, he stopped and faced Liza. There wasn't a twitch of mocking in her features, so she was being serious. "No, I'm not. All of my life I've grown up with women who had to survive insurmountable odds, who raised their daughters to be the same. And in my adult life, I've encountered numerous women who were thrown some pretty shitty cards their way, but they moved past it. I guess that makes me a damn smart man to realize the significance you ladies bring to any situation."

A flush deepened the tawny tone of her skin to a red-brown. Liza blinked, turning her head as the elevator dinged its arrival. "Guess that does."

The doors slid open. Shane and Liza took a few steps back as a new father bearing the load of flower vases with balloons shouting "It's a Girl!" and a soft, brown teddy bear exited. He was followed by a nurse pushing a wheelchair with the new mom and her baby.

Shane nodded, gave his most award-winning smile, then watched the little entourage roll down the hall.

One life taken, another born. The never-ending circle. How many babies were brought into this world the night Cheyenne's ended? That familiar ripping in his chest made Shane gasp for breath. Another piece of him torn away at the memory of her death. His gaze swung away from the newly formed family and landed on the woman next to him. Her attention was riveted on the family.

"I never thought to ask, is there a Mr. Bartholomew?"

Her head snapped in his direction. "Why would you have need to ask?"

He shrugged, stepping onto the elevator. "It's a thought that crossed my mind, and Boyce hasn't mentioned it."

Liza joined him, leaning on the wall opposite from him. "I still don't see how my marital status is of any importance to you. You don't even know me outside of being an agent."

"No, I don't. But if these surprise visits resume, it might be a topic to discuss." Pressing the button for the basement, Shane copied her stance. "Beam me down, Scotty."

Her features crinkled. "Isn't it 'beam me up, Scotty?'"

"Ahh, but we're going down."

With a shake of her head, she bowed it, but not before he glimpsed the smile. Gradually, she lifted her head to look at him again. "No, there is no Mr. Bartholomew." She held up her left hand, wiggling her fingers. "The ring finger has always stayed empty."

What a shame. He wasn't too caught up in his grief not to realize that Liza Bartholomew was a good lookin' woman with many fine traits. Her single status did beg the question, what kind of baggage was she burdened with? Or was her career a total time suck that didn't leave her with any chance to consider someone else in her life?

Dr. Jasper Drummond was waiting for them when the elevator spit them out. "Mrs. Higgins paged me when you showed up."

"She afraid I might get lost?"

Drummond's mouth cocked sideways. The good doc was a few years younger than Shane, but you couldn't tell it by the gray spreading through the man's hair. And like Shane, Drummond was as single as a good-lookin' guy could be. There had been speculation that Drummond wasn't into women, since the unmarried nurses who'd tripped all over themselves to get his attention had failed. Shane was of the mind that Drummond had his right to privacy just like everyone else. God knew Shane didn't want people—he was fairly certain they did already—gossiping on his reasons for being alone.

"She's doing as I asked. I needed to know that you were here." Drummond tilted his head as he took in Liza. "Agent Bartholomew, this is a bit of a surprise."

"I'm more surprised that you remember me. I was barely around you last time."

Drummond tapped his head. "I never forget a pretty face." He winked, then beckoned with a curt wave of his hand. "Our latest case has revealed more than I expected."

Shane gaped at the doc's back. Had the man just flirted with Liza? There was that husky chuckle again as she followed Drummond. Shaking out of his fog of shock, Shane caught up with them.

They walked the length of hallway to a room that Drummond had set up as an autopsy. Not so long ago, there had been no reason to have a morgue, as most of the unusual deaths—meaning anyone who hadn't passed away in a hospital or nursing home that wasn't health-related or due to advanced age—were handled in one of the funeral homes. Then Drummond was voted in as county coroner, and the unusual deaths moved into unexplained suicides and homicides. After some good ole politicking and fund-raising, Drummond managed to find some wiggle room in the hospital budget to get a morgue. The hospital renovated two storage areas in the basement and filled it with the equipment Drummond would need to examine bodies.

The room had gotten more use than the hospital board and the voters of McIntire County were expecting. When talking about the situations that called for autopsy, no matter how Drummond spun it, the people were buying it. The good doc was spending another stint as coroner.

Shane, on the other hand, was feeling like Frankenstein's monster, avoiding the villagers with their torches and pitchforks.

"What's the verdict on cause of death?" he asked.

"Well, I'm fairly certain it was the blunt force trauma to the back of the skull that killed him. By the size of the hole—and this is only a guess—it was either by a hammer or a crowbar."

"Hammer or crowbar? Weapons of convenience?"

"Not the first time someone got angry enough and took it out on a victim with whatever was handy. You know, I read that there was a woman who died of blood loss after she got into a fight with her sister. The sister stabbed the woman in the chest with a ballpoint pen, and neither one thought the injury was bad enough to go to the hospital. Autopsy revealed that the pen managed to nick the aorta, and she bled out in her sleep, never knowing she was dying."

Shane glanced at Liza, noting the green hue to her face. Oh, this had to be bad for someone who wasn't normally on the backside of viewing homicide victims. He cleared his throat and eyed Drummond. "Do you have to tell me weird autopsy stories every time I come down here with you?"

"You're a cop, Shane, these things should fascinate you."

"Yeah, well, I'm not that fascinated."

"Agent Bartholomew probably is."

She waggled a hand before pressing it to her mouth. Yeah, not fascinated.

Drummond shrugged and entered the room where Gene Avery's body, draped with a white sheet, was laid out on the special table. Avery's clothing had been packaged and sealed and placed in a box sitting on the counter. Shane and Drummond surrounded the table, but Liza hung back near the door, hand pressed over her nose and mouth.

"Anything to note on the clothing?" Shane asked, averting his gaze. Hopefully, he wouldn't make her feel more conspicuous.

"Other than the blood, nothing that I noticed. DCI will probably have better luck than I did." Drummond snapped on a pair of surgical gloves, then adjusted the bright lamp to point directly at the victim's left side. "You need to be on this side to see it."

Drummond rolled Avery onto his side. The man's pale skin was mottled by dark purple bruising.

"Lividity?"

"Mostly. Get the magnifying glass on the counter."

Shane grabbed the large round glass and held it over the first patch of bruises. The magnification revealed what he couldn't see at first: circular marks smaller than the size of a dime, less than an inch apart. He moved to another patch of bruising and found the same thing.

"Electric prod?"

"My second educated guess is whoever did this tortured him, or prodded him to the river. But I found no burn marks on his shirt."

Shane straightened. "His killer had it removed, then put it on afterward?"

"Possibly." Drummond laid the victim back on the table. "Here's a real kicker for you. Men like Gene Avery typically wear some type of undershirt beneath their dress shirts. Avery's is missing."

"The killer might have kept it," Liza piped up from her corner.

Shane looked her way. Damn, he'd completely forgotten she was here.

"Maybe the burn marks were on that undershirt, and the killer didn't want to give himself away," she added.

"Interesting," the doc said, jotting something down on a notebook he kept near the table. "I'll have to take a closer look at that."

"What about stomach contents?" Shane asked.

Drummond picked up a small tray with three plastic jars, sealed with red tape. "He had a heavy meal, partially digested, so I'd say death was sometime around three or four hours after eating."

Shane pinched his nostrils. The smell was finally getting to him. "Once they figure out what he ate, I might be able to pinpoint where he was. Mrs. Avery claims he was gone for the evening but didn't know where or with whom."

"Mrs. Avery? There's a wife?" Liza blurted.

"Does the FBI have some interest in our victim?" Drummond asked.

Sighing, Shane looked at Liza. "I don't know, does the FBI have some interest?"

Her hand creeping back up over her mouth and nose, Liza inched closer to the table. "Yes, I have some interest," she said from behind her shield, "but I can't go into details."

"Top-secret mission," Shane muttered. That little comment earned him an ugly scowl from Liza.

"You never told me he had a wife."

"You never asked."

Liza huffed. "My intel said this man isn't married, never was."

"Well," Shane dragged out, "apparently he decided he needed one for this new identity."

"That doesn't make sense. He works alone. Why would he risk bringing another person in who could expose him?"

"I have no idea. We can't exactly ask him, now can we? And how do you know this man is the guy you're after?"

Drummond cleared his throat. "Do I need to step outside the room?"

"No," they both barked.

Liza held up a finger and shook it under Shane's nose. "I don't know if he is. You're not giving me a chance to find out."

"You're the one hiding in a corner as far from the body as you can get." Shane stepped aside and gestured with flourish at the prone man. "Have a real good look, Agent Bartholomew. Is this the guy you're after?"

She blanched as she got a full-on view of the autopsied corpse. Her throat bobbed erratically, probably doing her damnedest to keep the bile down. "He looks nothing like him," she whispered.

"Then it looks like you might be in a jam here."

"Maybe not," Drummond said. He grabbed another magnifying glass and held it out to Liza. "Agent Bartholomew, I want you to take a real hard look at this man's hairline and behind his ear."

What the hell was the doc getting at?

Liza took the offered glass and then lowered herself until she was eye level with the side of Avery's head. Shane's pulse beat like a bass drum in his ears. He ticked away the seconds until she rose, her features stretched taut.

"Damn it," she muttered.

"What?" Shane's demand echoed in the small room.

"He had plastic surgery." She set the magnifying glass on the tray beside her. "And if those scars are telling, he's done it more than once."

Another mystery had come banging on Shane's back door. This was supposed to be a boring, peaceful county. He'd left violent deaths and destruction behind when he left the army. This was not what he wanted to come home to, and definitely not the reason he became a cop and then the sheriff. No wonder people were upset with him. Not that he had a choice in the matter. But when would the misery end?

CHAPTER FIVE

Liza took a bracing breath the instant she passed through the hospital's doors, and gagged.

"How do you stand it?"

Hamilton sauntered past her, heading for his truck. "I don't, but I've had to adapt with the amount of bodies that have gone through there."

"This is why I work in the fraud department." She hightailed it after him. No way was she getting left here.

Clambering into the passenger seat, she strapped in, then tried to meld her body inside the leather-covered seat. *Be one with the leather.*

"Ya know," Hamilton started the engine, "I'm feeling like a bacon cheeseburger and fries. How 'bout you?"

Liza heaved. Slapping a hand over her mouth, she turned the meanest glare she could muster at him. She lowered her hand, pressing it to her queasy stomach. "That's beyond cruel."

"I always get hungry after an autopsy. Sorry." He backed out of the parking spot and left the lot. "If I go slow, it might give your stomach time to settle down."

"I doubt it."

"And I doubt you'd pass up some of Farran O'Hanlon's fine cooking. You do remember her cooking, right?"

Oh, she remembered all right. Liza hadn't been able to find a single restaurant in Cedar Rapids or Iowa City that matched Farran's finest rib-eye steak. Her burgers were deemed the best burgers in the state of Iowa two years running. That was saying something. All this thought about steak and burgers was making Liza's mouth water. Guess she wasn't as grossed out after that autopsy after all.

"If you drive slow, I might think about something to eat."

That grin turned up the kilowatts. Wow, she couldn't think of a time in her life when a man who grinned like that could look so devastatingly handsome. Then again, her exposure to handsome men was severely limited. Not many of them parading through the foster care system or in the world of fraud. She pinched the bridge of her nose, got a whiff of decaying flesh and chemicals, and then slapped her hand in her lap.

"Here." Hamilton reached into the center console, pulled out a green, round tin, and held it out to her. "Put this on your hands. It'll pull the smell out."

She took the tin, eyeing the label. "Watkins medicated ointment?"

"Works wonders on the ole sinuses, too."

She pried the lid open and swirled her finger in the half-used ointment, gathering enough to rub into her hands. She returned the tin to the console and commenced with rubbing the eucalyptus-scented salve into her skin. The overpowering eucalyptus made her nose feel like a winter wind had passed through it. This medicated balm was doing wonders in removing the nasty odor of death. Pretty freaking amazing.

"Plastic surgery would explain why you had a hard time pinning this guy down when he runs."

Except for the fact he could be a real bore, Liza was actually enjoying this ride-along with Hamilton. Who knew? "I almost had him the last time." So close she could still see the flames licking the sky as the warehouse burned. Liza had been a few minutes too late. Ripley made damn sure no one could finger him. "He probably decided to change the game in his favor. The hard part is being able to prove to my supervisor he's the same guy."

"Don't you FBI types have someone working for you who does facial reconstruction or something like that?"

"Only if I want to wait forever and a day for one to come here to Podunkville, Iowa. I don't think my guy would reach the top of the priority list, not with all those unidentified remains backing up the system."

Hamilton grunted. "That bad, huh?"

Liza waved away this thread of conversation. "I want to talk with the wife." Good God, how did Mr. Ripley have time for a marriage? "You know, if you had mentioned her earlier, I might have moved along and never bothered with this."

"And you would have missed out on the tidbit about the plastic surgery. I'm still serious about him doing a change-up on the MO to throw you off his trail. When was the last time you had a bead on him?"

"Over two years ago, twenty-nine months if you want to get all technical."

No answer. Liza peered at Hamilton, who seemed absorbed in his thoughts. She distracted herself by trying to memorize landmarks as he passed through the town. Compared to Cedar Rapids, Eider didn't even scratch the surface in population size. And yet she couldn't find her way out of a coffee can around here. Put her in the heart of Cedar Rapids blindfolded, and she'd be home in five minutes. This was ridiculous.

"Twenty-nine months, you say?"

Flinching, she averted her attention. "Yes."

"Gene Avery was hired by the school late in July. He was coming on being the superintendent for two years this summer."

Liza dug out a notepad. "Late July, you say. From the time he disappeared on me until the school hired him, he had plenty of time to reconstruct his life and face, and apparently get married. Never would have pegged him for trying to be a school official."

"I'll pull the school board together and see if they have seen any funny business with finances."

She shook her head. "Not right now. I want to bring in a forensic accountant first. Ripley is good; the board members would have never seen it until he pulled his Houdini act. My accountant guy is better, knows how the suspect operated. I can't afford to have your average Joe messing with the books."

"Almost two years. Is this the longest he's stayed in one area?"

Liza noted a familiar sign up ahead. Killdeer Pub. What a name for a bar and grill. "It varied, depending on exposure or how long it took him to pad his bank account. One thing stayed the same: no record of his existence as soon as he packed up and left. Some of his victims were so embarrassed to be swindled, they wouldn't report him. I had to put the screws to a few just to get them to bleed information."

The radio squawked. "Sheriff, this is dispatch, over."

Hamilton reached out and took the receiver off the hook on the dashboard. "Copy, dispatch. What is it? Over."

"We have a 10-73. Concern it's a fire."

"Shit," Hamilton hissed, then pressed the receiver button. "Where, dispatch?"

Static garbled Deputy Jennings's answer.

"Dispatch, repeat."

"1801 Maple Leaf Drive."

Hamilton hit the brakes. Liza grunted as she jerked into the locked seat belt. Ouch! That was going to leave a mark. Better on her chest than a goose egg on her forehead from smacking into the dashboard. Wait. Her gaze flicked to the side mirror, and she heaved a sigh. No one had been behind them when he stopped dead in the middle of the road.

"Damn it to hell! You've got to be effing kidding me." Hamilton railed on like a marine drill instructor at Quantico laying into an inept recruit.

The significance of that address had certainly riled the unflappable sheriff. On second thought, he wasn't that levelheaded. She'd witnessed the man provoke her former partner to the point Boyce Hunt actually tried to throw a punch at the sheriff.

"Are you sure about that address, Jennings?"

"Sir, I couldn't be more certain if it had been my sainted granny reporting it."

"Copy that. I'm on my way, over."

"Roger."

Resuming his colorful cursing, creating words Liza had never heard in the whole of her life, Hamilton tossed the receiver at the dashboard, missing the hook entirely. "Hang on," he barked, flipping on the lights and siren.

Liza grasped the oh shit bar on the roof of the truck, braced her feet against the floorboard, and tensed as Hamilton whipped a bitch right there in the road. He gunned the engine, making the V6 roar with power, and the truck shot down the road. Liza chanced a glance in the rearview mirror, watching the Killdeer Pub sign fade in the background. Well, so much for getting food.

"So, it's a potential fire. I get it's bad, but why all the swearing?" she chanced.

"It's Gene Avery's house, that's why."

• • •

Shane spotted the black smoke rising above the trees two miles out. By the time the truck cruised around the last bend in the road, the fire was in full sight. The entire house was swallowed in a raging inferno. He fumbled with the radio receiver, missing it by a mile. It was suddenly placed in his hand, and he dared to take his gaze off the road to look at Liza. "Thanks," he rumbled and pressed the button. "Dispatch, this is the sheriff. Be advised it's a full out 10-70. House fire, fully engulfed. Send all fire personnel. Put a call out for any and all surrounding area departments, over."

"Roger."

Shane let the receiver fall from his hand, gripped the wheel with both, and veered off the pavement onto the gravel. The truck's rear end went squirrely, but he drove into the slide, righted the vehicle, and let the rocks fly as he spurred the F150 forward.

"Sheriff, someone is standing next to it," Liza said.

Shane looked where she pointed. A lone figure swayed side to side about fifty yards from the oxygen-licking flames. He drove the truck off the gravel road, through the shallow ditch, and tore through the immaculate landscaping. Slamming on the brakes, the truck went into a slide, spewing lawn and dirt until it lurched to a full stop. He rammed the gearshift into park and barreled out of the cab. Out of the corner of his eye, he caught Liza doing the same. Together they rushed toward the woman.

"Roslin!"

The brunette stiffened, her head snapping back as she came to attention.

"Roslin, are you okay?" he yelled over the rush of fire.

The heat battered his body in waves. Shane raised his arm, trying to shield his face from the onslaught.

Roslin shifted enough to show only her profile to him. In her left hand she gripped a nearly empty whiskey bottle. "Stay back, Sheriff," she slurred.

Slowing his pace, he gestured for Liza to do the same. The agent did, inching her way toward the right, and into Roslin's blind spot.

"What happened here?" he asked.

Roslin lifted the bottle to pink-smeared lips, then took a long gulp. The orange-red glow of the fire highlighted the dark smudges dusting her cheeks and the black trail along her jawline. She faced the burning house.

Shane took advantage of her back turned to him and inched closer. "Roslin, I need you to back away before you get hurt."

The widow spun, her speed surprising for one who was clearly as intoxicated as she was, her right arm coming up to level a six-shot revolver. "I said, stay back!"

He held up his hands. "Whoa, there. I'm just here to help."

"I don't recall asking for it."

Shane was kicking himself three ways to Sunday for not paying better attention. The fire and concern for Roslin's safety were big distractions. At the edge of his peripheral, Liza was easing along, staying out of the widow's line of sight. What was Bartholomew planning?

"You know," Roslin blurted, jerking Shane's attention fully on her again, "that slimy bastard cheated." She wobbled the revolver. "He cheated."

Sweat ran a course down his temples, smoke was clogging his airways, but Shane wasn't about to abandon this woman to her craziness. Straightening, he lowered his hands, palms out. "Roslin, I don't think burning the house was the way to get back at him."

Fury lit up her eyes. With the flames licking at the sky behind her body, it was like witnessing the coming of Satan's horde.

Pops and crackles led to a bang, then a boom. Shane and Liza ducked as a ball of flames rolled up into the sky. Fueled by the minor explosion, Roslin danced around and laughed at her handiwork.

"Let 'er burn!" she screamed.

Crouching down, Shane held up his arm to block the wall of heat that bowled him over. "Roslin! We need to move back before the house blows."

A screeching laugh burst from her, and she held up the bottle and gun in a victory stance. "Blow, baby, blow!"

The woman had come completely unhinged.

Shane tried to crabwalk toward her, but she did a little spin at the wrong time and caught him. The business end of the revolver was pointed at his chest. She dropped the bottle and cradled the weapon with both hands.

"Nu-huh, Sheriff. I aim to watch this place burn to the ground."

And kill herself in the process. Not on his watch.

The faint shrill of sirens reached him over the noise of the fire. He had to move fast. The last thing he needed was Roslin's crazy antics and his delayed response to be plastered all over the evening news, because this house burning was going to draw in the local stations. And if the pops and bangs continued, they could have a full-out explosion with a propane tank.

"Roslin! This is dangerous. If the place blows, it'll kill you."

Her gaze narrowed. "Then so be it."

Movement behind her was all the warning Shane had before Liza darted up. Roslin didn't have the luxury to react before Liza sacked her like Reggie White eating up a quarterback. The revolver flew from Roslin's hands and landed on its side, graciously not going off. With her arms pinned to her body, Roslin hit the ground with Liza coming down on top of her.

Shane scrambled over to grab the gun, emptied the chambers, and disengaged the cock before chucking the gun and bullets toward his truck.

On the ground, the women grappled, each trying to better the other. Liza struggled to get a good hold on the hysterical widow's arms while dodging thrashing legs and gnashing teeth. All through the wrestling match, Roslin continued to scream her maddening mantra, "He cheated."

Despite the warning at the back of his mind to stay out of it lest he get his balls kicked, Shane jumped into the fray. He managed to wrangle one of Roslin's arms and forced her facedown in the dirt. The woman's rage at being bested vibrated through her body.

Liza scooted around, jerked the other arm up behind Roslin's back, and then slammed her knee into the back of the woman's legs, successfully pinning her.

"Cuffs?"

Shane freed his pair from their holster and clapped them on Roslin's wrists, ratcheting them as tightly as he could without punishing her skin. The screaming stopped, and the widow went still.

At that precise moment, the volunteer fire department arrived. The trucks barreled into the yard, further tearing up the sod.

Roslin's silence was short-lived. Her body shook with a wicked cackle that increased in volume.

Shaking her head, Liza climbed to her feet, dusting off her now dirty and grass-stained jeans. "She's high as a kite."

"It would appear so." Shane winced as he struggled to his feet, pain stabbing his knees. "Let's get her out of the way."

Together they hooked their arms in the crook of Roslin's and hauled her upright, and then half dragged, half carried her to his truck. As thin as she was, Roslin Avery felt like she'd bogged herself down with all the whiskey in the county. They unceremoniously dumped her on the ground up against a tire.

Blowing her disarrayed hair out of her face, Liza arched, pressing her hands against her lower back. She nodded to the blazing inferno. "You can see that thing from space."

"I think that was her plan." Shane swiped the sleeve of his shirt across his forehead, mopping up the puddle of sweat. "The house wasn't exactly small, either."

"Burn, baby, burn," Roslin cackled.

Liza sighed. "Anything he might have had stashed away in the house is now gone." She groaned. "I'll never know for certain if he was my guy."

"We're not without options."

"Gone. It's gone. All gone," Roslin said.

Shane eyed the crazy woman propped against the tire. This was a woman who managed one of the banks in town. She dressed like a professional, polished and sophisticated, with an air of class that put her a cut above McIntire County. And for some damn reason, the hard-working women of the county didn't hate her for it—no, they admired her, wanted to be like her.

Now look at her. Roslin Avery was a raving lunatic. What had Gene done to knock her off her rocker?

"Sheriff?"

He turned to the head of the volunteer fire crew. "Hey, Jim."

"I've told the guys to spray the surrounding area. We're going to need more trucks and crews."

"I had Jennings put out a call for any and all available units."

Jim nodded. "Good."

"What about the propane tank at the back of the house?"

"We'll keep an eye on it. Seems like it's letting off the pressure fine, but we won't take any chances. I contacted the propane company as soon as the call came in. They're sending a crew this way."

"Boom!"

Jim jolted, gaping at Roslin. "What the heck?"

"Don't mind her." Shane gripped Jim's shoulder and squeezed, steering the fire crew leader away. "I'll be here. Keep me posted."

Touching a finger to his forehead, Jim returned to his men, bypassing Shane's young deputy.

Murdoch jogged up to him, her features strained. "Bossman, what happened?"

Glancing around, he beckoned her closer, then, putting an arm over her shoulders, guided her to Liza and Roslin. "I want you to take Mrs. Avery to the department and put her in a cell."

"Why?"

"Because I'm charging her with arson. She purposely set that house on fire. And I'm tacking on threatening an officer of the law with intent for bodily harm."

Murdoch stutter-stepped to a stop and gaped at him. "She set the house on fire?"

"Cheat me, you little bastard," Roslin blurted.

Murdoch's gaze darted from the irrational woman to him, and back.

"Oh, and she's high on something and drunk."

His young deputy scrubbed her face, and with a pop of her lips, she set forth to her task. With some assistance from Liza, Murdoch hauled Roslin to her squad car. Once the woman was tucked in the back seat, Murdoch gave him a two-fingered salute—a trait she'd picked up from Boyce—and then climbed into her car, driving off.

Liza rejoined him next to the hood of his truck. "What do you think she meant by 'he cheated'?"

"That I don't know. Could be she found something in the house she thought was proof he cheated on her with another woman."

The agent's mouth cocked to the side, and she seemed to work over his assumption in her head. "Mmm, I don't know." She shrugged quickly. "Then again, I didn't take him as the marrying kind, either." She shifted to face him. "Was she always that crazy?"

"Not even close. If she was a drug user, she hid it from everyone."

"And whatever secrets they were hiding in that house are burned up." Liza's eyes narrowed. "Like that was the plan all along."

Shane averted his gaze from the rigid woman at his side and focused on the fire crew as they battled the spread of the inferno. Were Roslin's mad ramblings a cover for something darker?

Was Gene Avery the embezzlement mastermind Liza had been chasing for years? If his schemes had finally caught up with him, the citizens of Eider were going to look for a scapegoat for their missing money. And sadly, in this county, anyone could become the scapegoat—Shane included.

CHAPTER SIX

Thankfully, the gas tank the sheriff was concerned about blowing didn't. The propane company was able to stabilize the situation and prevent any further destruction.

Liza studied the whole ordeal of putting out the fire like she was watching a TV drama—one part fascinated by the unfamiliar procedure, two parts bored that this was taking so long. But there was one bright spot, and he held most of her attention. Sheriff Hamilton took co-lead with Jim, the designated fire chief of the volunteer crew. Hamilton barked out commands and directed people where they were most needed, and warded off the curious public with a mixture of cajoling and sternness that sent even the most stubborn people on their merry way. His actions and conduct spoke of a man who'd long been in command of people, which was expected of a sheriff, but his movements revealed something deeper. Much deeper.

Was the cowboy sheriff more than he presented to the public?

Another vehicle joined the fray and parked near Hamilton's truck. From her post sitting on the truck's lowered tailgate, Liza waited as the driver emerged. Tall, dark-haired, and wearing an Eider police uniform, Detective Con O'Hanlon spotted her. His blue eyes twinkling with mischief so like the little men in green that his native homeland had once believed in, he gave her a wink, then strolled over.

"Agent Bartholomew, I was not made aware that you'd be paying the in-laws a visit."

"I'm not here in a visiting capacity." She shook his offered hand. "Boyce has no idea I'm here."

Con jerked his thumb over his shoulder. "Well, if he's watching the news, he knows now."

Liza peeked around the Irishman's muscular frame and cringed at the sight of the three news vans she hadn't noticed before. Too busy staring at a particular sheriff. "Damn it," she muttered, hopping down from the tailgate. "How long have they been here?"

"Who knows? So what brings you to our little town of mayhem and chaos?"

Mayhem and chaos—that about summed up what she'd witnessed so far. "Actually, it's a long story." Cupping the back of her neck, she waved her free hand at the dwindling fire. "And it hasn't gone exactly as planned."

"Par for the course in McIntire County, I'm afraid."

Better take another conversation path before Con got too curious about her unexpected presence. "How's the family? I heard you had a baby girl."

Beaming as only a proud daddy would, Con unearthed his billfold and removed a wallet-sized photo of a toothy toddler boy and a curly-top girl, both with dark hair and bright blue eyes. "Liam and Honor, both the apple of their mam's eye."

Liza chuckled. "Or is that the apple of their dad's eye?"

Con winked.

The green-eyed monster reared its head. Since Kurt and Stephanie had married and had Quinn, Liza fought her envy over Kurt getting what she wanted—a marriage and a family. Her job as an FBI agent was losing its luster. Despite a "mild" job in fraud, she had seen more evil and ugliness than she wanted. Then even Boyce got married and had a kid.

Everyone had a family but her.

But Ripley was still out there, and she couldn't let that business go unfinished.

Behind her, Hamilton hollered some incoherent order. Well, Hamilton didn't have a family, either. There was a little consolation in that. She shifted to observe the man as he strode to the fluttering yellow caution tape where a young woman was trying to duck under. Someone was obviously making an attempt for an exclusive shot.

"You and the sheriff are friends, right?" Liza asked Con.

"Since we were in school."

She made a noise of half-interest. "But you're not the same age?"

Con snorted. "Hell, no. He's older than me." He leaned forward. "That old fart's birthday is soon, and my mam is planning a party that will make him seriously contemplate becoming a drinking man."

"He doesn't drink?"

"Used to, back in high school." Con's forehead crinkled, like he was deep in thought. "I always wondered why he quit, but he's not one to do much talking." A grin broke out on the man's face. "I do enough for the both of us."

"That I can see." Liza's gaze drifted back to the subject of their new line of conversation. "I'm sure he has his reasons."

"We all do. Why so interested?"

She shrugged. "I'm an observer of people, and well, he intrigues me."

Humor lit up the Irishman's eyes. "Does he now?"

"O'Hanlon, what is your lazy butt doing here?" Hamilton interrupted before Liza could rebuff any thoughts Con might be having about her and his friend.

"Police chief wanted me to ask if you were in need of assistance," Con replied.

"Naw, got this under control. Was just contemplating leaving the cleanup duties to the fire crews. I've asked the state fire marshal to send down an investigator."

"This wasn't an accident?"

Liza slid her grimy hands into her back pockets and eased back a step. This was Hamilton's show, and in no way was she going to spill the beans about what Roslin Avery had done.

"Come to the office in two hours and we'll talk." Hamilton's attention swiveled to her. "Let's head out." He closed the tailgate on his truck.

"Sure thing." She flashed a smile at Con. "Later, Detective."

He returned her wave, then returned to his vehicle and climbed in. As Con backed out, Liza moved to the passenger side of Hamilton's truck. She popped the door and stepped onto the running board but hesitated before getting inside. Examining the immaculate interior, then her filthy clothing, she gnawed on her lip. Did she dare soil the man's upholstery?

On the other side, soot-covered, streaked with dirt and grass stains, Hamilton settled into his seat. He did a double take as he reached for the key. "Problems?"

"Uh, I wasn't sure if you'd mind my dirty rear end on the seat cover."

He shrugged, starting the engine. "I've looked and smelled worse than this and still drove it. I've got a detail guy who's been chomping at the bit to do another cleaning. Go ahead, make a big mess."

"If you insist," she said, sliding into her seat.

"Oh, I insist."

Liza snapped her seat belt. "You're one strange man, Sheriff."

"You don't know the half of it, Agent Bartholomew." He dislodged his big truck out of the ruts he created plowing into the yard. "You still hungry?" He maneuvered the vehicle onto the road while dodging people and obstacles.

Liza checked the time on her iPhone and groaned. Six thirty-three. "I'm starving." Her peppermint mocha indulgence had long burned up in her system. And her last remembered meal was the lone energy bar she'd eaten as she left Cedar Rapids that morning.

"I'll have Murdoch pick us up some food when we get back to the station."

"Why is she still running rookie errands for you? Isn't she a full-blown deputy?"

"Questioning my methods, *Agent*?"

"Damn straight I am."

The corner of his mouth twitched. "Never let it be said that you weren't persistent. I need to get back to the station, ASAP. Murdoch has more leeway to do a food run."

"Why the hurry to get back? You really should wait on the fire investigator."

"Should, but Jennings paged me. Apparently my prisoner is causing a ruckus, making demands my deputies won't listen to."

"So you go."

A lift of his chin was all the acknowledgment she got, which fit his persona. The good ole boy doing his sworn duty. More people could learn from Hamilton, and then maybe there would be less sexism and fewer problems.

What the hell? Was she bordering on worshipping him? Okay, time to backtrack this and get her focus back on her duty, watching the scenery flash by being the safest option.

Liza had given up trying to memorize any of it after Hamilton got the call about the fire. There were so many back roads and twists and turns that sent her head spinning. She'd bet her badge and Sig none of these gravel roads were on a map. Which explained why her GPS had fits, utterly failing her when she drove into town.

Short of admitting her little weakness to Hamilton, she was going to have to come up with an excuse to not drive around the county on her own. And any excuse she'd pull out of her ass would be lame at best. This few-hours jaunt had turned into a nightmare for a woman who was directionally challenged outside of Cedar Rapids.

"Must be some tough thinking you've got goin' on there."

Her gaze jerked from the window to him; she blinked as her nutrient-deprived mind tried to catch up with her quick movements. "Uh, yeah, sure."

He chuckled, a deep rumbling sound she felt all the way to her toes. It warmed her in those cold, dark places of her soul no one had touched before; not even her nephew Quinn managed that, and the kid was something special to her.

"I'd like to have a conversation with Roslin."

"I think that can be arranged. But I'd rather wait until tomorrow. Let her sleep off whatever craziness is going on up there in her head."

"Makes sense. However, what am I going to do in the meantime? I can't go back to Cedar Rapids tonight and let my SAC know I have nothing to show for this trip except a dead man and a burnt house."

"You could stay here in Eider. Tomorrow you can gather what you need before heading back."

"Where do you propose I stay? I didn't exactly put in a voucher for a hotel."

"Cassy and Boyce's house is empty for the time being."

Liza frowned. "Why's that?"

"Cassy is training as a K-9 handler, and Boyce and their baby went along."

Empty house, and if it was the same place Cassy had lived in the last time Liza was here, she knew how to get there, and from the sheriff's department, too. Only if the Hunts hadn't moved.

"I appreciate the offer, but will they be okay with it?"

"Considering I'm the one in charge of looking after the place, I don't think they'll mind. Only condition I have is you need to cover chores."

"Chores?"

Hamilton grinned but kept his focus on the road. "Cassy owns a pair of horses that need grain in the morning, and you check the water to make sure it's running okay."

"Horses?"

"It's easy. I can show you where the feed is and how much."

"Sheriff—"

"Shane."

She blinked. Wha—? Oh, he was just trying to be friendly. After all, she did mention that he should call her Liza. "All right, Shane, I haven't ever owned an animal in my life. Are you sure this is wise, having me feed horses?"

"They're mostly self-sufficient. If you forget to give them their grain once, it won't hurt them. Makes them grumpy, yeah, but they have plenty of pasture to graze on, so they won't starve."

It all sounded simple enough, and if he was going to show her how to do it, maybe he'd lead her there—she could make sure it was the same place as before—and she wouldn't have to worry about getting lost.

"Okay, if you're sure Cassy and Boyce won't mind."

"I can give them a call if it would make you feel better."

"Preferred." That solved that. Liza inhaled, caught the smell of her clothing, and grimaced. Oh, this so was not going to fly. She needed clean clothing. Was that emergency overnight bag still in the car? Had she checked to see if the clothing inside was clean after the last time she used it? "Oh, crapola."

"What?"

"I don't think I have a clean set of clothing with me. Damn it."

"I'm sure Cassy wouldn't mind if you wore something of hers."

Liza eyeballed the man next to her. "How are you so certain that her clothing would fit me?"

She didn't think it possible, but Shane Hamilton's face changed to an interesting shade of pink. Could it be? The man did get embarrassed.

"Well," he choked out, "uh … you two look similar in … size."

"I don't know how I should feel about that. I look like a formerly pregnant woman?"

His face flamed bright red. "Not what I was saying."

A wicked grin turned up the corners of her mouth. Oh, he made this too easy. "What was I supposed to assume, Sheriff?"

"That you needed clean clothing and Cassy's would fit you."

"How would Cassy feel about you pimping out her clothes?"

His mouth dropped and closed. If she gave him a few minutes, his eyes might glaze over and he'd have a fit. "I'm not pimping out her clothing."

"But it never crossed your mind I could buy something?"

Now he was utterly flustered. Ooh, he looked damn fine all tongue-tied and twisted.

"I just thought you'd …" He hmphed. "You're one wicked woman. You had me going."

"I thought for sure the smile would give me away."

"That was a smile? Looked more like you were baring your teeth."

Shrugging, Liza scooted into a slump in the seat. "Baring my teeth, smiling, it's all in the eye of the beholder." She closed her eyes. "I'll see what Cassy has. If nothing fits, I'll have to make a run to the store. No biggie."

"You didn't have to make a production of *Chicago* out of it."

"Oh, but it was way too fun."

CHAPTER SEVEN

After settling Liza in at the Hunts', showing her the ropes with the horses, and waiting for Murdoch to drop off Liza's meal, Shane returned to the office. Well, there was a moment of awkward shuffling of boots and silence right before he walked out the door. Damn, he hadn't felt so tongue-tied and gangly since he was a teenager about to steal his first kiss. There was something about that witty woman that turned him into a man he'd long thought dead.

Which was damn near impossible. He couldn't actually be attracted to Liza Bartholomew. No way, no how. No woman would take Cheyenne's place.

He was vulnerable at the moment. That was it. Normally after the anniversary night, he would still be secluded in his home, quarantined from all human contact for the next day or so. He wouldn't emerge until it was over and he could face people again. But this murder, Liza's abrupt arrival—it was throwing him all sorts of out of whack.

Nothing else explained his irrational need to open his mouth and insert foot. Or have weird pangs of embarrassment. And feel those funny little sparks in his chest. Or an uncontrollable need to experience the feel of her lips against his own.

Yeah, he'd completely jumped off the roof with only a red sheet tied to his neck.

Pulling into the department lot, he bypassed his usual parking spot behind the building and took an open slot next to a dark green truck. Leave it to Con to be right on time. Gathering his fatigued and aching body, Shane slid out of the cab and hauled ass to the front door.

The drone of conversation lured him to the open bullpen. Camped out at her desk with her red head bent over a binder, Murdoch was discussing something with Con. Once the young deputy had taken Shane's advice and became his budding investigator, she'd spent long hours learning how to do the job with Eider PD's lone detective. Con O'Hanlon was a good instructor, and Shane welcomed his experience in helping pull out Murdoch's natural instincts.

"Murdoch, don't you have somewhere to be?" was warning enough for the two to know he'd arrived.

Con nodded a greeting and pushed up from his seat next to the desk.

Murdoch flipped the binder shut then swung her chair around. "Took you long enough."

"Showing someone the ropes takes time. I'm back, so shove off. Go remind that Aussie bartender why he's going to marry you."

His deputy's features wrinkled in an expression that resembled a grossed-out teenager. "If I'm getting your implied meaning, that's wrong on so many levels." She vacated her seat and gathered her gear. "Later, Con."

Con's inquiring look gave Shane a twinge. Shit! He'd said something that put his friend on alert.

"What?"

"I don't think I've ever heard you actually tease her quite like that before."

Shane shrugged, heading for his office. "Doesn't mean I've never done it. You just weren't around to hear it."

"You didn't do it with Nic, or Cassy for that matter." Con took up his usual spot in the most comfortable chair in the office besides the one behind Shane's desk. Kicked back and looking all too relaxed with his right ankle resting on his left knee, Con interlaced his fingers and tapped the tips against his chin. Freud had entered the room. "So, what's the deal with Agent Bartholomew? And why did Roslin Avery burn her home to the ground?"

"Who told you that?"

"Murdoch. Then again, I didn't miss much coming from the jail when Roslin started in on her ranting about thirty minutes ago."

Now that he mentioned it, Shane hadn't heard a peep out of the woman when he arrived. "What calmed her down?"

"I think she passed out. Apparently, it's hard work being a crazy woman. Now, about Agent Bartholomew?"

Shane jerked open a deep desk drawer and rummaged for his emergency box of chocolate fudge Pop-Tarts. Bolting down that rib-eye sandwich as he returned from Cassy's might have been a mistake. He was still starving. "What about her? She's here for reasons I can't divulge."

"Any investigator worth their badge will be able to put two and two together on that one."

Aha! One packet left. Shane snagged the foil-wrapped sugary goodness. *Reminder, bring another box.* Ripping off a corner with his teeth, he freed the precious tarts from their cellophane.

"Boyo, you're about to turn fifty, and you're still eating those?"

"Your point being?"

Con's eyebrows rose. "If Nic caught me eating that garbage, I'd get my arse kicked three ways to Sunday. Two words: heart attack."

"When did you turn into an old nag?"

"Where've you been? I've always nagged. So says my wife."

Rolling his eyes, Shane took another bite out of the doubled tarts. Theirs was an unexpected friendship, Con being much younger while they were in school, and each having wildly different interests. The years Shane was away from McIntire County—aside from his aging parents—he'd maintained contact with Con, but the Irishman knew nothing about Shane's other life. Sadly, about the time he'd been working up the words to ask Con to be his best man, Cheyenne died.

"I have some interesting news on the untimely death of our superintendent," Con said, dropping his Freudian facade.

"Let's hear yours first."

Con dug out a notepad from his uniform pocket. Licking his forefinger and thumb, he paged through the sheets to the right point. "Apparently, a few school board members got suspicious about some activities Mr. Avery was performing."

"Such as?"

"Going to 'special' training classes for administrators that there are no records of him having attended. Trips for functions he claimed he was required to be at, and once again, no records of these functions."

"So, that's how he did it?"

Con's mouth quirked. "Did what?"

He knew. Shane never underestimated this man with his knowledge.

"Let me guess, all that money he claimed for reimbursement can't be found? The board has been trying to audit his finances and ran into red tape and hoops they have no hope of getting through."

Con's twirled finger encouraged Shane to continue.

"And now that he's dead, they're even more panicked, because the audit revealed that money has been shifted around in accounts that were previously unnoticed."

"Which begs the question . . . "

"How did Avery get access to those accounts when superintendents aren't allowed to even get a whiff of them without board and state approval?" Shane polished off the last of his chocolate fudge tart and leaned forward, swallowing the sugary bite. "The better question is, how did a conman convince a whole school board that he was qualified to run a school when he isn't even a real superintendent?"

"That's your tidbit of news?" Con asked. Then the light bulb blinked on over his head. "And that's why Agent Bartholomew is here."

"Gene Avery isn't who he claimed to be. He's been under investigation by the FBI for years."

"Do we even know what his real name is?"

Shane shook his head, rocking back in his chair. "Bartholomew hasn't revealed that to me yet. From what I gathered, she might not have a clue. The guy changed IDs like he changed clothes. Hell, he probably forgot who he truly was."

"How'd he manage to avoid capture this long?"

"Plastic surgery. The photo she had of him didn't even match the man in the morgue."

"But it caught up with him." The Freud expression returned.

"Someone in this county figured out who and what he was. Right now, my money is on Roslin."

"Because she burned down the house? While I'm not one to argue the matter, nine times out of ten, it would be the spouse. But that man gathered enough enemies in his lifetime; it could be anyone. And let's not forget, Roslin came with him. We don't even know her background. Let's get a clearer picture of who Gene Avery really was and how many people he screwed over in the past who are capable of murder."

"That will have to come from Liza."

Aw, shit, he opened the cunning drawer of his friend's mind on that one.

"Liza, eh?"

"Don't read anything into it." Shane pushed to his feet. "You keep working the school board and the money trail. If you can track down the funds he squirreled away, maybe we can locate his other ill-gotten gains. I'll focus on Roslin and the other personas of Gene Avery."

"How are you so sure I'll succeed where the FBI hasn't?"

Shane grinned. "I'm not. I'm playing on the hunch that your fresh eyes will catch something they've missed."

"That's a whole lotta wishful t'inking."

• • •

The food had been fabulous, the shower even better. Thankfully, she still had clean undergarments tucked inside her to-go bag, no awkward moment of "borrowing" something of Cassy's. 'Course that woman's taste in bras and panties was truly an eye opener.

What kind of panties did Hamilton like? *Oh, Liza, what kind of thoughts are those? Sweet mercy, don't you have any pride?*

Nope, not a bit. The cowboy sheriff was truly an interesting topic she wanted to explore. Forget whatever she'd learned before, Shane Hamilton was an enigma that deserved solving.

Oh, let it be me.

From the moment he'd shown her how to take care of the horses and then made sure she was set for the night, Liza wanted to know what a good-night kiss from him felt like. It was crazy thinking about him like he was an itch that needed scratching.

If she was honest with herself—and hell, when wasn't she?—Shane was the type of guy she could see testing the waters with again. He carried himself in a way that declared to the whole damn world that he was in charge and the world better take notice, but not in a way that was bullish. He was more unassuming, the whole silently assertive type, and it spoke to a part of Liza that she was just beginning to understand about herself.

She was tired of being alone and tired of making all the decisions, wrong or right. Of having her supervisor breathing down her neck, and Kurt dumping his crap on her shoulders.

She didn't know how much longer she could struggle under the burden of these loads.

Okay, let's consider this antidepressant commercial over.

Wearing a loose pair of athletic pants and a long-sleeved tee, she wrangled all of her clothing into the washer. There were just some things she was crazy grateful for, and spending time in someone's home with a washer and dryer rather than in a hotel was one of them. Now that she was satiated, Liza wanted to curl up in bed.

She peered into the Hunts' bedroom, then down the hall to where a new guest wing had been added but not completed, then to the living room, and back to the bedroom. It would be just too weird to sleep in the couple's bed. The couch did look comfortable. One night wouldn't kill her. With a shrug, she padded into the living room. After locating a fitted sheet to cover the cushions, a fluffy pillow, and a thick flannel blanket, Liza made a cozy nest and crawled in.

Clicking through the multitude of satellite channels, she found a music-only station playing the Eagles style of rock. She dragged her leather carrying case close, and, one by one, she pulled out the files, reviewing each header, though she didn't really need the reminders. Laying them out over the coffee table and the empty spot on the couch beside her, she took a deep breath.

There has to be something in them I missed. Something that can tell me who might have killed him.

"Sure, Liza, you know who wanted to kill him. How about everyone he's stolen from, or the friends and family of the people he so callously killed?"

The folder with the information on the warehouse fire was smack in the middle. That file she hadn't memorized. It was the black mark on this whole case, the catalyst for her wanting to leave the FBI. It was the part in the entire affair that didn't make sense. The warehouse fire was the only incident to her knowledge where Ripley had actually killed.

Liza reached for the file. If she skipped the photos of the bodies, she could read the report, revisit what she remembered. Not that she could ever forget the sight of the charred building and the smell of cooked flesh.

Don Henley sang out. Her hand spasmed, and she snatched it away from the file. Grabbing up her cell, she sighed. *For all that's holy and right.*

"Hello."

"What are you doing, Liza? Quinn saw you on TV tonight and freaked out."

Oh God, she'd hoped the TV crews hadn't gotten footage of her. "Kurt, I'm fine, as you can clearly tell."

"But Quinn doesn't know that, or understand. He's been banging on his bedroom door for the last two hours. I can't get him to calm down."

"Turn on your video chat and show him. Now."

"Liza."

"Kurt, do it!"

Damn him for waiting so long. Damn it, damn it, damn it!

Liza jerked her phone down, accessed the video chat app, and waited for Kurt to do the same. The peach walls of his home popped up on her screen. Repetitive banging echoed through her speaker, the only sound, other than Kurt's labored breathing. He entered the dimly lit bedroom and dropped down on the floor next to his son. Liza winced at the reddened fist. Blood smeared the white wood.

"Q, hey, buddy, Auntie Liza is on the phone."

The boy wouldn't acknowledge his dad; his fist kept up the steady cadence. Pain meant nothing to him; somehow his nerves and his brain wouldn't register the connection. So the doctors claimed. Liza's uneducated guess was that Quinn wanted something to feel, and pain had been the most logical choice in his jumbled mind.

"Quinn, baby, look at me."

His fist paused halfway to the door. A blood droplet splatted on his jeans.

"Quinn, it's Liza. I'm on the phone. Look at me, baby. I'm right here."

Slowly, in increments, Quinn's head swiveled toward the phone in his father's hand. A pair of beautiful brown eyes latched onto the sight of her, and a spark that he only had for her flared to life in those blank depths. His tenderized hand reached for the phone and ripped it from his dad.

"Hey, Q. See, nothing happened." She fluffed her hair. "Did I look beautiful for the camera?"

A wistful grin popped up. He nodded hard enough to give himself whiplash.

"Oh, good. I thought for sure they were filming my bad side." She tilted her chin left, tapping her cheek. "You know, this side."

She got a flash of the pearly whites. Her heart soared. No irreparable damage done. It was her own damn fault. She'd seen the news crews at the fire. And she knew part of Quinn's nightly ritual was to watch the six o'clock news; he had been an information junkie from the time he could sit and watch TV. Up until he lost his mother, he'd scream bloody murder if anyone disrupted the routine, but since her death, not a peep out of him. He'd replaced screaming with beating his hand against objects when he became upset.

"I heard you wanted to see me."

An eyebrow crooked.

"Sorry I can't be there right now, buddy. My job sent me on a trip. But I promised Dad I'll be back soon. Okay?"

The smile faded. His uninjured hand shot out and jerked hard on his father's shirtsleeve then pointed at something behind them. Kurt hopped up and went to get whatever Quinn wanted. When he returned, he held a dry-erase board and marker. Quinn yanked it out of his dad's hands; the kid had no regard for his rough behavior, something she needed to work on with him. He scribbled quickly, then pointed the phone screen at his board.

Will you bring me a rock?

The phone jerked back to his hopeful face. The kid loved rocks and was bound to be a geologist when he grew up.

"Yes. I know someone who can show me some pretty ones." She'd have to ask Hamilton if he knew of a good place to get the rocks.

That brought back the happy boy.

"Quinn, let your daddy take care of your hand, okay?"

Uncertainty painted his features, then he shrugged and handed the phone to Kurt. Liza heard the scuffle of a nine year-old boy scrambling to his feet before Kurt's pained face filled the screen.

"I can't do this, Liza."

"Yes, you can. He loves you."

"He loves you more. I'm just someone in his way."

It had been easy when Stephanie was alive to let her handle Quinn, the doctors, and the psychologists. Kurt could just sit there, letting her explain all the medical terms to him, show him how to handle Quinn's behaviors, and keep Kurt on track with a routine. Now her foster brother was alone and frustrated. There was no way he could quit his job working for the oil and natural gas company. The money was too good, and it kept the bills paid for Quinn's treatments. Liza had become his lifesaver, and it was irritating as hell. Kurt was a grown-ass man. He should be capable of handling his own family drama. After Stephanie died, Liza became too available to help with Quinn. Admittedly, she had been looking for an excuse to spend less time at the office and more time with her nephew, until Ripley resurfaced. Now Quinn, and Kurt, paid for her absence. But she had to catch Ripley before she could focus on them.

She ran her thumb over the screen where his cheek was. "Stop thinking like that. You're the only thing standing between him and an uncertain future. He's got everything we never had, and you keep telling yourself that. Every day."

"I don't know what to do any more. I do everything Stephanie taught me, what the doctors say, and I still can't reach my son. You're the only one he responds to." Defeat was starting to win.

"Have you talked to Mom and Pop Bartholomew?"

"Yes, but they're having some problems with a new foster."

Two wonderful people who took a chance on two rebellious teenagers and adopted them were saints in Kurt's and Liza's eyes. Mary and Michael Bartholomew were still trying to be saviors to kids in the foster system.

"Kurt, one step at a time. Go take care of his hand, get his pjs on, and give him his ice cream. Don't forget the cherry."

"I never do."

"I'll call you in an hour."

"Liza, hurry up down there."

"I'm trying. I'm really trying."

Her phone went black, the wallpaper of a beach scene replacing the blackened screen. Dropping the phone in her lap, she swallowed hard, but it did nothing to loosen the tightness in her throat. This phone call would set her back. How could she focus on the events happening in Eider and her case when she was bombarded by the reality of Kurt and Quinn's predicament?

The real question should be, how much longer could she hold out with her job in the agency before her need to protect Quinn and Kurt overwhelmed her? The unfinished business with Ripley or not, if there was one point that had been driven home to her as a foster kid, family was all that mattered. When you had it, you never let go.

Never.

CHAPTER EIGHT

Another night with less than desirable sleeping conditions left Shane twice as sore and stiff as he'd been the previous day. To be fair, he wasn't about to make one of his deputies pull overnight duty watching the prisoner. He'd put Roslin in jail, which made him responsible for her. At least he was spared the plague of memories. Instead of reliving those very short, sweet years with Cheyenne, he kept thinking about a raven-haired powerhouse with the wit of Will Rogers. He barely knew Liza Bartholomew, and yet she'd managed to find a way to consume him.

With an old-man groan, he eased himself upright and scooted around to sit on the edge of the dented sofa cushion. While more comfortable than the hardwood floor the night before, the sofa had too many miles on it. Time to consider a replacement if he kept this up.

Scrubbing both hands along his face, his callouses grating against the scruff, he grimaced at the taste of dragon's breath. That was something he didn't wish on anyone. Hoisting his body off the offending sofa, Shane staggered in his socks into the tiny bathroom, did his business, and gave his hands a good cleaning. He peered at his reflection in the black-spotted mirror. That was one ugly mug staring back.

Sniff test results concluded that he stank worse than his breath tasted. A quick rinse off in the locker room was in order before his underlings showed up for work. Grabbing a toothbrush and a small tube of paste, he headed for a file cabinet behind his desk.

He pulled open the drawer and snagged a clean uniform set from the two he kept there at all times.

Tiptoeing across the hall, he deposited his stuff in the locker room, then snuck down to the holding cells to check on his prisoner. Roslin was draped over the cot, lightly snoring. She hadn't made a peep since passing out. It would be interesting to see what came next with this woman.

The power shower wasn't enough to melt away the aches and pains, but it cleansed the stench. The scruff would have given any commanding officer a coronary, but there was nothing to be done about it. Shane had forgotten to replace his razor. Bad breath vanquished, he was ready for round two with Roslin, and more encounters with Liza.

Time to get the coffee going. As he scooped the grounds into the filter, his nose tickled with the scent of lemon and blueberry. Starting the machine, he thumbed open the cabinet above the pot and grinned. Eureka! Murdoch had left the rest of her mother's coffee cake. Breakfast was saved.

Dishing out a large square on a paper plate for himself and a moderate-sized one on another, he tucked the sealed glass baking dish back inside the cabinet. Once the pot had filled enough, he stole two cups' worth then left the maker to finish its job and carried his mug along with one Styrofoam cup and plate down the hall. As he entered the holding cell area, a disheveled Roslin, gaping at the bars, greeted him.

"What's going on?" she demanded.

"What's going on, Ms. Avery, is you got mind-numbingly drunk and high on something, then proceeded to set fire to your home. After which, you decided to threaten a sworn officer of the law with a loaded weapon."

Her eyes were perilously close to popping out of her sockets. "I did what?"

"See, that's the funny thing about substance abuse—it can wipe your memory."

She plastered her hands to her face. "Oh, no, no, no, no."

Shane tapped his mug against a bar. Roslin peeked at him between the flesh and bone prison of her own making.

"How's about you come get some food and coffee in you. When my female deputy gets in, she'll see to you getting cleaned up."

Rising on wobbly legs, she teetered over to the door and accepted the cup and plate. "I don't get a fork?"

"Less dangerous to let you eat it with your fingers." Shane raised his mug. "The coffee is dark, should knock that hangover right out of the park." He turned to leave.

"Sheriff?"

He looked over his shoulder.

Roslin glanced down at her breakfast, then at him. "I get my one phone call, right?"

"Your lawyer contacted the county attorney last night. They'll be in this morning, and we'll sort this all out."

Seemingly satisfied with that answer, she wandered back to her cot, sipping the coffee. Shane resumed his path back to his office but was waylaid by a resounding knock on the front door.

His stride shortened as the woman on the other side of the glass doors cocked her head to the side. A stray lock slipped free of the ponytail and laid against her cheek. Liza wore a different pair of jeans and a cream-colored shirt under a black jacket, with the same knee-high boots. One corner of her mouth tipped up as she held aloft a large, white paper bag and pointed at it. A bag that was all too familiar to him. She'd gone to Betsy Lamar's diner.

Sweet home Alabama.

He pushed open the door. "You're here early." What a great greeting.

Liza slipped past him, a light lavender scent tickling his senses. "I remembered that great diner Boyce took me to every morning we were here, and I decided I had to have some of Betsy's pancakes and bacon. I thought you'd like something." She stopped and turned. "I had a feeling you were camping out here while Roslin was in holding."

"What if I wasn't?"

She whisked the freed lock back from her face. "Oh, you were here." She tapped her cheek. "You need a shave, Sheriff." With a wink, she spun and flounced through the second set of doors into the building.

Flounced. The woman had actually flounced, like a flirting twenty-year-old. What the hell?

Shane proceeded with caution. It was one thing to entertain the idea of being interested in her. But if she started showing interest back and actually acted on it, what was he going to do? This was not territory he wanted to explore. Not on his life.

Liza bypassed the bullpen and paused at the coffee station to pour herself a cup. Shane approached her like he would a spooked filly, stopping within inches of her. He could still catch the scent of her shampoo, or lotion, or whatever the hell she put on, and it was creating weird little tightening sensations in his chest. He'd never expected to like something so … girly. Cheyenne had preferred this spicy number that had made him imagine—and eventually acting on—how he'd drive her wild. To this day, given the right conditions, he could still smell her perfume. But this floral scent Liza wore was sweet, innocent, the complete opposite of the woman standing before him.

She turned, the mug pressed to her full lips as she gently blew on her coffee. An electrical charge zinged through his body and zapped portions of his brain long dark and dead.

"So, where do you want to eat this?"

Jolting, he sucked in a breath. One of her eyebrows lifted.

Smooth, Hamilton. He gulped a mouthful of coffee. The shock to his system doused the sudden desire. He nodded at his office. "In there."

She headed to his office, and against his will, his eyes drifted lower, wanting another glimpse of what he saw yesterday, but he stopped at the small of her back.

What the hell are you doing, man? This is a federal agent. She's not here for you to stare at her ass and lust over her. Get your damn head out of the gutter and focus.

Yet shouldn't he be happy that his cold heart was finding a reason to beat again? No. No, he'd made a promise over Cheyenne's grave that he'd never love another. His heart and soul died that rainy night on the side of a road. His job and his county were the only things that deserved his devotion, like his country had before.

Refilling his mug, he snagged his plate with coffee cake and joined Liza in the office. She'd set out a large square container on his desk, a fork neatly placed on the cover, and then sat in the chair opposite him, her box open. The spicy aroma of sausage filled the room.

"That doesn't smell like bacon to me." He sat in his chair.

"I said I was craving bacon, but I decided I wanted sausage after I ordered you the biscuits and gravy."

His mouth salivated at those words. Damn, he hadn't eaten Betsy's sausage gravy and biscuits in a dog's year. He flipped the lid open and was blasted with the heavenly warmth of butter and spices. "You did good, Bartholomew."

"You seem like a simple man who enjoys the simple things in life, like a heavy morning meal with coffee."

Chuckling, he dug in. They ate in silence.

On occasion, Shane let his gaze drift her way to soak in the odd sight of a woman sitting across from him. Well, sure, he had two female deputies, but they came in to discuss duties and patrol routes with him. Liza wasn't his deputy, wasn't talking about work-related topics, and looked like she was right at home with her Styrofoam container balanced on her crossed legs, finishing her stack of pancakes and sausage links. With her focus absorbed on her meal, he let his gaze linger, taking in the curves and details of her frame.

She had a feminine quality that belied her tough exterior. Minus the makeup she'd worn yesterday, her face looked fresh and emphasized her cheekbones. Shane itched to smooth his thumbs over them. The ponytail didn't hide the fact that her hair was losing its sleekness. If she let it down, would it be a soft wave or coil? Damn, he wanted to know, to run his fingers through the locks. And that mouth …

"So, I was reviewing what we learned yesterday."

His brain slammed to a halt like a bronc throwing its rider into a wall. Shane dragged his attention off of her lips. She eyed him with a suspicious uplift of one eyebrow.

Shit! Nothing like getting caught gawking. Clearing his throat, he tried to hide his embarrassment behind a stilted cough.

"Uh, yeah, and what's that?" Why couldn't shop talk wait another thirty minutes or so?

Closing the lid on her empty container, Liza set it on the floor next to a satchel he hadn't noticed her carrying when she came in. "Well …" She flipped the flap over and pulled out a handful of manila folders, one with a red, arrow sticker flagging it. "I spent some time last night re-reading everything I had on my Mr. Ripley, and there's one thing that sticks out." She rose from her chair and placed the folders in front of him. "The fire."

Shane pushed his partially eaten breakfast aside and, with his gaze on her, pulled the files closer. "The fire was Roslin's doing."

"What if he told her to do it? What if, in the event something happened to him, he instructed her to burn it to the ground?"

His roughened fingers played with the red sticker. "The question would be, why would he insist on a fire?"

"Because he's done it before." When she grasped the flagged file, her fingers touched his, and a buzz of energy surged through his veins. She stilled, as if she'd felt it too, then slowly pulled the file from the stack. "Read this," she said breathlessly.

Ignoring the sensations coursing through his system, he took the folder out of the stack and opened it. The scene photos slammed into him. His hands thunked on the desktop.

"He killed?"

Her grim features said it all.

"What the hell, Bartholomew? From the way you talked yesterday, he was nothing more than a rogue thief who loved the thrill of stealing money and making the FBI look like a pack of fools. Not a killer."

"It's not 100 percent certain he's the one who did it, because it was so outside the realm of his MO. The one thing linking him to those victims and that fire was the victims themselves. They were the only people I could find who actually had the guts to see him behind bars. Were they ashamed of letting him scam them? Yes, but they weren't going to roll over and play dead." Liza flopped into her chair. "And I repaid their bravery by letting him get a hold of them and burn them alive." She turned green at that statement.

Breakfast roiled in his gut. Unbidden images of burning vehicles and the screams of men as they burned inside popped into his head. Shane jolted out of the memory. This was not war, and he was not in Iraq. It had been a long time since he'd even thought of his time there; no need to start again.

"Okay, so let's examine this from our standpoint. I got a call from the fire marshal last night. There were no bodies in the remains of the Avery home. So, you can ease your mind on that matter. From what he could tell in the dark, she'd used an accelerant, probably gas or diesel fuel, to get it going."

"What about the propane?"

"By all appearances, nothing was turned on that would leave valves open. And we can thank God for that, because if she had used the LP to burn the home, we wouldn't be here."

Liza's features slackened. Whatever tension she'd kept pent up was now slipping from her body.

"However, she burned whatever evidence I would have needed to close the book on Ripley's life and scams. Do you think it's possible he kept something at the school?"

"Hard to say. We can go look after Roslin is out of my hair."

Uh-oh, here it came. That perturbed expression could only be disastrous for him.

"Excuse me, how is it that Roslin will be 'out of your hair'?"

"Her lawyer has done an exceptional job of convincing the county attorney and our esteemed judge to grant bail. All of that is probably being finalized"—he checked his clock: 7:23— "at this moment."

"Who is her lawyer to have that kind of pull?"

Shane closed the file on the warehouse fire and pushed his creaky body out of the chair. "A very formidable woman named Pamela Frost." Skirting around his desk, he headed for the door. "If you want a chance to talk with Roslin before she shows up, now is your chance."

Liza vaulted from her chair.

"How are you so sure the lawyer will be here soon?"

"Did you know her husband ran against me in the election?"

"Boyce mentioned it, said the guy lost by a hair."

Shane nodded, grabbing another cup of coffee for his prisoner. "I didn't put much effort into my re-election—probably should have done better about that—but the only reason Donovan Frost managed to get so close was because of his wife. She's got the fortitude of a politician but no desire to play the field on her own. Likes her job stirring up trouble in the courts, thank you very much."

Liza made a sound in her throat that was akin to a grunt. "Maybe she should face off against my supervisor."

"Maybe . . ." Shane froze in place as Murdoch rounded the corner, a well put together brunette in a tan pantsuit with a mint-green blouse and heels tagging along behind her. This just got a whole lot more complicated.

"Sheriff Hamilton, I hope you're not planning to have a conversation with my client in my absence."

"Not one bit, Ms. Frost," he fibbed.

Liza's head bobbed down and then up, no doubt sizing up the woman before her. Liza's features relaxed as though she was bored, like she found Pamela lacking.

"Sir, I tried—" Murdoch was cut off when the dispatch line pealed out. "I've got it."

"I'd like my client released. The judge has accepted the county attorney's and my agreement. Bond was set and paid."

"That was fast," Liza muttered.

Pamela's cool, assessing gaze flicked to the agent and remained there. "And you are?"

"None of your business."

"Uh, sir," Murdoch waved.

Shane held up his "give me a minute" finger. "Ms. Frost, we'll gladly release her. But I need to ask her a few things before she leaves."

"That won't be possible."

"I do have the right to question her about the reason she set fire to her home."

Pamela crossed her arms and those eyes turned venomous. "Like I said, that won't be possible."

"Sheriff."

He held up his finger, which every deputy should know by now was code for "give me another minute." "Only if she says it's not. As of right now, with her sober and lucid, I believe I have the right to ask. And you have the obligation to sit in the room to advise her."

"That was not the agreement the county attorney and I came to. Mrs. Avery is to be released immediately, and questioning will be reserved for a later time as she will have been given proper time to grieve for her deceased husband."

"Pamela, the woman had ample time to 'grieve,' which brings me to my other problem. I need to question her further on the night of her husband's death."

"Is she a suspect in his death?"

Shane gave the uptight lawyer his own cool and assessing look. If she thought for one minute he was about to blurt out any information she could use to circumvent his investigation, she had another think coming.

"Sheriff!"

"What, Murdoch?" His attention snapped to his perturbed deputy.

"We have a problem."

CHAPTER NINE

"I drove by it twice a day, the last few days."

The woman next to Shane stared down at the lumpy, black plastic in the ditch. The tips of her brown shoes were damp from the three inches of water pooled in the dip. Her hand trembled as she lifted it to cup the back of her neck. She should be at work. She should be sitting behind a desk working at a computer, answering the phone, not standing here on the side of the road.

She shuddered. "It bothered me that it was just lying there. Who leaves a huge wad of black plastic sitting in a ditch?"

She wasn't familiar to Shane—she lived in one county and drove through McIntire to get to work in another—but she had to be aware of how folks in rural Iowa were used to seeing debris in ditches.

Carefully navigating the ditch's slope, Shane put himself between her riveted gaze and the makeshift body bag. "Why did you decide to stop this morning and check it out?"

Jerking, her gaze flew to his face and stayed there. "I don't know. I guess I'm too nosy for my own good." Her already washed-out features turned gray. "I should have just ignored it and kept driving."

Despite his strict protocol of avoiding physical contact with witnesses, Shane placed his hand on her shaking shoulder. "If you hadn't, maybe no one would have."

Her face crumpled, and tears leaked from her eyes. "It's awful."

Beckoning Murdoch over, Shane patted the woman's arm. "Why don't you go with my deputy, and she'll take your statement. Have you excused yourself from work?"

"Should I?"

"Might be best. I don't think you'll be able to concentrate."

Sniffing, she nodded, and his deputy escorted the commuter toward Murdoch's squad car.

Liza left her post near his truck and approached the edge of the road. "You've got a body?"

He sighed. "I've got a body."

Those golden-brown eyes stared at him expectantly. "Is this something . . . you know, you need . . . assistance with?"

"No, I'll handle it." He dug out a pair of latex-free gloves. "When Doc Drummond arrives, you wouldn't mind pointing him in the right direction?"

"I can do that." She flashed him a bright smile and thumbs up, then scurried back a safe distance, next to his truck, which was blocking the right lane.

Hitching up his fortitude to descend into the ditch, Shane snapped on the gloves. "Let's see who you are." He eased down the grassy slope.

The water was from the all-day rainstorm they'd had three days ago, run-off that hadn't soaked into the ground or evaporated. By the discoloration of the water, there was more in there than normal mud and decayed foliage. He was going to have to wade through that yuck to get to the body. How had the female commuter got only the tips of her shoes wet?

He grunted as the muck soaked through his leather boots and got to his socks. The sickly sweet stench of decomp blasted him. No matter how many years he'd done this job, his long life around livestock and animals, and that brief stint in the military during war, Shane never got past the gross-out factor of death.

Bending at the waist, he fisted a flapping corner that the commuter had dislodged when she made her discovery, and peeled back the heavy-duty plastic. Flies and blowflies took flight. White larva wriggled and wormed their way through the open orifices. Shane shuddered in revulsion. This was the sickest part.

He grabbed quick, swallow breaths, trying not to inhale too much of the nasty fumes, and yanked back the rest of the plastic to fully expose the body. Distended flesh was mottled and purple. Pieces of skin were missing, scavengers having found a way inside to feast. Despite the advancing stages of decomposition, Shane recognized the man trussed up like a corpse from the black plague.

"Shit."

The disturbing aspect to Donovan Frost's corpse, clothed in only a white dress shirt and slacks and missing his shoes, was the similarities to Gene Avery's. Shane would bet his best bucking stock mare that the back of Donovan's head was a crushed mess. The questions of the hour: Were there electric prod marks on his body? And with the state of decomposition on the body, would Doc Drummond be able to find said marks?

"Son of a . . . biscuit."

Shane glanced up at Nash, who had finally arrived.

"Sheriff, no offense, man, but Donovan Frost being dead is not going to go over too well for you."

"That's why I have the county pay you the big bucks, Nash, to state the obvious."

"Just sayin'." Nash crossed his arms over his lean chest. "I'm glad I don't have to be the bearer of bad news to his wife."

For the love of Pete. It would fall on him to corner Pamela and tell her. How wonderfully convenient that he was stuck doing it right after getting into a pissing contest with her over Roslin Avery.

"Take Murdoch with you," Nash said. "She has a knack for calming hysterical women."

"I'll handle it. I don't have to remind any of you to keep Donovan's ID to yourselves. I have to notify Pamela first."

Nash nodded his confirmation.

"We need to block off this road and detour folks to the side roads. Probably going to call in the staties for help, because I want a two-mile radius locked down. No one comes in or out without authorization."

"Only two, sir?"

"Any farther out will require more manpower. Unless we get assistance from the state patrol, we can't go any wider. You have your orders, Deputy."

"On it, sir." Nash took off.

Two bodies in two days, a fire, a whack-nut arsonist, and a venomous snake of an attorney who now had a dead husband, topped off by a tailing FBI agent, all while the anniversary of Cheyenne's death hung over his head. This was shaping up to be a week from hell.

• • •

Liza did her best to stay out of Hamilton's way while he worked. The man kept removing his cowboy hat and treating his scalp to a rough massage. His wet boots had to be uncomfortable, but he acted like he didn't care. So why should she? Because wet socks in wet boots gave one blisters from hell, that's why she cared. Liza was all too familiar with that feeling.

She shouldn't be here alongside the road while he worked a homicide scene. This was way out of her league. Since the warehouse fire and her brief stint with Boyce during the deadly bank robberies, Liza's aversion to murder had tripled. She could put on a brave face, but death, violent death in particular, did not agree with her.

The buzzing in her coat pocket came as a welcomed distraction from her dark thoughts. A text from her SAC.

Oh, joy.

There was no point in dragging this out via messages. Liza put in the call to her supervisor.

"Montrose."

"G'morning, ma'am."

"Agent Bartholomew, I believe I sent you a text asking for an update."

"And I got it, but I thought it best to call and debrief you."

There was some shuffling, and Montrose commanded someone to vacate her office. "I'm waiting."

Pinching the bridge of her nose, Liza resisted the compulsion to sigh. "First off, I was not avoiding you. Things got complicated, quickly."

"Complicated? Would you care to explain to me how things got complicated?"

Gulping down the metallic taste of trepidation, Liza braced for the full impact of SAC Ally Montrose's wrath. "Sorry—"

"Sorry isn't the answer I want from you, Bartholomew. I sent you on this search and recovery operation with strict instructions that you were to do it as quietly as possible. Nowhere in those instructions did I tell you to make a public scene."

"Ma'am, I did as you ordered, but things changed."

"Damn straight they changed. To my complete and utter surprise, I found myself watching a newscast last night that had you at the scene of a house fire."

"Oh God." Face, palm, face, palm. She should have known that the same reporting Quinn had reacted to would be something her SAC would also see.

"God won't help you out of this one. If our suspect has seen this, he's now long gone, and laughing his ass off at you, once again."

"That's just the thing, ma'am, beg your pardon, but I highly doubt that."

"Excuse me?" Montrose's tone would have frozen anything liquid within a mile radius.

"Hear me out. When I arrived in Eider, I discovered that the suspect was dead."

Chirp, chirp.

"You're certain it's him?"

"Eighty-five percent certain. He had plastic surgery, and I was about to confirm what we had on him with the body, but the fire interrupted."

"Attending a house fire is not part of your job description."

"Ma'am, I'm aware of that, but the house on fire was the last known residence of our suspect. It appears his wife went off the rails and intentionally started the fire."

"Wait, back up. A wife?"

"Yes, it was a shock to me as well. I wasn't able to interview her to learn more about my suspect. Unfortunately, her lawyer took the opportunity to block any attempts to question her."

Montrose groaned. This was so not going to dig herself out of the grave.

"What are you doing now?"

Liza's gaze flicked to Hamilton. He was approaching, a little too cautiously. "I'm with the county sheriff at another homicide."

"Bartholomew, that is not your job."

"Yes, I know. I just happened to be around when the call came in."

"And what, pray tell, is your plan?"

Liza had mulled on her next steps most of the night. She'd slept little, despite the exhaustion pulling on her. It didn't help that she worried about Kurt and Quinn, nor could she stop dwelling on Shane Hamilton.

"My plan is simple: confirm that one Gene Avery was our Mr. Ripley, document all I can, and hopefully return tonight."

Hamilton halted inches from her. That sizzling, electrified air returned. He was entirely too close, and too distracting.

"And the wife?" Montrose asked.

"If I heard the sheriff correctly, she's under suspicion for his murder."

Silence reigned supreme once more. Oh to be the psychic gnat on Montrose's shoulder, reading her mind. It probably went along the lines of: *Incapable screw-up. You're never going to make it. You're nothing more than a foster kid who nobody loved or wanted.*

Liza doused the voices of the past. They were wrong. If Montrose wanted to continue to make her pay for one slip-up, there was nothing Liza could do to stop the woman. Once this case was wrapped, Liza was gone.

"Keep to your plan. Get the information you need, and update me as you go. See if you can at least talk with the wife. If the lawyer roadblocks you, let me know. I'll find the right string to pull to get an audience with that woman. I want you on the road by 10 p.m., understood?"

"Completely."

"You have your orders."

"Yes, ma'am."

Dead air met Liza's answer.

Her body slumping against the truck, Liza let the hand holding her iPhone fall to her side. She'd gotten off easy this time, but not by much. If she didn't produce some results and return, she might lose the Ripley case for good, and she couldn't live with herself knowing he got away from her again. Kurt incessantly asked why she'd allowed herself to be pulled into a government entity that mistreated her as badly as the social services that jerked her around as a kid. Why did her foster brother have to be right?

"I take it that was not good news?" Hamilton asked.

"My supervisor is coming down hard on me for messing up my little mission in such a grand fashion. I've been ordered to wrap it up and get back by tonight."

"Oh, boy."

"Putting it mildly." Damn Gene Avery and all his damn aliases. He'd been a piercing thorn in her side since his file first came across her desk, right up until he slipped through her fingers. The stringing her along, the fire he set, killing her witnesses . . . *sigh*. She was nothing more than a screwed-up foster kid in way over her head. "What's next for you?"

Hamilton nodded his head at the black van with Coroner painted on the side panels crawling along the road. "Get Doc Drummond to work on the body and clean up this mess. Do you need to leave?"

"I should if I'm going to meet SAC Montrose's deadline. Do you know the victim?"

"Yes, and I don't relish my next death notice."

Liza's muscles twitched at the nervous energy rolling off of him. This had to reach a whole new level of bad for him.

The van parked beside Hamilton's truck, and Drummond and a younger man exited the vehicle. Hamilton's attention left Liza. She felt the void keenly all the way to her heart.

Now that was going just too far.

"Sheriff," Drummond said, "Agent Bartholomew, pleasure to see you haven't left our little corner of Iowa yet."

She gave him a pleasant smile. The doctor was handsome in his own right, but when compared to the cowboy next to him, it was no contest.

"Not yet. I need to complete my task."

Drummond turned to Hamilton. "Lead the way, Sheriff." The doctor seemed a bit too gleeful to be examining a body left in a ditch.

Before leaving, Hamilton touched her arm. An involuntary shiver coursed through her. If he'd felt it, he didn't act fazed by it, nor did he release her.

God, the things he could do.

"I can have one of my deputies take you back to the station if you like."

If she liked? Hell yes! Anything to avoid seeing the body when it was moved. "If you can spare one, that'd be fine."

He released her arm, and, flicking his wrist, he beckoned someone behind her. "I can spare Murdoch for a bit."

Liza glanced to her left as the young female deputy joined them.

"Sir?"

"Please take Agent Bartholomew back to the station, then come right back."

Hearing him use her professional title was like a pinch in her side after a long run. But why would it matter how he referred to her, especially when they were in a not-so-private situation? Maybe it was because she actually enjoyed hearing her name with his Midwestern twang.

Murdoch nodded, and then headed back to her car.

Liza's gaze met Hamilton's as she turned to follow, making her pause. He gave her a tight smile. This job had taken a toll on him, but there was something darker in that gaze now; something that spoke of terror and sorrow. And her urge to comfort was roaring to the forefront.

"Good luck, Agent." His voice more than his words spoke of finality. He didn't expect to see her after this. And he could be all too right in that regard.

She was going back to Cedar Rapids to put an end to her job in the FBI for good and be the surrogate mom Quinn needed. Suddenly, the thought of not seeing Shane Hamilton again was depressing.

CHAPTER TEN

Miracle of miracles, Liza managed to find the school building where the district office was housed without getting lost in the process. Mark that for the record books. From the outside, the building appeared to be running on a normal Monday schedule. Yet, inside, it looked anything but normal.

Liza gaped at the madhouse. A winding line of parents streamed out of the office and down the hall. Beyond the reinforced glass windows, two harried women tried to appease upset adults and answer the phone that wouldn't stop ringing.

Moving to the small gap between the metal doorframe and a squat, brunette wearing—oh good Lord—pink pajama bottoms with a black hoodie and flip-flops, Liza gave her a pained smile. "Excuse me."

Several pairs of angry eyes turned her way.

"Get in the back of line," the pajama-wearing woman snarled. There was a decidedly condescending lilt to her voice that Liza had heard all her life as an African-American female.

The veiled racism made Liza's blood boil. She itched to slap that tart mouth right off the witch's face. *Be the better person. She's so not worth getting a complaint filed against you.* "I have a scheduled appointment with the principal."

"Don't we all," another person—a man this time—remarked.

Narrowing her gaze, she gave the line a sweep of her authoritative gaze. "While I understand that we all believe our visits with the principal are important, when it comes to legal matters and the law, I hold the trump card."

Pajama Witch gave a derisive snort. "The law. Whatever. I don't see you wearing a uniform."

"Agent Bartholomew?" one of the harried secretaries called out.

"Yes, that's me," Liza said to the confused blinking from the line of stubborn people. She unclipped her badge and held it up against the glass for the secretary to verify.

"Would you *please* move aside so Agent Bartholomew can step inside," said the secretary.

"Who was stupid enough to give *her* a badge?" Pajama Witch muttered.

Oh, they thought they were so clever in their superiority. Liza looked down at the woman. It really paid to be taller than most people.

"The President of the United States and the U.S. legal system. That's who." With that, she brushed past the line and headed around the counter.

She followed the secretary who'd rescued her from the traffic jam down a short hall to the last door. Principal Charles Walker was painted in gold to stand out against the beveled glass of the door. The secretary knocked, then opened the door for Liza. She slipped inside, tensing when the latch clicked shut behind her.

Behind a set of cornered off desks, Charles Walker appeared just as harried and flustered as his secretaries. A pair of horn-rimmed glasses was perched on the top of his balding head, which had a bright sheen that reflected in the weak fluorescent glow. His tweed jacket had long been discarded, and the sleeves of his white dress shirt were rolled to his elbows. And it wasn't yet nine.

"Agent Bartholomew." He rose and held out his hand over his desk.

She grasped his slick appendage, trying desperately not to wipe the greasy feeling off on her pants. Then, at his gestured bidding, she took the sleek leather chair angled at the junction where the two desks met. "Thank you for seeing me, Principal Walker."

"I wish it weren't under the current circumstances." He rubbed his jaw line. "You said over the phone you were investigating Superintendent Avery. May I ask what for?"

"That's actually information I can't reveal."

"What can you tell me?"

"Not much, I'm afraid. Despite his untimely death, the investigation is still an active one."

Principal Walker gaped at her like she was a Hydra head about to eat him. "Then why come here at all?"

"As I said, active investigation. I need to get inside his office."

"You're the FBI. Don't you just go wherever you please and do whatever you want?"

"That's not how it works, Principal Walker. The TV shows and movies don't always get it right."

He slumped back into his chair, letting his arms recline on the desktop. "Oh." A tick started above his right eyebrow. He reached up to rub at it, but the tick kept a steady pace. If that's how fast his heart was beating, did the good principal have something to hide?

Liza eased to the edge of her seat. Spooking this guy was the last thing she wanted to happen. "I understand that you're under a lot of pressure right now. And there's a long line of parents who aren't very happy out there."

He released a cynical laugh. "Happy? What you ran into out there are the same parents who'd scream for a lawyer if their ice cream gave them brain freeze."

Oh, Mr. Principal, tell me how you really feel.

"I deal with some of that bunch on a daily basis, because they have nothing better to do than to harass me about their kids' entitlements. While that . . ."—his face turned beet red—"blockhead kissed their asses and allowed them to get whatever they wanted. You want new playground equipment at the elementary, sure, I'll see to that. School meals don't appease your kid's appetite, how about we offer seventeen choices in the lunch line? And who had to clean up after the fallout when none of this stuff happened?" Walker slapped a hand against the desktop. "Me, that's who. They hate me, and they want to see me burned at the stake."

"What kind of fallout are we talking about?"

"The kind that cost the district money it barely had in the first place. We're looking at severe funding shortages for the next school year, and it's left on my shoulders to work with the school board to figure out what to do. That could mean some teachers not having jobs."

Now we're cooking. "Is there anything else?"

He blinked as if confused, then his features sagged in defeat. "Every promise Avery made to those parents and the district is exploding in my face. I can't tell those people that there won't be any new uniforms for the sports programs. The parking lot will never be repaved. And the equipment for the science and math department is nothing more than a defunct idea."

"Principal Walker, if I may, how does that put the district in a shortage of funds? I'm mostly ignorant of how school budgets and funding work. But, aren't most of those things you mentioned fundraiser projects from the community?"

The man gave her a hard stare. "That's exactly what they are, Agent Bartholomew. The money the community and parents have raised is gone." He pointed at his door. "And once the public learns about it, all hell is going to break loose."

• • •

Despite their best efforts to circumvent Shane's roadblock, he managed to keep the drivers of McIntire County away from the site of Donovan's makeshift grave. Doc Drummond and his assistant had loaded the body and transported it out of the area. The last four hours of evidence collection and walking the whole two-mile area around the dump site left Shane feeling drained.

And the worst was yet to come.

What he wouldn't give right now to hear Liza's voice. She had a soothing quality that made him less likely to bite someone's head off.

Shane tracked down Pamela Frost at her office, a block off the town square. She'd chosen a prime location, and a pricey one. With the redevelopment of the square, rental prices for buildings around the town's star attraction would run the renter into the thousands depending on location, location, location. With the way she ruthlessly defended her clients and charged them for her services, Pamela could afford the cushy little office right beside a popular coffee and bakery shop.

The warm, yeasty aroma of freshly baked bread made Shane's stomach howl its protest at missing lunch. A stop for one of the bakery's roast beef and smoked provolone sandwiches on toasted sourdough bread was in order. After he delivered the devastating news. He'd need all the comfort food he could get after this.

A digital doorbell chimed his entry into Pamela's office. Shane removed his Resistol and hooked it over his right hand. The receptionist's chair was empty, but Emily Schofield's distinct Oklahoman drawl came from down the short hall leading to the back of the office space. Pamela's receptionist had met and married Derek Schofield while he attended Oklahoma State. Somehow Derek convinced Emily to move to Eider so he could help run the family farm. Derek's father was one of those men people loathed behind his back and smiled to his face. But the kicker of the year? Derek's mother, Annabeth, managed to land a spot on the school board. No one wanted her, but when she was the only option, what could you do?

It was no secret Emily despised her in-laws; she made it plain as the nose on her face. If the gossip mill was to be believed, Emily was trying to get Derek to convince his father to sell their debt-riddled farm. She wanted to move back to Oklahoma. None of it proved to be working.

While he waited for someone to realize he was here, Shane examined the photos strategically placed on the walls between some high-falutin' artwork. The pictures were mostly of Pamela and some of her prominent connections in McIntire County and Des Moines. There wasn't a single photo of her and Donovan. Maybe she'd left those for her actual private office.

The conversation from the back stalled. Shane took the opportunity.

"Pamela, it's Sheriff Hamilton."

Fifteen seconds later, the door at the end of the hall opened, and Emily emerged, followed by her boss. Pamela appeared just as coiffed and professional as she had that morning when she barged in demanding he release her client. Emily, with her wheat-colored hair and tall, athletic build, wore curve- hugging black slacks and a flowing turquoise blouse. The Oklahoman looked like she wanted to chew leather and spit bullets.

Uh-oh, everything in paradise wasn't peachy keen. 'Course, working for Pamela Frost had to be the furthest thing from paradise.

"Sheriff Hamilton, if this is about our conversation this morning, I believe that was officially settled with the judge."

"For now it's settled. But no, this is a different matter. Could we speak in your office?"

With an eye twitch—or was it more of a hidden eye roll?—Pamela sighed and gestured for him to lead the way. He moved past the receptionist's desk as Emily stiffly took her seat.

Pamela, who had been watching him this whole time, narrowed her gaze. Shane did his best to keep a passive face, and headed down the hall to her sanctum.

Pamela closed the door and rounded her gleaming black desk. "Why are you here, Sheriff?"

"When was the last time you spoke with your husband?"

Elegantly propping herself against a matching bookshelf loaded with law books and placed under a window, she crossed one arm across her abdomen and rested the elbow of the other on her wrist to tuck the upright hand under her jaw. "I'd say it was a few days ago."

"Could you be specific? How many days ago?"

The cold, calculating eyes turned wary. "Is there a point to this, *Sheriff*?" The emphasis on his title sounding as belittling as she typically made it.

Ironic. She had been the one to push her husband to run against him in the election. Yet, she acted like a civil servant was below her station in life. This coming from a woman who defended the very people she disdained.

"There is a point, Mrs. Frost."

The upright hand settled into the crook of her reclining elbow. "The exact time was four days ago. It was the day he left for a weekend conference."

"Where was this conference?"

"In Kansas City."

"What was the conference for?"

Pamela huffed. "Sheriff, these are tedious questions. What is your point?"

"Did you speak to him at any time over the weekend?" Ignoring her pushback was the only way he'd get what he wanted.

Her silence was . . . admirable. However, in his lifetime, Shane had long learned to out-stare, out-think, and outmaneuver any and all opponents, whether they be bronc, enemy combatant, or criminal.

"No," she finally said. "When he goes to those mindless conferences, it's to get away from me."

"I ask again, what was the conference for?"

Pamela shifted her shoulders, then rose from her perch. "It was an agricultural trade conference. Satisfied?"

"When was he due to arrive home?"

"Not until late this evening. This line of questioning has gone on long enough, Sheriff. What is your point?"

Shane looked down at his hat, studied its swoops and curves, the tightly woven weave of the white straw. No use putting it off any longer. He met her irritated gaze. Too bad Donovan was dead—a man Shane had felt no ill will toward—but hell, he'd like to strangle the guy for leaving him with this task. He sighed.

"Pamela, I came here to inform you . . ." He swallowed hard. "Donovan is no longer with us."

Her frown deepened the permanent scowl lines around her eyes and mouth. "What is that supposed . . . oh, good God." Her eyes widened. "He's dead?"

"I'm sorry."

She stood rooted, gaping at him. One hand reached out, patting for the chair in front of her, connected with the top, and then pulled the chair closer. Her normal stiff elegance fled as she flopped into the seat.

"H-how?"

"We're not certain."

She lost her stunned look. "What is that supposed to mean?"

"Pamela, we discovered his body in a ditch. Here in McIntire County."

Her features paled, the makeup giving her a sickly yellow appearance. "That's not possible. He was in Kansas City."

"I don't think he made it."

His other words must have hit home. She mumbled *body* and *ditch*. "Wait. Are you saying . . .? Was he . . .?"

"Pamela, we think he was murdered."

Shane didn't think it was a possible, but her eyes widened further. She bolted out of the chair, slamming her hand on the desk.

"Get out!"

"Pamela."

"I said, get out!"

With a slight nod, he rotated on the heel of his boots and, donning his hat, headed out the door. He made it as far as Emily's desk when a scream and the crash of something breakable made him flinch. Emily shot up out of her chair, but Shane held out a hand.

"I wouldn't right this minute. Let her wind down before going in there."

She gave a wobbly head wag then sank into her seat once again. Her gaze lingered on him a moment and then shifted to the hallway as multiple muffled thumps came from the back office.

It was no secret around Eider that Pamela was ruthless, but she hadn't crossed Shane as a hothead who'd lose it after getting upsetting news. First Roslin burning her home to the ground and now Pamela destroying her office, both over the deaths of their husbands. What had gotten into the professional women of McIntire County?

Neither woman reacted normally. Not even he had lost his marbles when the ER doctor gave him the horrible news that Cheyenne was gone. Shane went numb inside, but he didn't cry. He'd stared at the doctor, trying to wrap his head around what the man had told him. Even during her funeral, Shane hadn't shown any emotion. His world had been a block of ice.

At the next violent outburst from Pamela, both he and Emily shuddered. It was time to go. There was nothing more he could glean from Pamela.

Another scream and a *thunk* followed him out the door. Good God Almighty, he needed that sandwich now, with a jolt of pure caffeine.

CHAPTER ELEVEN

Nothing. Not a damn thing in this office to prove Gene Avery was stealing money. Or who he actually was.

Liza slapped the leather portfolio against the desktop. Pushing away from the knee hole, she spun the chair to face the three-panel window.

"Where'd you stash your reports, Ripley?" *Please not in the house your* wife *burned down.*

She had jack squat in physical evidence that the man known as Gene Avery had taken any of the money that had been given to the school for his pet projects. There had been money, of that Liza had proof. Principal Walker had the secretary who handled incoming funds give her copies of all the receipts given to the parents and community that donated money. But neither one of the secretaries knew where all that cash had gone after it had supposedly been turned over to the accountant.

The accountant was not available for questioning until tomorrow.

Outside, birds flitted from the tree branches to the flower garden below them, pecking for insect meals. The bright spring morning had turned gray and cloudy, the promise of more rain to come. Had Shane and crew finished up at their crime scene? The shower could cause more problems than he already had.

The investigator in her was curious to know who they found in the ditch. And did it have any connection to Gene Avery, a.k.a. Mr. Ripley?

She turned from the view at the sound of a tap on tempered glass. The office door opened a crack, and the secretary who had escorted Liza to the principal's office poked her head in.

"Sorry to interrupt you, Agent Bartholomew, but the school board president is here, and he wants to meet with you."

Yay! One less person to track down. "That's fine. Show him in."

Liza gathered the portfolio and file folders she had scattered across the desk and tucked them inside the banker's box on the floor by her feet. A creak of hinges was all the warning she had to straighten before a tall man with dark-brown hair and deep brown eyes entered. He wore khaki slacks and a light blue polo with brown business loafers.

He gave her a tight smile as he held out his hand. "Agent Bartholomew? I'm Neil Lundy."

Liza rose and gripped his hand—smooth palm but roughened fingers; a man who worked, but kept himself professionally presentable. "Thank you for coming to see me, Mr. Lundy. You were, in fact, next on my list to speak with." She pointed at the chair opposite her.

He settled in the squeaky pleather chair. "Principal Walker called me at work and asked me to come meet with you. I'm extremely baffled that an FBI agent is here investigating our deceased superintendent."

"Correct me if I'm wrong, but the sheriff informed me that the school board had recently become suspicious of Mr. Avery and a case of missing funds?"

"Yes, that's true, but we haven't even begun to investigate the matter ourselves. Our school accountant has been sick the past week and a half. Once she returned, we were going to review the books."

"If it's all the same to you, I'd rather have our accountants from the Bureau do the job. They're better equipped to find irregularities that a normal accountant won't."

Mr. Lundy's frown deepened. "FBI accountants? Which brings me back to my original question: why on earth is the FBI here?"

Liza knew her subterfuge would eventually irritate then anger anyone involved with Avery, but the integrity of her case was at stake here, and the last thing she needed was gossip flying and more evidence hidden or destroyed. Her ass was already walking a tightrope with Montrose.

"I apologize, Mr. Lundy, but I'm not at liberty to reveal my true reasons for being here. Those in the know have already been informed."

"Meaning the sheriff and the police department." The strained tone of his voice set off a tinkling bell in the back of Liza's head.

"Yes, the proper authorities."

Lundy leaned forward. "Then what would be the purpose of you meeting with me?"

Try to assert any authority you want, dear sir, but it'll get you nowhere but on my bad side. "For you to give the authorization to hand over any and all accounts that have school funding."

"Are you out of your mind? The state would have my head if I did that."

"And the state has given me the right to request them. If you'd like, I could get a warrant to make it official and save you the trouble of having to explain yourself to the community."

The agitation fled. Lundy fidgeted, running one hand along his pant leg. "Well, we should follow proper procedure. Get the warrant, and I'll make sure you have the access you need." He shot up from the chair. "I should return to work."

"Certainly, by all means. I'll have the warrant here within the hour. Where is it that you work?"

"At Thayer Lotts engineering firm."

That would be on a city street, which meant Siri could lead her right to it. "Would you prefer I call you?"

Lundy rammed his hand into his back pocket, and after some rummaging, pulled out a wallet and then a business card. "Call that number. I'll meet up with you."

Taking the card, Liza gave him a relaxed smile. The man about-faced and stiff-walked to the door.

He paused before opening the door and turned to her. "Just a word of caution, Agent Bartholomew, since you're not familiar with our town. People talk a lot around here, and not all of it is true. The school has had a lot of problems in the past, and we're trying to prevent any further incidents that would cause harm to the district's reputation. Please exercise extreme care with what you're doing."

"Rest assured, Mr. Lundy, I will do everything to be most discreet. However, I'm somewhat aware of how things happen around Eider and McIntire County, and I can't guarantee that someone, somewhere, hasn't already made their own conclusions and started talking."

His nostrils flared, but the man remained mute. He gave her a curt nod and then showed himself out the door.

Once she was certain he was long gone, Liza pulled out the iPhone and brought up Montrose's number. The SAC answered on the fourth ring.

"Status, Bartholomew?"

"Still digging, ma'am. Seems Mr. Ripley did a fine job of covering his tracks here. I'm afraid the fire might have destroyed what I need."

"He probably learned his lesson from the last time and secured his chances of never getting caught."

"Well, he didn't do as fine of a job if he got killed."

Montrose sighed. "Pursue that avenue. See what you can learn about his death and who might have had a hand in it. And talk to the wife. She's connected more than we know."

"Yes, ma'am. I also called to request a fast track for a warrant. The school board president is being a stickler. I'm not sure which had him more flustered, that I mentioned a potentially bad rap with the community or that I pushed to see the state of the district's finances."

"Small-town people don't like their dirty laundry aired for the world to see."

Don't I know it. "Ma'am, if I may, could I have information pulled up on a . . . " Liza looked closely at the business card, "Neil J. Lundy, civil engineer at the Thayer Lotts firm?"

"Your reason?"

"Something about him feels off to me. I just want to ease my mind."

"I'll see what I can do. I'll have that warrant for you within the next half hour or so."

"Thank you."

"Don't thank me yet. You wrap it up down there and get back. Your former partner did enough damage to the FBI image in that county. I don't need any more."

The typical silence followed Montrose's final orders. Liza stashed her phone and glanced down at the banker's box. It was going with her. Avery-Ripley had to leave some kind of clue behind. Grabbing the evidence off the floor, she vacated the chair and tucked the box under her arm.

Pursue Ripley's death. Oh joy.

Still, if that's the route Montrose wanted her to go, it meant another encounter with Shane Hamilton.

That in and of itself was worth jumping into a homicide investigation.

CHAPTER TWELVE

Shane stared, dumbfounded, at the dashboard. He had returned to the department to hide out in the back lot to eat his sandwich and savor his coffee. Lunch started to slosh around in his stomach. "Come again?"

"I repeat," Doc Drummond said over their phone connection, "Donovan Frost was dead before Gene Avery. The insects can tell us more, but after the quick assessment from the forensic entomologist expert at DCI, she says the larvae are about four days old, and that was going off what she could see of the larvae through video chat. Once she has them in her possession, she can give me an exact timeline. Either way, Donovan has been dead longer than Gene."

"Yet both men exhibit the same exact markings and causes of death?"

"Short answer, yes."

Shane dug his stubbed fingernails into his scalp. "I'd hate to hear your long answer."

"I could give it."

"No," Shane barked. "I'm fine with what you've told me. Thanks for the info."

"Do you want me to call you on your cell if I find any anomalies?" Drummond asked.

"Yeah. I still have no idea where I'll be at any given point today."

"Will do. By the way, is Agent Bartholomew with you?"

"No," Shane drew the word out. "Why?"

"I think I have a break in her case. Do you have a way to contact her?"

"Maybe."

The crunch of gravel under rubber drifted through the open window. Shane twisted in his seat. An Eider police squad car rounded the corner of the building and parked haphazardly next to his truck. Through the tinted window, Shane made out Con's form before his friend opened the door.

"Doc, I've gotta go. I'll let Agent Bartholomew know you want to talk with her."

"Got it."

Ending the call, Shane set his phone aside. Unlocking his stiff muscles took some work, but he managed to push past the aches and pains and climb out of his truck. He met Con as the detective rounded the tailgate.

"Heard through the grapevine you've got another homicide," the Irishman said.

"Please tell me you don't know who it is."

Con shook his head, hooking an arm over the side of the truck bed. "It's why I'm here. The police chief decided I was a safe bet right now to have that discussion with you."

"Because he's not on friendly terms with me since the election?"

Con lifted a shoulder. Noncommittal answer. Yep, all the answer Shane needed.

Word got around that the police chief let it slip to the wrong person that he wasn't all that impressed with Shane's performance as sheriff and someone more capable was needed. This coming the day before the election. Shane wasn't the type to let something so trivial bother him, but when it came from a man who was supposed to be working alongside him as an ally, it burned. Normally he'd ignore it, but three days after his reinstatement as sheriff, an unexpected encounter with the chief at the courthouse led to an exchange of words and Shane pushing the man into a wall.

"I regret nothing," Shane muttered.

"I'd expect nothing less from you." Con sighed. "Doesn't make this any easier." He squinted at the department. "Is Agent Bartholomew here?"

"She's trying to wrap up her case and get back to Cedar Rapids. Why?"

"Aw, no reason." Con clapped Shane's shoulder. "Now, about that homicide."

"Let's not have this conversation out here."

They entered the building through the back and headed for Shane's office. Halfway there, the front door opened, and she walked in.

Shane came to a screeching halt, gaping as she bypassed the always vacant receptionist counter and paused long enough to catch sight of him.

"Liza, did you forget something?"

"Don't for one second think I didn't notice that, boyo," Con whispered.

"Can it," Shane said.

He gave Liza a pained smile as she joined them. She frowned for point zero two seconds at that.

"I thought I wouldn't need to return here, but it seems Gene Avery made certain I wouldn't find even a crumb. I'm following up on his death and seeing where that leads. Also, I was hoping I could make contact with Roslin's attorney, at least see if I could speak with the woman."

"Getting a hold of Pamela right now will be problematic," Shane said.

"Why, pray tell, is that?" Liza asked.

He gestured at his office. Both Liza and Con stepped inside, with Shane bringing up the rear and closing them inside his sanctuary. None of them sat. Taking up his position behind his desk, Shane faced the two.

"First, Pamela is in no state to be dealing with her duties as an attorney. I gave her a death notice a few hours ago."

"Saints alive," Con muttered, "you're not saying . . .?"

"The body recovered this a.m. was Donovan Frost."

Con followed up that statement with a colorful spiel in Gaelic.

"It gets better," Shane interrupted. "His death appears to be exactly like Gene Avery's."

"You've got to be kidding me," Liza said.

Shaking his head, Shane picked up a pen and twirled it between his fingers.

"There's more?" Liza asked.

"Donovan was killed before Gene. Almost three days before."

Liza sank into the chair. "Unbelievable."

"Are you insinuating there's a connection between the two men's deaths?" Con asked.

"Doc Drummond swears on the Bible that both men were bludgeoned to death. The size of the holes is nearly identical, which could mean the same weapon. He located bruising from the suspected electric prod on Donovan's back, even through all the lividity and decomp."

"We have to find a connection to these two men," Con said.

"We don't have to look far," Liza said. "Frost's wife is Roslin's attorney."

"But for how long? If I'm reading it right, this popped up overnight when Roslin burned her home to the ground," Shane said. "Besides, that doesn't connect the two men. Donovan had nothing to do with the school, so there was no reason for Avery to run into him through that channel."

"We have to tear their lives apart." Liza sighed. "There's no way I'm going to make Montrose's deadline now."

"You don't have to stick around for all of that."

"Shane, I do. If there is any connection between them, then whoever killed them might have the evidence I need to prove

Gene Avery is my Mr. Ripley. Far as I'm concerned, that takes priority over meeting some ungodly deadline."

And this is what it boiled down to for her: getting her man. Not that two people were dead. This was why Shane took issue with the FBI. There was a callousness to the agents who came to his county. They didn't care about the people who lived here, or the repercussions their visits left behind that he dealt with. McIntire County was his home, the good and the bad, and he wasn't about to let Liza Bartholomew plow through here like a pissed off cow destroying fences. He worked hard to mend those fences.

"Okay," Con's voice shattered the silence, "just so we're on the same page here. Agent Bartholomew, would you explain exactly what it is that has brought you here?"

She opened her mouth and then clicked it shut. Her features were a mix of indecision and stubbornness. Apparently it was one thing to tell Shane everything she could, but another when it came to revealing her true mission to someone else.

But if she didn't tell Con, he would. This subterfuge was pointless, considering the fact that Con had it mostly figured out.

Her deep brown eyes landed on Shane and didn't waver, as if she sensed his sudden shift in loyalties.

When had his loyalties changed tracks? The safety and well-being of the people of McIntire County had always come first. It's why he'd won this last hard-fought election. The public knew he was looking out for them, despite the gossips who talked just to hear their own voices.

Agent Bartholomew, on the other hand, was only a temporary distraction. And, boy, how she had distracted him. Shane was a Grade A prime idiot. The ring burned against his skin, a reminder of what he'd lost and what he'd vowed. Cheyenne had been his everything; no woman could replace her.

"You might as well tell him," he said. "The sooner we get through it, the sooner we can figure this out."

Liza closed her eyes. Her shoulders slumped, the weight seeming to drag her down. When she opened her eyes, they were focused on Con.

An electrified zap burned across Shane's chest. *Stupid, stupid emotions.*

Gradually, she walked Con through her case, pausing to answer his pointed questions, until she was up to the point where she'd arrived in Eider yesterday only to learn that her potential suspect might be the one and same deceased Gene Avery.

"That would explain the school board's sudden panic. They were duped by a career conman," Con said.

"Speaking of the school board, the president came to see me," Liza said as she rifled through her coat pocket, pulling out a business card. "Neil Lundy."

Shane whistled. "Now ain't that something. Neil Lundy came to you?"

Liza frowned. "Why is that such a big deal?"

"Lundy thinks pretty highly of himself. If you want an audience with him, you typically make an appointment. The fact that he sought you out tells me he's worried. Really worried."

"He should be," Con said. "The entire board was hoodwinked, and Lundy's the fall guy in this case if it gets out that Gene Avery was not a legit superintendent."

"The perfect Mr. Lundy will now be over the coals for the whole county to roast." Shane shouldn't feel giddy at the thought of that egotistical man being gutted and fileted like that, but sometimes karma was a bitch. "I have a feeling there will be a major switching of the guard in the next school board election."

"That explains Lundy's advisement to me to keep this whole ordeal discreet," Liza said.

"Too late for that." Con pointed at her. "I've already fielded a few questions from 'concerned' citizens. Seems some remember you from the last time you were here."

"I did warn him it was too late for discreet. He didn't take that too well."

"We need to arrange a meeting with the entire board. Think we can pull them together early this evening without a battle?" Shane asked, Con specifically.

"That's being arranged as we speak," Liza said.

Both men frowned at her.

"How? you ask with your faces." She checked her watch. "I should be receiving confirmation that my warrant request has been approved and the paperwork will be here soon."

"Well, isn't that interesting," Shane said. "A warrant can be a real motivator."

"Especially with that lot." Con slapped his thigh. "I've done my due diligence. Should get back to the department and debrief the chief before he starts calling. When you get the board together, tell me, and I'll help with the interviews."

"Appreciate the assist." Shane watched his friend leave the office. Once Con's footsteps faded, Shane's gaze swept back to Liza. "What's next for you?"

"I was hoping to have a lengthy chat with Dr. Drummond."

"That would be perfect, since he requested that I let you know he needs to talk with you. Seems he might have a break in your case."

Her features lit up, making her eyes spark. "Good." She turned as if to leave, halted, and then faced him once more. "About Pamela and Roslin?"

"Let me see what I can do. If Roslin's willing, she could force Pamela to allow her an audience with you. Learning that her husband was dead set off Pamela something fierce, but she's always been a lawyer first."

"Roslin is the only solid lead I have to Avery. My SAC is insistent I speak with her, and I tend to agree. Let me know as soon as you set something up." She headed for the door.

He fought the urge to let his gaze drink in the sight of her swaying hips, but it was a losing battle. He couldn't do this. Damn it. They both had a job to do, and the moment she completed hers, she was gone.

"Liza?" *You damn fool!*

She paused outside the doorway and turned back to him. "Yes?"

"What are you going to tell your SAC?"

She seemed puzzled by his question.

"The deadline she set. What are you going to tell her?"

"Oh." She shrugged. "I'm fairly certain once I tell her I've got some compelling evidence that keeps me here, she'll have to reconsider."

If her SAC did reconsider, it meant a few more encounters with Agent Bartholomew. That was good and bad. Good, because it gave him a chance to explore this inexplicable urge to be near her and to get to know her a bit more. Bad, because he shouldn't want to be near her and get to know her more.

If his past was any dire warning, satisfying his curiosity was never good for the county or his job status.

CHAPTER THIRTEEN

For six miles, a small gray-silver SUV had been tailing Liza. She hadn't noticed it when she first left the sheriff's office, but a few miles out she got an odd, creepy crawly feeling up the back of her neck that led to her glancing in the rearview mirror more often than not. It wasn't following real close, like some drivers were apt to do, just hung back the recommended two car lengths. Yet with every turn she made, the SUV turned as well. She couldn't see the driver, couldn't get any details of who it might be. And the vehicle itself was simply an SUV, the same type of automobile any soccer mom or middle-aged professional man would drive.

She shouldn't be worried about a tail. It's not like she was in some spy movie where every vehicle held a potential threat. This was Eider, Iowa, for God's sake. But there was a killer out there. Someone had taken the lives of two men. That alone set her senses on high alert.

In reality, she was seeing shadows where there were none.

So, let's test the theory.

Instead of taking the street Siri suggested to get to the hospital, Liza drove past it and headed down a hill. The SUV stayed on the same path with her. After driving another half mile, she slowed to turn left onto a street heading toward the epicenter of downtown. Siri was having fits. Liza sped forward, glancing in the mirror. The SUV didn't follow but continued straight, and she lost sight of it in a small grove of trees lining a yard.

"Okay, so you were being paranoid. Good one, Liza. See what happens when you see things that aren't there?"

At the next stoplight, she headed left for a roundabout way back to the hospital. This was a beautiful side street that spiked off the town square. Like sentinels on watch, black, ornate streetlights decorated with hanging flower baskets bursting in red, blue, and white flowers lined the sidewalk in front of shops and business. Art deco clashed with Victorian era, but all showed the buildings' histories. Most of her views in Cedar Rapids were more modern buildings that were plain and boring to her eye. Maybe one of these shops would have that one spectacular rock she could take back to Quinn. Liza's gaze swept across the mirror, and she stiffened.

There it was. The same SUV.

Or was it?

"Damn it, Liza, knock it off. There could be fifty cars like that in this town."

Yeah, right.

She slowed and took another side street, zipping past a three-story building that looked suspiciously like apartments. Her perceived tail followed.

"Okay, maybe I'm not paranoid. Screw this." She needed to get to the hospital, and messing around on the streets would only get her lost.

If the person tailing her followed her right into the parking lot, she'd do the sensible thing and confront the little prick. Siri was recalibrating and happily announced that at the next street Liza should turn and she'd arrive at her destination. She drove the suggested distance and whipped into the hospital parking lot, all the while keeping an eye on the vehicle in her rearview mirror. Liza found a spot facing the street and parked.

To her utter shock and relief, the gray car continued on its merry little way down the street and out of sight. All she was able to see of the driver through tinted windows was a shadowy form.

Liza waited. Her body hummed; the nervous energy left a metallic taste in her mouth. Crap! She'd bit her cheek. Gently sucking the blood from the small cut, she watched.

The car never returned. Liza sagged against her seat. Her muscles slowly unwound. She'd been tenser than she expected. This! This was what she hated about this job. She was always on alert, and her body was wearing down from the constant tension. "I'm so done with this."

Now that that little excursion was over, she had to get back to the job at hand. She'd keep her eyes peeled for the car when she came outside. Hopefully, whatever Dr. Drummond had for her was something she could report back to Montrose to get out of the unreasonable deadline and this town. Liza hadn't experienced this much suspense—if she discounted the warehouse fire and going after Ripley—in the entirety of her career in the FBI. Eider, Iowa was one weird place.

The same gray-haired woman who had put Shane in his place yesterday was on duty as Liza stepped through the sliding glass doors.

"Good day, Ms. Bartholomew."

"You remembered my name?" She glanced at the attendant's nametag. Gladys Higgins.

The woman's shrewd gaze held Liza's as she tapped her temple. "This brain doesn't forget. Especially when you arrived here with our bachelor sheriff."

Liza's face heated to unbearable levels. Clearing her throat, she broke eye contact with the help-desk attendant. "That's not why we came together."

"Oh, I know you were here to see that body in the morgue. Only reason the sheriff would have come to the hospital. Well, one of the reasons."

Gulping, Liza's throat managed to slip free of its shackles. "I came to see Dr. Drummond. He's expecting me."

Mrs. Higgins reached around to snag a visitor's tag and passed it over the countertop. "Do you know where you're going?"

"To the morgue?" Liza asked as she clipped the tag to her coat lapel.

"Actually, he should be in his office." Mrs. Higgins stood and shuffled over to a floor plan display board. She pointed at an orange-hued floor plan. "Take the elevator up to fourth floor. Hang a left out of elevator bay, and go five doors down. His is the one on the right side of the hall." She turned to Liza. "Got that?"

Giving the older lady a thumbs up, Liza headed for the elevators.

"Ms. Bartholomew."

She paused and peered at the woman over her shoulder. "Yes?"

"Our sheriff is a man of many talents, but he's been alone for a long time. Think long and hard about that."

What in the world does she think she saw going on between Shane and me? "Again, Mrs. Higgins, it's not that kind of situation."

A sly smile pulled at the corners of the woman's mouth. "Sure." She turned back to her duties as the doors whooshed open again.

Liza bolted for the elevator bay. She lucked out as one emptied its passengers. Slipping inside, she punched the number four then tucked herself into a corner. A nurse in vibrant scrubs joined her, pressing the two button. Once the doors glided closed, Liza relaxed against the adjoining walls.

It was one thing for her to entertain thoughts about Shane Hamilton. It was a whole different ballgame when someone else voiced them. How had that Mrs. Higgins come up with the idea she and Shane could be a couple? Ever? It was crazy.

The elevator stopped, and the nurse exited on her floor. The faint sound of a baby's lusty wail brought to mind the memories of Quinn as a tiny bundle. Before his precious little brain altered. Before his parents' world was turned upside down by a diagnosis that changed everything. The doors slid shut, cutting her off from the maternity ward.

Liza relieved her jacket pocket of her iPhone. Thank God for the geniuses at her wireless network who managed to give her great coverage. Tapping the call icon, she pulled up Kurt's name and put the call through.

He answered on the fifth ring. "Is this you calling to tell me you're on your way back?"

"Not quite. I was checking on you and Q. How'd he do last night?"

"He punched me when I tried to wrap his hand. I think he broke a bone this time; it's all bruised and swollen."

"Did you take him to the doctor yet?"

"I got an appointment this afternoon. He's pacing the floor by the front door."

The elevator dinged. "Will he let me talk to him at least?"

Kurt sighed, then said in a lowered voice, "Liza, I got a call from my company. They're moving up my ship-out date."

She halted at the edge of the elevator bay. "To when?"

"Next Monday."

Stiffening, she turned to put her back to the hallway. "Why that early?"

"The powers that be were able to green-light all the permits and crap, and they want us to get going now before certain people in certain positions change their minds."

"Where are you going?"

"South Dakota."

"South . . . Are you going where I think you're going?"

Kurt's silence was deafening.

"Kurt, you'll be there for months."

"Liza, I'm sorry, but I have no say."

She slammed the side of her fist into her thigh. "Your child should have all the say in the world right now. You can't leave him for that long."

"Do you think I want to? Do you think this is easy for me? Damn it, Liza, if his medical bills weren't piling up a mile a minute, I'd leave that job in a heartbeat and do something else. But I can't afford to."

"There are other jobs that pay just as well."

"Not for an ex-foster kid with nothing to show for his life except some crummy military service and dirty fingernails. Not all of us were as lucky as you to get a college education and a chance to kiss the government's ass."

In the background there was a large crash.

"Sonofabitch! Quinn!"

"Kurt, what happened?"

"Liza, I've got to go."

"Kurt—?" Nothing.

This was too much. Kurt had stipulated with the oil company that he couldn't be gone for long periods of time or leave the state of Iowa. This was horrible. Horrible.

"Is everything all right?"

Her body convulsed. Gasping, she turned, coming face to face with Dr. Drummond. "Good Lord, you scared me."

"Apologies. I didn't mean to."

Her heart back to its normal rhythm, she put her phone away and wrapped herself in a cloak of professionalism. "That's okay. I was taking a personal call."

"I could sense that. Is it something serious?"

She pasted on a false smile. "It's being handled. Uh, weren't we meeting in your office?"

"Mrs. Higgins called to let me know you were coming, and when you didn't arrive at the expected moment, I came looking for you. I wondered if you were lost."

"She sure does like to call ahead."

Drummond beamed. "I think I'm the only one she does that with. I haven't heard of any other doctors in the hospital getting the same special treatment." He looked up and down the hall. "Let's step into my office. Unless you'd rather go to the morgue."

"No, that's okay. One trip to see a dead body in the last twenty-four hours is enough for me."

He beckoned for her to follow. Liza composed herself during the trip down the hall. Right now, Kurt and his problems would have to wait. Damn it, she had to wrap this case. Confirm Ripley was Avery, find the money, write this whole affair off, and be done with it. If Kurt couldn't get his shit together, Liza had to think about the better good for Quinn.

As Mrs. Higgins had directed, Drummond's office was five doors down and on the right. Drummond allowed her to enter first, and then he shut them inside. His office was spacious and bright, with wide, four-paneled windows making up the whole of the south-facing wall. The windows were double paned with the shades between the panes, currently half drawn to let in a minimal amount of natural light. Drummond sat behind his small desk with his back to the windows. The desk was one of those new contraptions where the user could raise it up to stand or lower it to sit.

"I don't think I've seen one of these desks before," she said as she took a seat in a comfy armchair.

"Being a doctor, I spend a lot of my time on my feet anyway, so it seemed logical to get a standing desk." He riffled through a stack of charts and files on a cabinet next to his desk and pulled out the desired file. "I was going over my autopsy on Gene Avery again. In fact, I've done it several times now since discovering the plastic surgery scars." He pulled out x-ray films and rolled his chair over to a small viewer, propping the film into a clip. "He has done extensive facial reconstruction, more than once."

He flipped on the viewer, the bright light highlighting the film. Liza leaned forward in her seat and studied the x-ray of Ripley's skull.

Drummond pointed at the hairline marks along the forehead and the nose bridge, and then traced similar marks along the cheekbones. "Do you see those?"

"Yes. It does explain why we've had a hard time catching him, and why none of our witnesses were able to pick him out."

"That's not all." Drummond removed the film and pulled out another, clipping it to the viewer. "Do you see it?"

Squinting, Liza studied the image of the side of Ripley's skull. There was a small strip of black on the backside of his jawbone. "What's that?"

Grinning, Drummond switched that film with another, that showed the back of Ripley's skull. Liza's eyes widened.

"A serial number?"

"Yep. That part of his jaw was not actually real. With all the surgery he had done, I didn't notice it at first. At some point in his life, he had that portion of his jaw replaced. That serial number is your key to finding out who did it and if they have any records on him."

"Doc, you're good."

Drummond grinned. "Hold on, it gets better." He rolled away from his x-ray viewer. Flipping through his autopsy file, he produced a single sheet of paper. "Your man had hepatitis C."

Her hand froze halfway to taking the page from him. "Wait, what?"

"If my prelim is right—I'll know for certain once the full results come back—Gene Avery had hep C. Whether he knew it, it's hard to say. But his liver was showing signs of inflammation, and it led me to check."

A chill raced through Liza. She'd touched the body. With a glove on, but still, she'd touched Ripley's body. "Please tell me you made sure you didn't get any—"

"Please, Agent Bartholomew, I'm a stickler for procedure. There was no chance anyone was getting it in my morgue."

"But his wife might have it."

"And his other partner."

Slam that baseball bat right to her face.

"Come again?"

"Consider me thorough, but after seeing the results for hep C, I had to do a little more examining. Unless Roslin's hiding a kinky side we didn't figure on, Avery had another sexual partner. And he liked it," Drummond's features turned contemplative, "I guess the best term would be fast and furious."

There was such a thing as too much information.

"Agent Bartholomew, you're looking a little green."

"Yes." She bolted to her feet. "I think I've heard enough."

Drummond rose as well. "Do you want a copy of my findings?"

"Uh, um, sure, I guess." Oh, wouldn't Montrose just love this new turn of events. Liza winced. Why did she have to be the one to tell her SAC the case was getting more complicated rather than unraveling?

"I'll take care of that right now." Drummond busied himself with making copies.

So far, nothing should shock her about Mr. Ripley, but learning he was possibly bisexual did. Nothing in her files gave any indication of his sexual preference, or at least none of his victims said anything along those lines. However, sex was a private issue, and Iowans loved their privacy.

Could that be the reason Avery was killed?

"Here you go."

She took the copies from Drummond. "Thank you. This should help greatly, especially that serial number."

"Let me know what you find on that. With my new homicide and my patients, I barely have time to sleep these days."

"That I can do." She hightailed it out of his office and out of the hospital as fast as her legs could get her.

Once outside, she took a bracing breath of clean air and shuddered at the flashing thought of Gene Avery going wild. Pinching the wrinkle in the middle of her forehead, Liza groaned. "I'm never getting that out of my head as long as I live."

She took off for her car.

Reaching for the car fob, Liza flinched at another thought. Her feet stuck fast to the pavement, as if huge wads of gum were stuck to the soles of her boots. If Avery had hep C, his partner or partners might have it, too. And if he'd been having sex with his wife, Roslin Avery could have it. Hep C was nothing to mess around with. Who would be the lucky person to tell her that? Somehow Liza got the feeling Hamilton would shy away from being the bearer of bad news on that front.

A car horn blared.

Startled, Liza skittered to the side, looking over her shoulder at the blue Ford SUV stopped in the middle of the lot, a perturbed woman behind the wheel. Ignoring the anger, Liza waved to the driver and unlocked her car door as the SUV's revved engine swept past. Settling behind the wheel, she placed the copies on the seat next to her and went to start the engine. A square of white paper fluttered under the wiper.

Liza froze. The gray car? This is why she couldn't mix family problems with the job. It was going to get her into some serious trouble, or worse, killed.

Liza stepped out and tugged the paper loose, her gaze scanning the area around her car. Not that the person who left it would still be around.

Riker's Club, 9:30 tonight. I'll find you.

Now this was an interesting turn of events. Who from this town would want to meet with her? Was it the crazy person tailing her? Liza shivered. If she decided to honor this meeting, no way in hell was she doing it alone. She was going to have to pay another visit to Shane in order to even learn what Riker's Club was, and its location. No matter which way she turned, fate kept throwing her back into Shane's path.

Why was that?

CHAPTER FOURTEEN

"Riker's Club? Are you sure?"

"That's what the note told me."

Shane took the scrap of paper from Liza. The handwriting was neat and tight, all in upper case—and unfamiliar. "How did you say you got this?"

"Left on my car. I'm beginning to think by whoever drives a gray/silver SUV."

"And you would think this why?"

"Because, *Sheriff*, I spotted that type of vehicle tailing me. I came to the natural conclusion someone wanted to find me but didn't want me to see them, so they followed me to the hospital. Which is beyond odd in a small town like Eider, Iowa."

The note crinkled in his fist. "Liza, just because this isn't Cedar Rapids or Des Moines doesn't mean people around here won't attempt to purposely follow someone." Damn it, she could have been hurt. Under his watch.

"Don't act like I can't take care of myself. I'm more than capable of handling situations that turn dangerous."

So she thought. But Shane had been witness to one too many dangerous situations in the last five years that made his skin crawl, and got his people hurt. "If you see that car again, call me." He handed the note back to her.

"I will."

If he could only shake some sense into her. But, he had to stop and remind himself, she wasn't one of his deputies, and she didn't have to listen or work with him on any of part of her case or his. Liza Bartholomew was a federal agent, and she had the right to do whatever the hell she pleased to wrap up her job here and leave. If Shane were a smart man, he'd make every attempt to help her along, so he could get back to pursuing a mundane life in McIntire County.

"I don't understand why your mysterious note leaver would send you to Riker's for a meeting."

"Why's that?"

"Riker's Club was opened by a couple of millennials with high expectations. They took an abandoned factory and turned it into a microbrew bar and dance club. It's a popular place, but not many of the locals go to it."

"So how is it popular?"

"It's attracted a lot of attention from the nearby college towns and the Iowa City sect. I'm just glad I don't have to patrol it. Eider PD gets that job."

Liza studied her message. "Why send me there? On a Monday night? If someone wanted to keep their ID secret, going on a Monday night won't give them much coverage."

"You might be surprised how busy that club gets. Especially on a Monday night." Shane propped open the toolbox he used as a makeshift crime scene kit. He'd been replenishing his stores of gloves, evidence baggies, and swabs when Liza pulled into the department lot. Never one to be caught shorthanded, he continued with the resupply. "What did you learn from Drummond?"

"He hasn't told you yet?"

"Nope." Shane stuffed a handful of gloves in their designated plastic baggie, then sealed it. "He was tight-lipped on that portion. I'm still waiting for final results on my other homicide."

Cocking a hip against the tailgate and crossing her arms, Liza watched him. She was too close and looked way too comfortable there beside him. If he took one step to the right, would she be offended?

"This new development might lead him to a more thorough examination of the other guy," she said. "And we *cannot* let anyone know outside of this department."

Shane set the box of individually wrapped swabs on the tailgate and shifted to face her. "Stop beating around the bush and tell me already."

"Gene Avery was having an affair." One etched eyebrow lifted. "With a man."

"Say what?"

"This guy, Ripley or Avery, whatever you want to call him, was bisexual. Well, at this moment it's only speculation until I talk with Roslin. Maybe she knew, maybe she didn't. Speaking of Roslin, were you able to talk with her lawyer about an interview?"

Shane's hand went up to halt Liza's subject jump. "Whoa, one thing at a time here. First, how does Drummond even know Avery was bisexual?"

"Best way to explain, there was evidence. Ask Drummond."

"Okay, secondly, there has to be more."

"There is. At some point in his life, Avery had his jawbone reconstructed. The replacement has a serial number. I'll be researching that, hopefully learning who he really was. And the kicker that led Drummond to discovering the bombshell news: Avery had hep C."

Removing his Resistol, Shane scratched the top of his head. Good God Almighty, these details were not what he was expecting. Shifting to sit on the tailgate, he resettled the hat on his dome.

"What are your thoughts?" he asked Liza.

"About what?"

"Why Avery was killed."

With a sigh, she hopped onto the tailgate next to him. Gripping the edge, she let her legs swing back and forth. She was acting like they were pals and had known each other forever rather than a short period of time. Shane wanted to keep this professional. But she was sure making this damn hard.

"I think whoever killed Avery knew about this affair and possibly learned about his embezzling. With the marks on his body, his killer might have been exacting revenge for either of the infractions or was torturing the truth out of him."

"Do you think it has a connection to Donovan Frost?"

"By the nature of his death and what you told me about the similarities with both men, it could be. Which," she looked at him, "is why I need to talk with Roslin. Did you have any luck in that department?"

"Not yet. Pamela isn't answering her phone, and her receptionist has no idea where her boss went. I sent Murdoch out to the Frosts' home. If Pamela is there, I'm to be notified immediately."

"That means I'm at a stalemate. Best I can do is research the new developments and check out what the sender behind this message wants."

"You do realize you're not going to make your SAC's deadline now."

Her face scrunched in a cute version of sheer pain. "Oh joy. She's going to blow a blood vessel."

"I'd call her now."

With a shake of her head, Liza pulled out her phone. Then hopping down, she headed for her car. Her body was like a country road, winding and scenic, making the driver want to go slow and enjoy the view. And did he ever relish the view. She could walk away from him any time.

What am I doing? Every time she was near him, he turned into a horn-dog. Liza Bartholomew deserved respect and professionalism. Not the lustful stare of a man who was sixteen years celibate. Thumping his thigh, he slipped off the tailgate and let her have her privacy while he packed away the supplies.

With a glance over his shoulder to check on her—she was gesturing as if punctuating her words—he entered the building, leaving the door propped open for Liza. After putting the supplies back in the metal cabinet, he headed for the bullpen. Jennings was tapping away at one computer, while another appeared to be downloading something.

The kid seemed to be bursting with more energy as of late than he had in the months since he was shot in the knee. And the particular appendage didn't seem to bother him like before. Was his deputy finally taking a turn for the better?

"What are you doing?"

Jennings's gaze darted up to Shane then back to his screens. "Agent Bartholomew's warrant came through." He jerked a thumb over his shoulder at the fax machine. "I was given another copy via email." He pointed at the printer next.

"Then what are you downloading?"

"A big-ass file I was told in not-so-friendly terms not to look at and give to Agent Bartholomew."

The back door banged close, and a few seconds later Liza breezed into the bullpen. "My warrant's here?"

Both Shane and Jennings pointed at the fax machine. She headed for the contraption that Shane loathed as a necessary evil.

"I've got . . . 10 percent left on a file that's downloading for you, too," Jennings told her.

Liza snatched the stack of sheets from the fax and rerouted to Jennings's computer bank. "Who's the file from?"

"Your boss."

She nodded. "Good."

"What did Montrose say?" Shane asked.

Liza tilted her head up. "I have to follow the trail. She's extended my stay indefinitely."

A rush of excitement, like the first time he'd straddled his first bronc, filled him. Yet, she didn't seem as elated to have more time. Shouldn't that be a good thing? To not have her supervisor breathing down her neck to get back?

"What's on the file?"

Her phone buzzed. "Something I asked Montrose to send me." She pulled out her iPhone, checked the screen, and sighed. "I need to take this. Mind if I borrow your office?"

"Go ahead."

She slipped inside, closing the door in her wake.

"She didn't give you a straight answer," Jennings said, his fingers still flying over the keyboard.

"FBI." Like that was the final answer. "What are you typing?"

"Code."

"For what?"

A wry smile curled up the edge of Jennings's mouth. "You'll see."

Grunting, Shane left his deputy for the coffee machine. The sludge in the bottom of the pot smelled charred. Emptying the glop in the sink, he rinsed out the pot. Should he start a fresh round of coffee or actually drink something caffeine-free? Maybe Con was right. Shane was getting too old for his bad habits.

"What do you expect me to do?" Liza's voice came through the door.

He stilled, straining to hear. A twinge plucked at his morals for eavesdropping, but the timbre in her voice wasn't one he'd heard her use with her SAC.

"Kurt, this is my job. Damn it. I shouldn't have to argue with you over this every time we talk."

Kurt?

"Your first priority should *always* be Quinn."

This was beyond wrong. Shane shoved the empty pot back on the cold burner and backtracked away from his office. Whoever Kurt and Quinn were, they were obviously important to Liza, and private. Why else would she shut the door? And Shane had trampled all over his number one rule: don't be a nosy prick.

Absorbed in his work, Jennings didn't glance up as Shane passed the dispatch station and headed for Cassy's desk. He was about to sit down when the phone rang. Without missing a beat, Jennings answered.

"Sheriff's department, how can I help you?"

Sinking into Cassy's comfortable seat, Shane's bones could have melted from the luxury. This was a nice chair. He should get one, too.

"Sir, it's Murdoch."

"Patch her through to Hunt's desk." Shane rocked forward as Cassy's phone rang once. "What do you have for me, Murdoch?"

"Pamela Frost isn't here, sir. I've waited for an hour, and she hasn't shown up. I called her office again, and Emily still hasn't seen her. Do you want me to check the places she might go?"

The dispatch phone rang again.

"No. Return to the station. We're going to have to give Pamela some time to process what happened to her husband."

"Might be easier to just go to Roslin herself."

"Sheriff," Jennings interrupted, "there's another call for you."

"Hang on, Murdoch." He cupped the receiver. "Who is it?"

"Uh, it's Roslin Avery, sir."

The office door opened at that moment, and Liza exited. She hesitated near the dispatch station and looked at Shane expectantly.

He gave Jennings the signal to hold. "Murdoch, I've got Roslin on the line. Head back to the station."

"Copy."

Shane hit the cancel button. "Patch her through."

Liza inched closer to Cassy's desk. "Speaker," she whispered.

He obliged as the sound of a radio came through the connection. "Roslin, it's Sheriff Hamilton."

"Oh, Sheriff, uh . . . hi."

"Is there something I can help you with?" he asked.

"I don't know if I should be calling you. I'm at a loss, actually."

Liza's features scrunched.

"Roslin, I'm here to help, even if there's been a problem between us."

An upbeat song pulsed on in the background. "I guess it would be okay," she said, hesitantly. The music faded. "Sheriff, I can't seem to find my lawyer."

Join the crowd, lady. "Have you tried her office?"

"Everywhere. The gal that works there for her said she hasn't seen her boss in a long time. And she couldn't tell me why Ms. Frost is gone."

So, Emily didn't divulge Pamela's tragedy. Good for the Okie.

"Sheriff, is something wrong with Ms. Frost?"

"Why do you think I would know?"

That remark earned a grin from Liza. Damn, he liked it when she smiled like that. He had to make her do it again.

"Because, you're the sheriff. You know everything."

Liza rubbed the tip of her brown nose and rolled her eyes. Shane had to swallow down a chuckle. The woman's humor knew no bounds.

"Now, Roslin, I wouldn't say I know everything."

"Well, do you know where my lawyer is or not?"

"No, I don't."

Tell her, Liza mouthed.

"I'm afraid that Pamela has been given some tragic news and is probably trying to process through it. She just needs some time alone."

"Oh."

Liza picked up a pen and paper and scribbled out something. She turned the page for him to see.

Ask her to come in.

-

"Roslin, would you mind coming in to the department to have a chat?"

"A chat about what?"

"There's . . . someone here who wants to ask you questions about Gene. It has nothing to do with what I arrested you over."

"I don't know, Sheriff. I don't think Ms. Frost would like me doing that."

"It's your decision. If you wanted to do it, your lawyer would have to comply."

"Would I have to have my lawyer there with me?"

"That's up to you."

Silence deadened the connection. Shane wouldn't push Roslin; this had to be of her own choosing. But watching Liza pinch and twist her full lips, while her whole body vibrated, was an interesting study in the woman's anxiety idiosyncrasies.

"I guess I could come in and talk to this person. But can I do it in the morning? I kinda need to find some place to stay."

Liza's head bobbed hard.

"That would be fine. Just give us a call when you're coming in."

"Okay. If you hear from Ms. Frost, would you tell her I'm needing to talk to her?"

"Can do, Roslin."

After the expected conventional partings, Shane set the phone on the cradle.

"That was easier than I expected," Liza said.

"Until Pamela learns what she's doing. She'll have to allow Roslin to do what she wants."

"Agent Bartholomew," Jennings cut in, "the file is done."

"Good. Do you have an empty flash drive?"

Jennings dug around in a drawer, producing the drive. He did whatever it was his magical fingers could perform and gave the file to Liza. She smiled her thanks and tucked the little yellow stick into her coat pocket.

"Now that I've got my warrant, I can get into those school accounts."

"Are you sure his embezzling activities will show up in the accounts?"

"If the information the principal already gave me doesn't mesh with what the school has accounted for, it most certainly will."

She had the most memorizing eyes. He couldn't think of any time he'd seen anyone with that shade of dark brown, and Shane had traveled the whole country and most of the Arab countries. He would know.

The creak of a chair startled him out of his trance.

"Agent Bartholomew, Deputy Nash can handle the warrant. Your SAC actually authorized anyone in the department to assist you with it," Jennings said. His sharp gaze drifted to Shane. "You two should prepare for that meeting tonight."

"What's to prepare? I show up and wait for the . . . Wait a minute. How do you know about that? And what do you mean, you two?"

A sly expression passed over the deputy's face. "Your conversation carried through the back door. Nobody could miss it." Meaning, he was eavesdropping and away from his station. "Ma'am, you're not familiar with Eider and our county. It's best that the sheriff go with you. But you two walk into Riker's dressed like that, they'll kick you out."

"Why would they do that?" Shane demanded of his deputy.

"No offense, sir, but those millennials don't want oldies in that club. You need to look less authoritative if you want to get through the doors."

"Makes sense," Liza said. "My only problem is, I don't have 'less authoritative' clothing with me."

"That would be a problem Joles can fix. She'd know just where to go to get you the right look. And, Sheriff, you need to look more retro cowboy, not ass-broke-poor cowboy."

Shane glared at his smart-ass deputy. Sometimes having the most intelligent people surrounding you was more of a headache than a help.

"Define retro cowboy."

That cocky grin plastered on Jennings's youthful face always worked in getting what he wanted—out of trouble. "Try the '90s. Or maybe a little more Luke Bryan."

"I'm not wearing skin-tight jeans just to appease some twenty-year-old girl into letting me in a bar."

Out of the corner of his eye, Shane caught the little twitch on Liza's part at the mention of skin-tight jeans. His body warmed. It had been a long time—a real long time—since he made a woman turn into a sexually quivering mass, but he damn sure didn't forget what it looked like. And Liza's flushed face and rapid breathing was indication enough of her wayward thoughts. Damn it! She was making it hard for him to focus.

"Do what you want, sir," Jennings's voice ripped through Shane's head, "but I'm warning you, you want into Riker's, you're going to have to look the part."

So be it, but Shane drew the line at tight jeans. He had something that would work to appease the so-called dress code of the less authoritative. One thing was certain: there was no way in hell he was going to let Liza do this meeting alone. Independent woman and a trained FBI agent she might be, but no one went anywhere alone without backup in his county. His deputies had paid a price for trying to fly solo. There was a killer on the loose, and Shane wasn't about to let him or her get a crack at any law enforcement officer.

CHAPTER FIFTEEN

Liza, with Jolie Murdoch's help, found what she hoped was the ideal outfit to gain her access to Riker's Club. If she were home, or even in Iowa City, she would have paired the hip-hugging white capris and buttery yellow blouse with flashy yellow heels, but she was in Podunkville, and her choices were limited to strappy sandals. Not that either type of shoe left her with the option to give chase to any human being who chose to escape her.

That was why she would take the good sheriff with her. She pulled into his driveway—Siri was finally working out her kinks—and parked beside a battered, brown Ford truck. After checking her iPhone—no new messages from Kurt—she exited her car and wandered along the gravel drive toward the house.

Kurt was angry—to the stratosphere angry—with her over the extension on her stay in Eider. There wasn't a damn thing she could do about it. He would just have to get over it and find other means to have Quinn taken care of while he was gone. Why then was her heart hurting over the thought of someone else being around Quinn? Someone who didn't know all of his quirks and patterns.

No, stop it! You can't be Kurt's savior every time he can't get his shit together.

This wasn't about Kurt. It would always be about Quinn. Maybe she should put in a call to the therapist's office and see if he could recommend a caretaker for a day or so. Okay, three, tops.

"You look like you've got a thousand-pound bull stomping around in your head."

Jerked out of her brooding, Liza took a quick assessment of her surroundings; she was standing on the porch and getting an eyeful of the man before her.

Someone find me a fan.

Shane leaned on the doorframe, one jean-clad leg crossed over the other, his arms crossed in front of his chest. His curls were damp and looked finger tossed. He wore a white T-shirt that was snug in all the right places. And was that a silver chain peeking out from under the collar of his shirt? *Good Lord, he's barefoot.*

Liza stiffened her hand before it shot out to touch the contours of those bulging biceps. This was not a man looking at the wrong side of fifty. No, this was one fine wine, and Liza wanted a sample. Swallowing, she found her voice. "Uh, you're not ready."

Nice one, Liza. What a comeback.

A corner of his mouth tilted up. "We've got some time. There's no rush." He stepped back, allowing her access to his home. "Come on in."

Slipping through the gap, her skin prickled at the kiss of heat from his body. The scent of cedar and patchouli overwhelmed her with the desire to stop and lean her cheek to his and breathe him in. *Get a grip, Liza.* But his sanctuary, too, carried his distinct scent and leather.

The clap of the screen door sent a shiver down her back. Her body tingled with awareness as he approached. For a second she closed her eyes, waiting for the press of lips to the back of her neck. He hovered behind her, and then she felt him move around her. She opened her eyes and met his as he passed.

"Want anything to drink?"

"A beer would taste good."

He frowned. "Sorry, I don't have any."

"Wine?" Her hand flashed up, and she shook it. "Never mind, you don't look like someone who would have wine."

"Actually, I don't have any alcohol."

"None?"

"I don't drink."

"At all?"

He shook his head. "You know, I might have a few cans of Dr. Pepper."

Liza blinked, letting her mind catch up. How was it that a man like Shane Hamilton, the epitome of a cowboy, did not drink? "A Dr. Pepper would be fine."

With a nod, he padded down the hall to a door on the right then disappeared.

Liza wandered to the first doorway on her left and discovered a quaint living room. This was where the smell of leather originated. A well-loved brown recliner/rocker was angled to get a great view out of the two lone windows and the TV—the only new thing in the whole room. A red-brown and white cowhide rug covered the middle of the floor. And flush to the wall stood a lamp made of deer antlers. Under that sat a loveseat with a brown and white cowhide pattern. Liza ran her fingers over the armrest; it was leather as well. Weird.

The crack and hiss of a can opening made her turn. She left the living room and returned to the hall, examining the picture frames hanging on the walls as she inched along. They were mostly photos of Shane when he was younger with a man who Shane favored in looks and height and a woman who smiled adoringly at both men. His parents. What had it felt like to have two people who loved you unconditionally always there for you? Liza stared at a picture of the couple with their arms wrapped around a beaming Shane holding an enormous belt buckle.

The whisper of movement and the clink of ice against glass pulled her gaze from the photo. Shane held out the drink.

With a smile of thanks, she took it and sipped. The bubbles tickled her nose. Ahhh, the sweetness of Dr. Pepper, a cola like no other. She tipped her glass at the picture she'd been studying. "What was that all about?"

Shane tilted his head to get a better look at what she was pointing at and then stepped back. “I won the saddle bronc event that sent me to the NFR.” He chuckled at her frown. “You don’t know what that is?”

“It’s all foreign to me.”

“Saddle bronc riding is when I ride a bucking horse in a saddle and a special halter with only a rope attached to it. I have to stay on for eight seconds. NFR stands for National Finals Rodeo—it’s like the Super Bowl of rodeo.”

“Ahh.” Liza sipped more of the soda. “How long did you do that before you decided to be a law officer?”

Cupping the back of his neck, he massaged the thick cord of muscle and sinew. “Most of my younger years. I retired before I was too torn up to walk.”

“So, you became a cop and then sheriff?”

A darkness shrouded his eyes. He avoided her gaze, turning to return to the kitchen. “What were you thinking about doing for supper?”

Liza’s brain felt like it had slammed into a brick wall at high speed. What was he hiding? Her gaze swept over the remaining pictures on the wall as she followed him into the kitchen. Nothing stood out, just more of the same kind of photos of him or his parents.

“I don’t know,” she said as she entered the room.

He stood at a cramped counter, facing the wall, and fiddled with something near the knife block.

The kitchen was small and functional, with a round table sitting in the middle of the floor and four chairs circled around it. She glanced over her shoulder and spotted the bathroom across from the kitchen. Then the remaining doors at the end of the hall should be bedrooms. One of those rooms was where he slept and dreamed . . . an electrified zap ran through the center of her body.

Shane ceased his fiddling and faced her. “Mind if I grill some steaks? And we can have baked potatoes with them.”

Her mouth watered at the mention of grilled steak. "Sounds wonderful."

He moved closer, hesitating between her and the table. Liza peered up at him looming over her, her chest constricting at his nearness. His gaze flicked down and then jerked back up. He was close, so, so close. Would he kiss her? Oh, would he just do it. She had to know if her wild daydreams were anywhere close to reality.

"Excuse me."

She stumbled back, allowing him to continue on his path to the fridge. Turning, Liza rolled her eyes at her stupidity. She was reading too much into his actions. Everything he did had a purpose, and it sure as hell wasn't about seducing her.

Positioning herself next to the doorway, out of his way, she leaned against the wall. While sipping the Dr. Pepper, she watched him work his way around the kitchen. The sight was a novelty for her. Growing up in one foster home after another, Liza had never witnessed any man in any home, even Michael Bartholomew, cooking. Half of them wouldn't have known where a frying pan was located.

Shane glanced at her over his shoulder and then looked at her. "What?"

"It's nothing."

"Nothing? You were staring at me like you were witnessing a miracle."

"Maybe I was."

"Agent Bartholomew, a man in the kitchen isn't a new phenomenon."

"Where I grew up it is. And look at you, using high-falutin' words like phenomenon."

He stilled at that and gradually turned to face her. "Because I'm a cowboy from a small town in the middle of nowhere in Iowa, you automatically assume I'm uneducated?"

Shit! That was not even a million miles close to what she meant. "No. Sorry. I . . . You know what, I put my foot in my mouth. That's not what I meant."

A smile crept along his mouth. "That was too easy."

The creep. "Don't enjoy yourself too much, Sheriff. Tease all you want, but I'll repay in kind."

He winked. "Looking forward to it." He resumed his food dinner prep.

Liza couldn't recall seeing this side of Shane Hamilton in her previous visit. He'd been serious, no nonsense, and in charge, all with military precision. Teasing and joking didn't seem part of his vocabulary. How wrong she'd been.

"Do your parents live nearby?" she asked.

"No, they passed on some years back."

"What about other family?"

He shook his head. "Nobody left except me."

"That has to be . . . lonely."

Shrugging, he wrapped the potatoes in aluminum foil. "It's not bad. I've got friends and my job."

Yet there was a hint of sadness in his voice. Friends and jobs weren't enough, as she knew from firsthand experience. If it wasn't for Kurt and Quinn, Liza would have no one to keep her sane. She rarely saw her adoptive parents, though she chatted over the phone with them on a weekly basis. It wasn't the same.

Kurt needed help, she was capable of helping, but she'd tossed his concerns and needs out the window in lieu of closing the most difficult case of her career. The longer she kept at this impossible quest to bring Ripley to justice, the more she was beginning to second-guess her decision to stay with the FBI to see this case through to the end.

"There's the bull again," Shane said.

"What bull?"

"The bull that seems to drag you into some deep, deep thoughts." Shane picked up a metal tray with two thick slabs of T-bones, the two potatoes, and a pair of metal tongs. "You hanging here or coming with me?"

"Don't you need to start the grill?"

He beckoned with the tray. "Follow me."

Follow she did, right outside to a beautiful deck, stained a rich, dark-red varnish. In the center was a stone fireplace with smoldering coals. A grill rack balanced on the circle of rock. It was like he expected her to agree to a steak dinner.

"What would you have done if I said I wanted to go out to eat?"

Shane shoved the foil-wrapped potatoes onto some of the coals. "Convinced you otherwise. I had a good feeling you preferred the home-style approach."

"Oh, you did, did you?"

His smile warmed her. How could he possibly guess about her preferences and be right, and she still couldn't crack his shell?

Taking her half-empty glass of soda, she settled on one of the deck chairs and studied the landscape. Off in the distance she spotted a small herd of horses, grazing on the lush grass spread across the hillside. To the left of the house, she could just make out the edge of what must be a barn. It was peaceful out here. Far enough away from the town limits to avoid the bustle and noise, but close enough for Shane to respond in a hurry for an emergency.

Once he had the steaks sizzling, he padded over to a chair set close to the pit. "What was the meeting time, again?"

"Nine-thirty."

"We should get there more than an hour earlier. Give you a chance to scope out the place."

"Me a chance, or you?"

He gave a nonchalant shrug, like a roguish Matthew McConaughey. It made her breath hitch. "Both."

A horse whinnied, drawing her attention to the herd. Had they moved closer?

"How many horses do you have out there?" Hopefully the distraction and change of subject would keep her mind off her reaction to him.

Shane twisted in his chair, the action tightening his shirt and revealing a taut network of muscles along his torso. So not helping.

"There's five out there," he pointed at the group that wandered down the hill. "I have another pasture past this one with fifteen mares and foals."

"Twenty horses. How do you ride them all?"

"I don't." He untwisted his body to look at her. "Hell, I hope no one does. They're mostly bucking stock. I've got one of the top bucking mares in the nation under my care."

The shell had a crack. *I'll be damned. I better exploit it as long as I can.* "If they're used for rodeos, how do you get them there?"

"I only breed them. I've got some strong connections to contractors who come test out what I've got and buy what they want. If the new blood won't buck, they're sold for riding and working purposes."

"Have you seen your horses in action?"

"Plenty of times. We've got professional rodeo stops in a few towns around here."

"And you have nothing to ride yourself? You don't strike me as a man who doesn't have a horse or two to ride."

"I've got three out there to ride. And I have two studs for breeding." Shane rose from his chair, a little slower this time, and flipped the steaks.

"And in all of that you find time to be a sheriff."

"Don't sound so amazed." He returned to his chair.

A comfortable silence settled between them. Liza gazed into her glass. She could use a refill, but she loathed disturbing their peace.

"Who's Kurt?"

The out-of-the-blue question threw her into a tailspin. Like a car chase scene in a Dwayne Johnson movie, Liza's brain sped through a hundred different variations of "how the hell did he find out about Kurt?"

"Wow, you have that same expression you get when you have some deep thoughts." One eyebrow peaked. "I'm beginning to think a thoughtful Liza is correlated to this Kurt."

The only way Shane could have learned about Kurt was overhearing her argument with him while she was in Shane's office. Or Doc Drummond had said something—after he, too, eavesdropped. Setting her glass down with a thunk, Liza scooted forward in her seat. "You had no right."

Any lightheartedness in him evaporated. "No, I didn't, and I won't make excuses. However, you weren't exactly quiet, either."

"Then you should have continued pretending you heard nothing."

"I might have, if I hadn't noticed how this Kurt fellow, and Quinn, seem to be affecting your capabilities as an LEO."

"You, of all people, should know that in our line of work, keeping our private lives private is paramount. Especially in my job. I don't need criminals finding out the names of my loved ones so they can use them as leverage against me."

They stared at each other. Unable to take the scrutiny, Liza hoisted herself out of the chair and headed back inside the house. This was a mistake. A monumental one. She should have known her personal life would spill over into this case. Having Shane call her out on it was bad form. And damn it, he was right.

The sliding patio door was her only warning.

"Liza, I wasn't pushing for a fight."

Turning, she crossed her arms and glared. "Then explain to me what you were trying to do."

"Understand. I was trying to understand."

"There's nothing to understand. My personal life is that, personal. That means you have no right to pry or convince me otherwise."

Shane didn't have a comeback, though his intense stare had a lot to say. Her backlash and insistence on shutting him out had triggered . . . what? His suspicion? Great, she hadn't deterred him one iota, and if memory served her right, she'd given him a damn good reason to get nosy. And if he ever got the itch to call her SAC, Montrose could reveal more than Liza wanted.

How could she have ever thought any of this was a good idea? She should not be going to Riker's Club with him. Taking along one of his seasoned, younger deputies would have been the better choice. Liza put a clamp down on her scattered thoughts and raging hormones. She had a job to do, and it wasn't getting done. Shane had been right about one thing: she was letting her personal life get in the way of her job. And it wasn't only Kurt and Quinn distracting her.

"You might want to attend to our food before it burns."

"You say that as if you're not planning on leaving."

With a tilt of her chin, she eyed him. "I should, but I've come this far, might as well finish it. We did agree to go to this club together, and I don't back out of a commitment."

He seemed to consider her reasons, gave a slight nod, and then headed for the patio door. Pausing, he looked back. "You don't have to hide away in here on account of my prying. There is more to discuss before we leave."

Yes, there was more. She wanted a solid plan in place with this mysterious meet-up. This whole setup had the potential to end badly, and she wasn't about to let that happen.

"I'll be out in a moment. I need a refill on my soda."

He pointed at the fridge. "Help yourself." With that, he slipped outside.

Her shoulders weighed a ton. This burden was beginning to take a toll on her. She opened the door and located a fresh Dr. Pepper. Setting the can on a narrow counter next to the fridge, she started to crack open the tab when a small picture tucked in a corner caught her eye. Glancing over her shoulder to ensure her nosiness wasn't about to be called out, she bent down and pulled the curling photo close. It was Shane, a buffer, dustier, grizzled, uniformed Shane. He stood next to a tan Humvee holding an M4. He was in the army? When the . . . Wait! What the hell was she doing? Hadn't she just chewed him out for prying into her personal life? Shoving the picture back into its place, she grabbed the Dr. Pepper and made a beeline for the door.

Erase what you saw from your memory. Yeah, like that was going to happen. The image of a battle-weary Shane was burned into her mind. Yet, it begged the question, why was that picture just lying around for her to see? And why did she get the sense that no one knew he'd served? From the way Cassy talked, Shane had been a cowboy and was now the sheriff, nothing in between.

But there had been something between. Something huge. No one served in the military and didn't get some kind of recognition. Did they?

Liza Bartholomew, leave it alone. You have enough problems to worry about. Digging up Shane's past is not one of them.

Opening the patio door, she hesitated before stepping outside. Shane hovered near the firepit, his backside turned to her. The fading sunlight glinted off the silver chain hanging around his neck. He peered over his shoulder at her. Those dark brown eyes carried a weight she had seen in her own eyes after Ripley had burned the warehouse and killed those innocent people. It was guilt over a wrong that could never be made right. Whatever had sent him into the army was more than huge— It was something terrible. And it had shaped his every thought and move.

Who are you, Shane Hamilton?

CHAPTER SIXTEEN

It had been a legit question and reason. So why did he feel like a huge hypocritical ass? Hadn't he dodged one of her innocent questions about his personal life?

Did it really matter? He shouldn't be interested in her other than how to solve their adjoining case. Once they got what they wanted, she would be gone. Back to her FBI position and her Kurt and Quinn. Hell, for all Shane figured, Kurt was a boyfriend or husband and Quinn their child. She could have lied to him about being single—she was an FBI agent, for God's sake. Just because she didn't wear a ring didn't mean she wasn't married. A lot of law enforcement officials hid their married status as a precaution to protect their families from criminals exploiting them. It made perfect sense for her to keep it secret and to get flaming mad when he pushed it.

Yet, the thought of her being married stabbed at him like a pair of spurs. He spared a glance her way then returned his focus to the road ahead. Silence had ruled most of their ride, and for good reason. Gone was the easy camaraderie they'd developed in the last twenty-four hours. She drove with stiff, jerky movements, avoiding eye contact.

He'd done pissed her off. The deathly silent meal was a big giveaway. Everything had been going fine, and he had to open his pie hole and ruin it all.

It was for the best. Nothing could ever come of them. Ever. She had no place here in McIntire County. And he had no reason to even imagine any type of relationship with her outside of a professional one. He was a man past his prime and dedicated to a dead memory.

"Up here, you'll want to turn right at the stop sign," he said softly.

They'd chosen to take her car to Riker's since it fit the type of vehicle a millennial would drive. Shane still couldn't see how his looking less like a cowboy would hide the fact that he was a man about to turn fifty walking into a bar for twenty-somethings. Liza would have better luck walking in unnoticed. Although, after seeing her approach his home earlier in those form-fitting pants and the delicate blouse, he'd been unable to tear his gaze off her. She'd been a sight, and it had taken his breath. How would any virile buck be able to keep his eyes and mitts off her when she passed over Riker's threshold?

The old factory came into view; pulsing multicolored lights streamed through the windows. Liza directed the car into the full parking lot.

"This place is busy."

He spotted a lone empty spot along the edge where the lot met the small grass patch. He pointed it out to Liza. "I warned you. Riker's has a certain appeal to its preferred client base." And he was about to regret every minute of this.

She whipped her car into the small space like an expert stuntwoman yet with a little more caution. Impressive. As he exited the vehicle, Shane grabbed his black leather jacket and slid into it. He hadn't been sure he'd wear it, but he was going to need something to conceal his weapon. The shirt wouldn't be enough. Liza had foregone wearing her weapon and had it tucked inside the purse she slung over her shoulder.

The faint thump of bass pulsed across the parking lot. The owners had done a respectable job of soundproofing their business.

Liza stared up at the historical building. "How in the world did they convince the powers that be to let them open a place like this so close to a residential area?"

"Lots of money and promises to keep the noise way down." He offered his elbow. "Ready?"

She looked at his arm, pursed her lips, then hesitantly threaded her hand inside the crook of his elbow and gripped his arm. The coat blocked the feel of her hand, but his hyperactive body could sense it.

Lock down, Hamilton. You're on the job.

Escorting her to the main entrance, they passed a handful of smokers getting their nic fix. The rancid stench of cigarette smoke hit Shane's memory like a ton of bricks. Oh God, this was too much like the last time he was with a woman in a bar.

June 2001

Cheyenne pushed him away. "You're being a prick." She flipped her honey-wheat hair over her shoulder and backed up.

Shane followed. "Babe, I'm being anything but. He's trespassing on my territory."

"Damn it, Shane. I'm not your possession."

"That ring says otherwise."

"Shane, dude, drop it. Nothing's happenin'."

He jabbed a finger in his traveling partner's chest. "Go to hell, Trigger. You've got your hands all over my woman."

"I'm dancing with her because you're too damn drunk to stand."

Weaving, Shane pushed at Trigger's chest. "Am not." He stumbled forward.

"Whatever, dude." Trigger reached for Cheyenne's hand. "Come on, sweetheart."

Shane grabbed Trigger's hand and flung it back. "I said to leave her alone."

"Shit! I always knew you were a horse's ass."

Shane swung. The next thing he knew he was standing over his buddy and his hand was throbbing. Trigger came up off the floor with a roar.

"Shane?"

Blinking, he stared at the double doors and then the woman next to him.

"Are you all right?" Liza asked.

The bass was somewhat louder this close to the building. Shane could just make out the music, and it was nothing like what had been playing that night in the bar.

"I'm good," he said, then pulled open one of the doors.

Any rebuttal Liza might have made was drowned by the blast of music. Thank God for small miracles. This was the first time in a long, long time outside of his ritualistic anniversary that he'd had a flashback to that night. He was not about to explain himself to Liza.

They descended a short flight of stairs and pushed through another set of doors. The music was louder yet as they entered what was once the factory floor where the machinery had stood. Now it was crowded with bar tables and stools and people, some dancing while others hovered around the tables, drinking and talking. All the grinding bodies and energy pouring from the room made it look like a mosh pit.

The music switched, and this time a song with a beat Shane was more familiar with started. The crowd screamed their approval and began jumping around with their hands raised over their heads.

"Is that supposed to be a country song?" Liza yelled over the noise.

"It's the new country." He spotted an emptied table. "Hurry before it's taken."

Settled on a stool, Shane leaned closer to Liza. The intoxicating scent of cinnamon and vanilla filled his senses, electrifying his nerve endings. Oh, how he wanted to lip the hallow of her neck and drink her in.

Liza cocked her head. "Do you see something?"

He cleared his throat. “Not yet. Do you want something to drink?”

“If they have it, a coconut water would be great. If not, ginger ale or whatever they have that passes as fancy water.”

“I’m sure they’ve got something along those lines. Right back.” He slid off his stool and plowed his way to the bar.

As he passed a quartet of young women dancing together, he stiffened as someone squeezed his rear. The group gave him a few seductive winks.

“Hey, cowboy,” a dolled-up brunette said. “Come dance with us.”

They horseshoed him, beckoning for him to step into the center. He shook his head at the women and then pointed at Liza. The group peered over the crowd to see his “date.”

One woman shrugged. “Bring her over.”

“Maybe later. Ladies.”

He escaped their siren call and made it to the bar unaccosted. Good God, the younger they were the bolder they got. He couldn’t recall the women of his generation being this gropey. Then again, he was a horny male at the time—what did he care what a woman did or didn’t do to him as long as it led to a night of tangled sheets and sweaty bodies?

A smiling pixie with wild pink hair and an eyebrow ring leaned on the counter behind the bar. “What can I get ya?”

Used to seeing a tattooed and heavily muscled Xavier Hartmann in the bartender position, Shane was taken aback by the young woman in front of him. Shaking free of the shock, he gave her Liza’s order.

“We’ve got coconut water. And do you want anything?”

Why not? “Make it two of those.”

“Sure thing.”

Glancing down the bar, Shane did a double take. Next to a blonde woman, who was definitely not his wife, was Derek

Schofield. The two looked chummy. Real chummy. As the couple shared a kiss, Derek wrapped an arm around the blonde's waist, pulled back, and then guided her out into the dancing mob. Shane watched them get right cozy until they disappeared in the sea of writhing bodies.

"Here ya go."

Shane gave Pixie an appreciative nod, tossed a ten on the bar, and, taking the tall glasses of mostly ice, he headed back to the table. Liza was conversing with a young African American male who leaned much too close to her, probably to look down the front of her blouse. Shane's blood simmered at the kid's audacity. However, Liza seemed interested in chatting with him. There was no logical reason for his jealousy. None. She was a colleague, not his girlfriend.

The young man placed a hand over hers and bent closer, and that's when it all fell apart for the poor sap. Liza flipped her hand out from under his, grabbing his wrist in deft move that made Laila Ali look slow. Liza twisted the kid's arm around and bent it in a painful, awkward position. His knees buckling, the kid folded away from her. Liza leaned with him and spoke into his ear. There was a vigorous head nod, and the kid was free. Rubbing his wrist, he took off like a man in desperate need of the bathroom. As he passed Shane, their shoulders bumped.

Juggling the glasses—hell, this stuff was too expensive to slosh on the floor—Shane spun to frown at the young man.

"Watch where you're goin'," the kid barked. He clamped his mouth shut, and his eyes bugged when their gazes locked. "Sheriff, I'm sorry. I didn't know it was you."

Well, there went his disguise. "Hey, Ziggy. Aren't you supposed to be in Iowa City at school?"

Ziggy grimaced. "Uh, we have a few days off."

Translation: *I'm here where I'm not supposed to be; don't tell my mom.* "Sounds good. Tell your mom I said hi."

"Uh, sure thing." Ziggy made like Houdini and escaped.

Shaking his head, Shane finished his trip to the table. Liza's perplexed expression was enough to tell him she saw the exchange with Ziggy.

"You know that kid?"

"All his life. He's a local. Good kid, just makes the typical dumb male mistakes." Shane placed her glass in front of her. "Your coconut water."

"Did you get some for yourself?"

"Had to see what all the fuss is about."

Shrugging, she pressed her lips around the straw and sucked. Shane about lost his marbles. Ripping his gaze off her, he bypassed the damn straw and gulped down the sweet liquid. Not much of a coconut person, he thought it was just okay.

"So far, I've found about five different ways to get in and out of here," Liza said. She pointed at the red neon exit sign. "Bathrooms are that way. Do you want me to check those out?"

"In a minute." He set his glass on the table and drew closer to her—a mistake when he caught a whiff of her scent, but he powered through the desire. "I spotted someone here who shouldn't be."

"I'm pretty certain there are a lot of people here who shouldn't be here and are."

"True, but not when he's with someone other than his wife."

Liza's brows rose. "Do tell."

"Pamela Frost has a receptionist from Oklahoma. The gal married a local boy, and they live around here. Rumors have been flying that there's marital strife. I think the rumors aren't rumors anymore."

"Does this local boy have a name?"

"Derek Schofield; his wife is Emily."

"Are you sure it was him?"

"Liza, I know the people in my county. That boy is fooling around on his wife, and she's figuring it out."

Her features wrinkled into a perplexed look. "I wonder. . ."

"What?"

"I don't know if this is any correlation to my mysterious note or not, but could it be possible that I was sent here to see that?"

"How would your note leaver know this?" Shane held up a finger and wagged it back and forth. "Scratch that. I can't discredit any possibilities. Nothing about our cases has made sense. Why not send you here to spy on Schofield."

"But how does his affair connect with our cases? Outside of the fact that Emily works for Pamela, whose husband was murdered, and who represents the widow of a scam artist, who was murdered, too."

"One more thing, his mother is on the school board that connects with Gene Avery. We're going to have to see how your meeting plays out."

"I guess." Liza stood, smoothing out her blouse and pants. "I'm going to scope the bathroom exits." She gave him a nod and then left.

Against his will, he watched her strut away. Well, damn it, she was too fine looking not to stare at.

A hand ran across his back. He flinched and damn near whipped around and throat punched the threat. His muscles seized, screaming for release, relaxing the second the owner of the hand came into view.

The dolled-up brunette who had boldly grabbed his ass smiled. "Well, cowboy, you're all alone. Why is that?"

Her friends joined them, swarming the table like a horde of honeybees.

"Howdy, again, ladies."

They all grinned, baring their canines. Shane's neck tingled.

This was not going to end well.

CHAPTER SEVENTEEN

Liza examined the exit door. A wire ran up alongside the frame and connected with a black box overhead. The whole thing was rigged to sound an alarm if the door opened. Probably a way for the owners to keep people from entering uninvited through the back way. She liked to hope that they weren't trying to keep people in.

Rubbing her chin, she turned to face the hall and the four doors that marked her path to get here. Two of the doors were for the men's and women's restrooms, one was a storage closet—marked as such—and the other was an employee's only room. Both of those doors were locked. So were the other exits rigged with sensors?

The women's bathroom opened, and two giggling girls spilled out. When they saw Liza, they sobered and straightened up. One wiggled her skin-tight dress down and avoided eye contact. With a shake of her head, Liza left the two to their guilty consciences and headed back to Shane. She didn't have time, nor the desire, to deal with whatever activities they might have been engaging in inside the bathroom. Not her circus, not her monkeys.

She cleared the hallway, did another scan of the building. Above the old factory floor, protruding from the walls, was a wide walkway. There had to be a staircase or an elevator to reach that level. If Liza had to take a guess, there were offices and such up there at one time. It could be that the Riker's owners turned those into special places for VIPs, or party rooms. Liza had to get up there.

It wasn't lost on her that a building such as this had become the death trap for her witnesses. Her lone consolation: Mr. Ripley was dead, and he wouldn't be setting any more traps.

She checked the time on her phone. T minus one hour until her mystery person came looking for her. She wasn't ready for this. She hated the unknown, despite its consistency in her job. The unknown had never been kind to her.

Shouldering her slipping purse strap, she entered the fray of people. The sheer mass of bodies surprised her still. Didn't these kids have classes or work tomorrow? Coming upon the table, Liza halted.

"What the hell?"

A quartet of women had trapped Shane in his seat. The look on his face was utter panic. One of the women seemed more insistent than the others as she was all but crawling into his lap. He clutched one of her arms, keeping her at bay, and said something to her. The others were enjoying the struggle but let their friend make all the moves.

Liza should go to his rescue, but her inquisitive side wanted to see how he got out of this. He was a big boy. That twig couldn't be more than 110 pounds soaking wet. Yet when that twig leaned forward enough to lick Shane's cheek, Liza snapped.

"Oh, no, not on my watch she ain't."

Liza was on the table in two shakes of a tail. The other women took one look at her and backpedaled. Twig, however, was too absorbed in her struggle with Shane and didn't notice a pissed off black woman until Liza took a firm grip on the scrawny shoulder and yanked her back.

"That'll be enough, ya li'l tart."

Twig threw up her hands and gave Liza the once over. "Excuse me. I didn't see your tramp stamp on him."

Liza scoffed. "Oh, honey, is that the best you can do?" She prowled closer to Twig. "You best be gettin' your skinny li'l ass outta here before I snap you in two."

"Ladies …"

"Hush!" Liza snapped at Shane. "What's it gonna be, honey?"

Twig's eyes darted to her friends, who had deserted her, and then back to Liza. Twig's chest rose and fell in rapid succession, she swallowed, then took a side step. "You can have him. He's an old fart anyway."

"Hey, now!" Shane came out of his chair.

With a snap of her finger, Liza made him freeze in his tracks. "Scat, li'l cat."

Twig gave Liza a disgusted sneer and bolted. Keeping an eye on the skinny bitch's backside until she merged with the dancers, Liza used the time to calm her temper. When she faced Shane, his eyes were bugging.

"What was that?"

"A rescue operation by the looks of things."

"I had it handled."

Rolling her eyes, Liza hooked a hand on her hip. "Oh, did you now? I'm pretty certain if I hadn't stepped in and you'd managed to dislodge Twiggy's arms, one of her three friends would have pounced."

For the briefest moment, his features turned contemplative, then it faded. "You know, it's not that important. We avoided a disaster."

The fast and upbeat music ended, and the DJ moved the crowd into a slower pace. Couples were now pressed close, arms draped around waists and shoulders as they swayed seductively.

"We should keep up our appearance of a couple on a night out," Shane said.

"What? And dance?"

"Might as well. We're not drinking, and if we stick out here, we're going to attract more unwanted attention."

She shouldn't want it. He was an exasperating man and not her type—if she had a type. Did she have a type? God, who knew? She was the queen of non-dating.

"I don't know, Shane, this . . . "

"Have you ever done an undercover operation?"

She frowned. "Sort of."

"In this situation, you've got to blend in and not cause waves. So far, we've done a poor job of it. Besides, if we don't go out there and dance, someone else is going to come asking either one of us. And we can't turn them down all night."

He had a point. That Ziggy kid had been insistent that one did not come to a dance club and not dance. It was possible, though Shane hadn't confirmed it, that Twiggy had been trying to get him on the floor in order to convince him she wanted in his pants. Liza's body warmed. Her gaze started to move south, but she brought that to a screeching halt.

Be a professional.

"No dirty dancing."

He grinned. "Wouldn't think of it."

They left their table and headed for the edge of the dancing couples. Facing Shane, she stiffened. Up close, she was acutely aware of how tall he was. No slouch in the height department, she could easily drape her arms over his shoulders, but he would still look down. And . . . she peeked at the top of her blouse. Yep, this shirt had been a mistake to wear.

"Liza, I'm not a pervert."

After a little crazy twitch of her eyes, she stared at him. He had an uncanny sense in reading her mind. No not uncanny . . . disturbing.

He held out his hands. Sighing, she stepped into his personal space, took his offered hands, and found herself drawn close. Shane led her into a slow two-step instead of the almost middle school kind of dance like the younger couples around them were doing. The pace had a sexy quality to it, and Liza liked it.

"You're a man who knows how to dance."

"My momma said there was nothing sweeter in the world than a man who knew how to lead a lady. She taught me everything from the waltz to the two-step."

"Bet you were a hit at all the school dances."

He chuckled. She could listen to him do that all day.

"I was at that. Though what passed as dancing in those days was a disgrace."

"I wouldn't say it was all bad."

"Watching rural kids head bang to punk-grunge is not pretty."

It was her turn to chuckle. She was comfortable with him. Exclude his nosy moment at his home and she actually relaxed around him. A rare feat indeed. The only people in her life who had ever managed that were her adoptive parents, Kurt, then Stephanie and Quinn. In her lifetime, people didn't bother being pleasant to a foster kid. Why worry about it? All foster kids were disrespectful, damaged goods. They didn't last long in homes, and if they didn't run away, they were bounced from place to place.

Her steps faltered. The scars of her past were a hurtful poison.

"I'm losing you again," Shane whispered in her ear.

His sudden nearness brought her out of the painful memories. His scent wove a gold thread of calm through her. She wanted to crawl into his arms and let him hold her. As if sensing her need, he brought their dancing dangerously closer. Liza let him. Now that she was flush to him, she could feel all the hard, lean contours of his body. The warmth of a moment ago turned into a raging fire.

Tilting her head to lay against his shoulder, she half nuzzled the juncture of his neck and shoulder. This produced a rumble from him, which sent a bolt of awareness through her. Swallowing against the tightness, she let her hand slide down his chest and then slip around his lean waist. For a man who loved his sweets, he was fit, and oh so damn fine.

After a subtle shift of his hips, Liza got the full scope of how much he was enjoying their little dance. Her knees weakened. How she wished it were just the two of them, somewhere private where she could freely express how much she appreciated his interest.

"Liza," he rumbled in her ear.

"Hush. Don't ruin it."

"Look at me," he persisted.

Grudgingly, she lifted her head from his shoulder and met his heated gaze. Hers drifted to his lips. *Kiss me, you fool.*

His head bent toward her.

Here it comes! Finally!

His lips were a hairsbreadth from hers. His breath feathered her face. His arms tightened around her, trapping her to his body.

Do it! Kiss me!

Liza's eyes shuttered. She was going to savor every second of this. She angled her head for better contact, brushing her lips to his. Shane drew back slightly, dipped in to lightly press his lips to hers, then drew back once more. Desire for more burned a path straight to Liza's heart. Rolling up onto her tiptoes, she moved in for the kill.

The gun blast shattered both her moment and her hearing.

CHAPTER EIGHTEEN

Chaos erupted in an instant. Shane clutched Liza to him as he scanned the now screaming and surging crowd for the shooter. People bumped or slammed into him, desperate to get out of the building.

Liza squirmed, breaking free of his vice grip. "I'll get the shooter!" she hollered over the noise. She swung her purse around and pulled out her weapon. She split, heading toward one of the exits.

There were people to rescue; he had to make sure no one was hurt. And, like in his army days, he geared up and headed for the threat as others fled from it. Drawing his sidearm and turning his body sideways, he sliced through the sea of terrified humans, moving toward the place where he thought he'd heard the original shot.

No further weapon fire occurred, but the panic was in full throttle. People were pushed to the floor and nearly trampled before being rescued by good Samaritans. Shane moved onward, his progress hindered as he came to a wall of immobile bodies.

"Sheriff! Move!"

The command startled a few out of their stupor. They stumbled away, opening a gap wide enough for Shane to fit through. He breached the ring of bodies, entering the center of their circle.

"Damn it."

Lying on the floor, blood pooling beneath him, Derek Schofield's body twitched its last. His date sat next to him, her shock evident by the pallor of her skin and the frozen expression of horror on her face.

Shane turned to those still lingering, his gaze roving over the stupefied group. No one held a gun. The shooter had escaped, unless Liza managed to get lucky. Highly doubtful with all these people scared out of their minds. This was the perfect night and place to pull off a homicide.

"Damn it." It had happened under his nose, no less.

A few of those too dumbfounded to leave were turning green.

"If you're going to throw up, do it away from my crime scene," he barked.

His order had the desired effect, and those looking bad staggered to the bar.

"Help him."

Shane looked down at the blonde. Her whole body shook, but she managed to hold Derek's limp hand.

"Please. Help him."

If it had been anywhere else and he was any other person, Shane might have made the attempt to pretend to save Derek. But the bloodstain on the front of his once dark blue plaid shirt was proof enough that no pretending was going to save this man's life. He'd taken the bullet straight to the heart.

Shane removed his cell. Dispatch picked up. "Jennings, there's been a 10-35 at Riker's Club. Send all emergency personnel and Eider police. Copy."

"Roger."

Hanging up, Shane returned his phone to his pocket. *Damn it to hell!*

"You've got to help him," the blonde sobbed out.

Careful to not disturb the scene any more than it had been, Shane navigated around Derek's body and crouched next to the woman. "Ma'am, are you hurt?"

She blinked up at him; her pupils were huge. Her shock-riddled brain took its time to process his question. "No," she whispered.

"Can you stand?"

More time passed before she silently gathered her legs under her and then wobbled up onto her feet. Once she was upright, she turned and collapsed.

Shane grabbed her before she hit the floor. Hoisting her into a cradle, he carried her over to the bar. She didn't utter another sound as he laid her on the floor under the massive counter. Shane instructed those who had remained to look after her, and to sit down themselves before they passed out.

Pixie, the bartender, popped up like the weasel from behind the counter. "Is the shooter gone?"

As if the question magically conjured her, Liza materialized beside him. "I couldn't see anyone who might be the culprit. Do you have security cameras?"

"Yes," Pixie nodded, "in the manager's office."

"I need to see those, now."

"Liza."

Her gaze slashed to him.

"There's a victim."

Pixie gasped. "Oh no."

Liza frowned. "Do you know the victim?"

He looked down at the now uncontrollably sobbing blonde with her arms wrapped about her in a sorry attempt of self-comfort, and then back at the prone form under the darkened lights. His unspoken answer dawned in Liza's eyes.

"Eider police and EMS are on the way." He pointed at Pixie. "Take Agent Bartholomew to the office and show her the footage. We may still be able to catch this shooter yet."

The weight of Liza's grip on his arm was a solid reminder of how close he'd come to making a huge mistake. Dancing with her, she'd felt like heaven in his arms. And when she laid her head on his shoulder and he could feel her lips brushing against his neck, he came undone. The thought of kissing her had consumed him. Now he'd be forever haunted about how close he'd come to destroying his vow to Cheyenne.

"Shane, I'm sorry this has happened again," Liza said.

He gave her a squeeze on the hand. "Go. I need to protect the body." Outside, the wail of sirens pierced the night.

Here came the cavalry, but they were too late for Derek Schofield. Damn it, if he hadn't been so wrapped up in kissing Liza, this never would have happened. He couldn't afford to have anyone else hurt on his watch.

• • •

If he were still a drinking man, he'd crack the cap off a few beers right now. The throbbing behind Shane's eyes was a blatant reminder that he hadn't slept well three nights straight, and it was nearly twenty hours since he rolled off the couch. He checked his watch for the hundredth time in the past fifteen minutes. The hour hand was inching closer to one a.m.

Arching his aching back, Shane groaned. Shouldn't have left the aspirin at home. His gaze swept the club floor, pausing on Drummond. The doc had already released Derek Schofield's body. Now all that remained was repacking his kit. The few Eider police officers allowed to assist at the scene were busy calming club patrons and patrolling the area. Con was in full out investigator-mode, interviewing everyone involved. It was odd not being the one in charge and asking the questions. Shane was itching all over from the lack of responsibility.

And it wasn't from a lack of trying. Before Con arrived, Shane had tried to get the woman with Derek to talk. Had she seen the shooter? Did she know why—except for Derek's obvious philandering—someone would want to kill him? The more Shane probed, the more the woman shut down, bordering on catatonic. He backed off. Hopefully, he hadn't hindered Con's investigation.

Liza had been as unsuccessful in her video viewing. The shooter had used the melee to escape. Liza had mentioned that it was too difficult to distinguish anyone with a weapon. It hadn't helped matters that those people dancing around Derek and his date weren't able to give any information. No one saw a thing.

And the killer got away.

Sequestered in a corner, far from him, Liza spoke with Con. Shane and Liza had both gone over what they knew about the situation and why they were there a few times already. Tedious, but effective, and now Shane understood why witnesses got irritated with repeating their story. Typically, he gave a person some space and time to let the events soak in and regurgitate. But that wasn't how Con rolled.

Giving Con a curt nod, Liza left and rejoined Shane. "If you're ready to go, he said we're free."

He rubbed the back of his neck. "I should head out, but . . . "

"But you're not used to sitting on the sidelines and watching someone else do your job."

"Nail on the head."

Liza smiled. "Sheriff, *get over it*," she sing-songed.

First the Desperado ringtone and now the reference to another song. "Are you an Eagles's fan?"

"Something like that." She reached out, took his hand, and gave it a tug. "Come on. I'm your ride, and if you don't leave with me, you're stuck."

"You know that's a piss-poor excuse? I've got plenty of options for getting home."

"And Con told me to tell you, and I quote, 'get your sorry ass home before he calls Nic to come get you,' end quote."

Shane shuddered. "He would use that threat." He slid off the bar stool and hobbled forward a few steps. "Damn those things are uncomfortable."

"On purpose, so no one will stick around longer than they should."

They left.

"Do you think my meeting was nothing more than a way to get me here to see Derek Schofield killed?" she asked.

Shane's steps faltered and he stopped. "I hadn't considered . . . " He scratched his right temple. "What color did you say that car was that followed you?"

"Gray, silverish."

Too vague. A lot of people in this county drove SUVs about the same color; it was damn popular option. "Model?"

"Buick. And no, I didn't get the plates. I was a bit distracted."

Well, the model narrowed it down. But it didn't match up with the reason Derek was killed or who had done it. "Why would the killer want you here to see that?"

"Maybe it wasn't me that they wanted to see it." Liza stared at him knowingly.

If he was the reason, then Shane had created a whole new problem, because someone was using Liza to get to him. And it begged the question, how did the death of Derek Schofield have anything to do with the deaths of Gene Avery and Donovan Frost?

With a huff, Shane continued on to Liza's car, with her hot on his heels. He caught her hand as she unlocked her car and held out his other. "Let me drive."

She drew back the key, her fingers curling around the fob. "Why?"

"I know a faster way out of here that avoids the mess of police and gawkers." And he wanted to test a theory.

"Just show me how."

"It'll be easier if I drive."

"You do realize it's my car?"

"My town, my county."

Stalemate. Liza stared at him with a half-lidded glare that made him want to reconsider his request.

"My car, Sheriff." The cool, yet firm tone of her voice was all kinds of seductive.

Liza Bartholomew had some strange hold on him, and he couldn't shake it. She had a man in her life; she was off limits. Or should be. If he wasn't mistaken, Liza had seemed particularly urgent in trying to kiss him herself. Hadn't she been the first to graze her lips to his? Who was this Kurt guy to her if she was all too willing to get in a lip lock with Shane?

A car door slamming jolted him. He released her hand and shoved his own in his jean pockets. "Look, I have an ulterior motive to driving."

"Oh, do tell."

Shane assessed the parking lot: the cops were too focused on their duties to even give Shane and Liza a second glance, which meant no one would squeal to Con. None of the Riker's Club patrons seemed overly interested in them, either. Beckoning Liza closer to her car, Shane draped his arm over the roof and leaned forward. Big mistake when he recalled how close they had been dancing in the club. He wanted to rip back through time to those precious minutes when he had her in his arms and was about to taste her lips. Except holding her had created another hellstorm.

Clearing his throat, he banished those wayward thoughts. "As I said, it's my town. Con hasn't lived here long enough to know all its secrets."

"You do?"

"Agent Bartholomew, I know where the founding members of Eider put their outhouses."

Her face screwed up in disgust. "TMI." Sighing, Liza shifted her body weight. "And you don't want Con to know what?"

"I think the shooter knew everyone would be looking for him or her to disappear out the front door with the flood of escaping clubgoers. Didn't you scope out the exits?"

"Yes, there was one back with the bathrooms." Her features lit up. "Dang, I didn't think of it. If the shooter ran out that door, it would have sounded an alarm."

"I didn't hear an alarm."

"Maybe it was a silent one that could only be heard in the manager's office."

"Did you happen to see anything on the video that would prove that?"

She shook her head. "There was a steady flow of people going through all the exits. No one stood out to me. Maybe Con will have better luck."

"And that's where my thought plays in." Shane turned and pointed at the back of the old factory. "Behind this are a few acres of trees. It opens into an old unused field. The shooter might have used that as an escape route to avoid detection on the roads."

"And you want to drive back there? In my car?"

"Don't worry, I won't hurt your car. There are roads."

"Shane, it's zero dark thirty. Shouldn't you think about doing this with daylight?"

"Liza, this is the best time to do it."

With a huff, she reached out, grabbed his hand, and slapped her keys in it. "Don't scratch my paint." Off she scooted to climb into the passenger side of the car.

Shane gazed at the keys in his hand. That was . . . strange. He half-expected her to continue to argue.

He drove out of the lot as if heading home, and then circled around on a side street.

"I didn't get a chance to ask before the police arrived—were you able to get that woman with the victim to talk?" Liza asked as she craned her neck to see where he was taking them.

"No. I'm pretty certain Con won't have any luck, either. I wouldn't be surprised if they end up taking her to the hospital to sedate her once reality hits."

"That poor girl. She'll be scarred for life."

"This is going to get ugly real fast. We have three dead husbands in the span of a week." His body felt weighted. "Damn, I'm going to hear about this for a month or more."

He stiffened as she placed her hand on his arm. Though his jacket kept them from skin-to-skin contact, he burned at the warmth that managed to seep through.

"Why do you keep doing the job if you can't stand how people talk about you?"

Forcing his gaze to remain on the lighted gravel road, he waited for his thumping heart to calm itself. If he pulled this car over now, he would not be held responsible for his actions. "I might not like people's opinions on what they think I, as the sheriff, should or shouldn't do, but I've never been one to give up in the face of gossip and speculation. Humans in general seem to think they can always do a job better than the people actually in the position, but give them the option to do it and they turn coward."

"You know, I never looked at it like that." Her hand fell away from his arm. His body ached at the absence. "When you live your life trying to survive, you don't get philosophical."

The grassy outlet for the field appeared at the edge of the headlights. Shane pulled in, parked, and killed the engine, her statement echoing in his head. Liza opened her door and moved to exit. His hand shot out and snagged her elbow. Stilling, she looked back at him.

"What do you mean 'trying to survive'?"

In the glow of the dome light, her dark features turned rock hard, just as they had when he brought up Kurt and Quinn. Liza had some ghosts haunting her.

"Where are we going?"

Damn, she was as good as he was at changing the subject. Okay, if that's how she wanted to play it. Shane exited the car, paused, and then ducked down to look back inside. "Do you have a flashlight in here?"

One exasperated sigh later, she produced a heavy duty Maglite from under the passenger side seat and thumped it in his outstretched hand. "I'm seriously considering using that thing up side your head."

"That would hurt."

"That's the point." She vacated her vehicle and met him at the front of the car. "Am I expected to follow you?"

"Well, that would be preferred since I don't think you have another flashlight in the car and you don't know where we're going."

"I could just wait here for you."

He flicked the beam on her sandaled feet. "Actually, you might want to do that. The ticks will make a feast out of you."

"Ticks? Already?"

He smiled at her. "Welcome to rural Iowa, m'lady." Moving out to make a path through the tall grass, Shane swept the beam ahead of him.

"Shane."

"Yeah?"

A heartbeat later, "Be careful."

He took in the sight of her, standing in front of the headlights, the glow accenting her curves. For one second, he considered abandoning this idea and going back to her to complete what they'd started on the dance floor. Another second flashed past, and he realized how stupid that would be. His heart was not free to give. Nor was she free for the taking.

"I always am." Setting out, he headed for the trees.

Closing in on the much darker tree line, he drew his weapon, holding it at ready. After a double pass with the flashlight, he breached the leafy overhang and entered another world. The heavy scent of hickory and cedar mingled with mustiness and decayed leaves. Shane took care to tread with a light foot as he eased through the sparse stand of trees. From where he walked, he made out the faint light from the old factory.

Back and forth, in a slow sweep, he passed the flashlight over the ground, looking for signs of disturbance in the padded timber floor. A hurried person could get careless, leaving a trace of their path behind. It was also possible that he was out of his mind and the shooter had not come this way. Hesitating, he rotated and passed the light over the path behind him. Yeah, he could see a faint impression of his footprints. He checked his watch. Too much time had lapsed since the shooting. If the shooter had indeed come this way, any trace of their escape was long gone.

Screw it. He had to check, if nothing more than to ease his mind. He pressed forward, taking the time to examine the area as best he could with the flashlight. The closer he came to the end of the stand of trees, the brighter the lights were from the factory. He would need to turn around and head back soon, before someone spotted his light and sounded an unnecessary alarm.

About to give up on this futile search, Shane moved the Maglite to the left; the beam glinted off something metallic. Adjusting the light, he could make out something cylindrical. *What do we have here?* He approached the object and crouched down. With the tip of his weapon, he eased the tuft of grass aside. Shit. A discarded Busch Lite can. Panning the light over the area, he found more discarded beer cans and a few empty liquor bottles. It was party central out here. The prime place to hide from the authorities and hold an underage drinking party.

"Damn it," he spit.

Rising, he kicked at the can. This had been a stupid idea. Turning to leave, he froze.

"You shouldn't have come," the hooded figure said before the gun went off.

CHAPTER NINETEEN

Liza broke out into an all out sprint. More shots echoed through the night, kicking her heart and legs into overdrive.

Don't trip. Don't break anything! Don't get lost!

Easier thought than done. She was going in blind, trying to gauge her path by where she thought she had heard the last gunshot. Weaving around the trees, she used the flashlight app on her phone to avoid a collision with the trunks. Wonderful, she remembered her damn phone, but not her gun. She could hear Montrose saying, *This is how an agent gets dead, Agent Bartholomew.*

Bite me!

She was Shane's last line of defense. But she'd be no good to him if she couldn't find him. No way in hell was she calling out and drawing enemy fire. Slowing, Liza took stock of her surroundings. Through the pitch blackness, she made out a faint light straight ahead of her. Closing the flashlight app on her phone, she opened a line for 911 and picked a path through the overgrowth and tangle of tree roots, her gaze darting around. At this point, if the shooter appeared out of nowhere, Liza didn't know who'd be more surprised, but she wasn't about to let them get the upper hand. She might be weaponless, but she wasn't without resources.

The faint light brightened with every inch, and Liza could make out voices. Squinting through the gloom, she could see the outline of something large and looming in the distance, backdropped by more light. Was that Riker's Club?

At the rustle of leaves, Liza spun and reached for a gun that wasn't there. She crouched down. There was no further sound. Liza remained in her spot, her gaze scanning each dark form to make out if it was object or foe. But there wasn't enough foliage here. She was a sitting duck. She awkwardly waddled away from her spot.

Beyond the trees the voices gained volume, and bobbing lights joined the crescendo of noise. The police were coming to investigate the fired shots.

"Liza," a pain-riddled voice hissed.

She swiveled on the balls of her feet, gasping. "Shane." She scrambled over to his position, propped against a twig of a tree. Placing her hands on his upper body, she stiffened at the sticky wetness that met her right hand.

He sucked in a breath at her touch.

"What happened?"

"Someone wasn't happy with me checking back here."

Liza pulled her hand away, her stomach roiling at the heavy metallic odor. "You're shot."

"It's a scratch."

"Bullshit." Liza wiped her hand on his jeans. "Where's my flashlight?" She peered around the tree to spot the single dot of light that must be her Maglite. In the distance the bobbing lights were gaining. Help was closer. She tried to crawl over Shane's legs, but he gripped her arm.

"Don't. I don't think the shooter has left yet."

Cold dread turned her stomach into a lump of coal. Liza rocked back on her heels. "The police are coming from the club."

"Let them." Shane groaned, then set to panting.

"Where are you hit?"

"I can't tell."

Opening the flashlight app on her phone once more, she held it up.

"Liza, no."

She swatted away his good hand as he tried to reach for her phone. "Stop it. If that shooter was still here, they'd have finished you off by now."

Her boldness plummeted when the light from her phone fell on Shane's torso. His jacket was flung back, exposing the bloodstained shirt. Liza's throat tightened as bile threatened her bulwarks. With a shaking hand, she tugged the shirt hem upward and released her pent-up breath. Just above his waistline a good-sized hole gushed blood.

"It's not that bad."

Her gaze snapped to his pain-filled face. "Are you whacked? You're bleeding buckets."

"It didn't hit anything vital."

"I think a doctor should determine that, not some cowboy sheriff." She rolled the hem back over the wound. "How did you not get shot in the gut?"

"Cat-like reflexes." His chuckle was cut short by a groan. "Ow, guess I shouldn't be funny."

"Police!"

Liza hopped up and waved her arms as she was blasted by flashlight beams. Using her arm as a shield from the blinding light, she squinted at the group. "It's the sheriff, he's been shot."

She was spared the further assault on her eyes as all the lights dropped, but the spots were still there.

"Damn it, Shane!" came Con's voice.

"Ah, shit," Shane hissed.

• • •

"He'll be okay."

Liza gnawed on her thumbnail, eavesdropping on Dr. Drummond's discussion with Con and Nic.

"I had to stich up his side. The bullet passed through, missing the organs. He's lucky."

"He's a damn lucky idiot," Nic growled. She had arrived not long after the EMS unit unloaded Shane. Apparently Con's mother was watching their kids.

Nic's piercing hazel gaze swung to her husband. "And you let him."

"Woman, I sent him home on the threat if he didn't, you'd come and get him. How was I supposed to know he'd sneak around my back and do his job?"

Apparently, Drummond found something on the ceiling to study. Liza's gaze followed his, and then she snapped hers back down. What was she doing? Drummond was trying to let the couple have their moment. Heck, they probably argued like this in front of everyone.

"What was he doing there in the first place?"

Liza stiffened like the deer in the headlights of a speeding car when three pairs of eyes swung to her.

"Care to explain, Agent Bartholomew?" Con asked.

She scowled at him. The sneaky Irishman knew damn well why she and Shane had been at the club but not why they were behind it. She swallowed the Rock of Gibraltar. "It was his idea, not mine."

Nic blinked, her features puckering. She scratched her forehead. "So, you let him talk you into stumbling through the dark after a shooter? Alone?"

"I didn't say it was the most sensible idea ever. We weren't expecting anyone to be back there."

"She's not wrong there," Con said.

Nic swatted his arm. "Are you insane? If one of his deputies had done something that stupid, Hamilton would rip them a new one. Hell, he did it to me."

"Guess the rules change when it's the boss," Liza said.

Nic's ire turned on her. "Why are you even here, Agent? Aren't you way out of your expertise?"

"Enough, Nic."

The barked command snapped the former marine sniper to attention. Liza wanted those mad skills.

Shane tottered out of his exam room and paused in the doorway. A blue doctor's scrub top replaced his blood-soaked shirt. His gaze slid to Liza and back to the dark-haired woman and his best friend. "Leave Liza alone. Anyone's at fault here it's me."

The use of her first name wasn't lost on the trio if the expressions of bewilderment were an indication. Liza's face heated.

"Doc, I'd like your opinion. Am I free to go home, or are you going to confine me to a hospital bed?"

Drummond frowned. "My 'expert' opinion would be you should stay and rest. But we all know that won't happen. My advice is that you go to bed and rest. Take the day off and let others handle your duties."

"Good to know." Shane gave Drummond a salute then hobbled over to Liza. "Would you mind giving me a ride home? I promise I won't bleed on your car."

When he worded it like that, how could a girl resist? "Uh, sure." She glanced at Nic.

Thoughtfulness filled the woman's eyes.

Shane turned to Drummond. "Doc, got my release papers?"

"Give me a moment." Drummond vacated the little powwow.

Con sidled up beside his friend and lowered his head to whisper something to Shane. Liza picked up the radar signal and scooted off to give them privacy.

It was probably about her.

However, her singleness left her open for Nic's counteroffensive. Cornered near the nurse's station, Liza's hackles rose.

"Don't get your panties in a wad." And this was Nic being mild. Boyce had always snarked about Nic's mouth giving a dumpster a run for its money.

"What?" Liza bit back.

"When you get Shane home, make him go to bed." Nic's gaze roved down and up. "To sleep."

Oh, no, she didn't. "What are you insinuating, *Mrs. O'Hanlon*?"

A slick smile appeared. "I don't insinuate, *Agent*." With that, she walked away, joining her husband as he left the ER.

Liza gaped at their backsides. What the hell? Did Nic honestly think she would attempt to jump Shane's bones after he'd been wounded? Warmth spread through her at the thought of sex with Shane. Sure, maybe she wanted to kiss him, nearly did that while they were dancing, but sex was . . . huge. The next question begged, as the O'Hanlons left the hospital, what did Nic see to even give her the idea that something, anything, could be going on? Hell, Liza couldn't figure out what was going on between her and Shane.

A finger poked her shoulder. Turning her head in increments, she peered up at Shane. *God, even hurt, you're sexy.* Wait, hold it, back up the car. These kind of thoughts and actions were what got another person killed and Shane seriously hurt tonight. People were counting on her to come through with results.

"Let's get out of here before someone changes their mind," he said.

Nodding, she started for the exit.

Shane cleared his throat, putting a halt to her feet. "Um, could I get some help?" He grimaced. "These stiches hurt . . . like a bitch."

Now this was a first for her, a big, strong man like Shane Hamilton asking for assistance. "That can be arranged."

"Much obliged, ma'am."

"Don't go all 'shucks, ma'am' on me, cowboy."

The twinkle in his eyes was matched only by the big smile. God, it was good to see his humor hadn't bled out in the tree grove. He hooked his arm around her shoulder, and Liza tucked herself snugly to his uninjured side, grunting under his added weight. For someone as rail thin as Shane, he sure weighed a ton.

"Don't let those two see you doing this," he whispered.

She winked. "We'll make like spies and disappear."

Their path to her car was slow. Once she had him in the seat, she aided him in reclining it back.

"Better?"

He sighed. "Much. Who knew standing and sitting would hurt like hell?"

"Anyone who's taken a bullet to the midsection. Didn't Dr. Drummond give you any pain meds?"

He lifted his hips awkwardly to reach into his jean pocket and pull out a prescription bottle. "My dealer supplied me."

"Smart ass."

"I'm here all day."

Rolling her eyes, Liza shut the door with a clap. A drugged Shane Hamilton could prove interesting. A sly thought slipped through her mind.

And maybe a drugged Shane was a loose-lipped Shane, too.

CHAPTER TWENTY

After a drawn-out argument—Liza knew better than to dispute with the doped-up sheriff, but the stubborn ass wouldn't let it go—she relented and picked up her things at Cassy's. Now she was toweling off water from her shower, but only after she made damn sure Shane wasn't trying to make her breakfast.

With slow, practiced strokes, she wrung the water from her springy hair. The waves were tightening into their natural coiled state. It sucked that she had none of her hair products with her. And none of the stores in Eider carried her preferred brands. There was one hair stylist in town—according to Jolie Murdoch—but it was a white woman who had never worked with African American hair. No way in Hades was Liza letting inexperienced hands touch her head. Looked like braids and ponytails were the norm.

Satisfied with a loose braid draped over her shoulder, she slipped into her clothing. It was too bad about the ruined pants and blouse she'd bought yesterday. Between the grass stains, dirt, and Shane's blood, there was no salvaging the outfit. A crying shame. Wadding up the mess, she shoved it into a plastic bag, and then carried everything out of the bathroom. She padded barefoot into the kitchen—good, Shane hadn't disobeyed orders—and dumped the ruined clothing into the trash.

Liza peeked around the corner, noticing the door to the left of the hall was partially closed. Curiosity killed this kitty-cat. Setting her stuff down, she tiptoed to the door and gave it a soft push. The door glided away from her, revealing the bed.

Shane was asleep on top of his covers in only a pair of athletic shorts. The bandages were stark white against his tawny skin. How had he stayed so tanned through the winter? His chest rose and fell in an even rhythm, but it was the twinkling object draped over his right pectoral that drew her attention. She crept closer to the bed.

The mystery of the silver chain was solved. The diamond in the ring wasn't something to shout from the mountaintops, but it was beautiful just the same. And it screamed that he'd been in love with someone enough to be engaged.

So what happened to change that?

Did it have something to do with the picture of him in army gear she'd found on his kitchen counter?

Easing her body onto the bedside, she stiffened when her weight shifted the mattress, causing Shane to stir. Two seconds later, he resettled. Breathing once more, Liza reached out and gently plucked the ring from his chest, her fingertips grazing his warm skin and sending jitters tracking through her nerves. If only she could touch more of him.

Don't go there, Liza.

She twirled the ring to examine the band. Eureka! There was an inscription. Squinting, she leaned closer to read: *Cheyenne . . .*

Shane's hand wrapped around her wrist and clenched. Liza's mouth went as dry as the Sahara.

"What are you doing?" he rumbled.

The ring flipped from her fingers and thunked against his chest. Their gazes clashed, his filled with pain and simmering anger.

"I'll show you mine if you show me yours," she whispered.

Rapid blinking was his response. Releasing his hold on her, he moved to roll away. Liza pressed her hand into his shoulder, stopping him.

"Kurt is my foster brother. Quinn is his autistic son." God, had she just blurted that out? "They're as close to family as I'll ever get."

Wariness crept into Shane's haggard features. "What are you trying to do?"

"Get you to talk to me. Open up."

"About things that are highly private?"

"That's what Kurt and Quinn were. Now what?"

• • •

He wanted to be furious with Liza, but he couldn't muster up the strength to let her have it. Must be the drugs dulling his senses.

Or the weight of carrying his secret for such a long time had finally become too much to bear.

Some portion of his non-drugged mind felt relief that Kurt wasn't a husband or boyfriend and Shane hadn't crossed any ethical lines by trying to kiss her.

"Cheyenne? Who was she?"

None of her business. The words were there, tickling his tongue, ready to explode from his mouth. But he held back. He couldn't tell her, wouldn't tell her.

"Shane." Liza's sweet whisper raked across his heart.

He shook his head. "Don't. I can't."

She touched his bicep then ran her hand down the length of his arm. The caress sent ripples of pleasure through him, killing the pain, emotionally and physically. Yet it hurt him. Ripped him apart. He didn't deserve the tenderness of a woman.

"Tell me," she said softly. "I'm not going anywhere."

Reaching up, he brushed his knuckles along her jawline. Liza's eyes shuttered, and he sensed her body melting under his touch. Twining a loose coil, he rubbed it between his fingers, delighting in the silkiness. Her eyes fluttered open, and she tilted her cheek into his hand. Releasing the lock, he cupped her cheek, smoothing his thumb over the high point. God, she was beautiful. Too damn beautiful for the likes of him.

"I have never told anyone." His voice sounded rusty to his ears. It made sense. The subject matter was old, ancient, and God knew he had no desire to unearth it. "What makes you privileged to know my darkest secrets?"

She bent over him, her gorgeous umber eyes burning holes through his fortifications. "Is that what Cheyenne is? Your darkest secret?"

"You don't give up, do you?"

"Not by a long shot." Strands of her hair tickled his face, setting his blood on fire. Her breath feathered him as she leaned closer. "If I'm reading you right, you don't, either. I'll wager you that I'm the only woman in a very long time you've wanted to kiss." She gave him a light press of her lips. "And a kiss can be a powerful motivator."

Every muscle in his body went rigid. *Damn straight.* His hand snaked around to the back of her head and dragged her to him, their lips colliding. She angled her mouth to his as she, *she*, deepened their kiss. She was turning him into a raging inferno. He wanted to feel every inch of her against him, to get a taste of the passion that smoldered inside of her.

The bed shifted under him as she carefully crawled over him, never once breaking the kiss as she straddled him. He moaned against her mouth, his left hand skimming to her backside to cup the back of her thigh. With a gasp, she nipped his bottom lip. A stronger spark ignited as her tongue delved into his mouth.

Son of a bitch, she was a tiger.

As he slid his hands up her hips to her waist, they snuck under the hem of her shirt. When his fingertips grazed the sensitive skin of her lower back and stomach, she shuddered. Shane started to roll up the shirt and hissed in pain.

Liza stilled, her mouth pulling back from him. "Oh no. Your wound."

Pain like fingernails being dug through his skin radiated out from the gunshot wound into the rest of his body, effectively dousing the desire and leaving him panting.

She scrambled back, sighing when she was sitting at his side once more. "You're not bleeding."

"It's nothing," he ground out.

"Says the man speaking through clenched teeth."

"Physical pain I can handle."

"But emotional pain you can't."

"I'm a man, Liza. We don't show our king of hearts."

"So," she rose from the bed, "is that the excuse you're giving me to avoid explaining who Cheyenne was to you? That you have no heart?"

Whoa! Wait one minute. How the hell did she get . . .? Ah shit.

With a shake of her head, she added, "Don't answer that. I don't want to know what's going on in that head. And, honestly, if I were half the investigator I claim to be, I could piece together the truth on my own. Cheyenne was your fiancée, something tragic happened to her—I'm guessing she died—and now you're left with only a bad memory and an empty engagement ring." Liza's eyes narrowed. "And if I could go a step further in my skills, I'd say you did a stint with the army—post 9/11—as a means to help eradicate her memory. Or maybe it was in the hope that you'd die so you wouldn't have to live with the pain of her death."

Son of a bitch, it was like she'd reached inside his head and ripped out every twisted, dark memory he'd had.

"Well, look at that. I must have hit the target somewhere close to the bull's-eye."

"Liza, stop."

"Oh, believe me. I'm done." As the curtain closed on her act, she exited his bedroom, the door shutting with a clap.

This wasn't over.

After a few failed attempts—damn these stitches and his injured side to hell—Shane managed to roll out of the bed. Big mistake lying down. The recliner might be the smarter choice for sleeping arrangements until his side healed enough. With measured steps, he exited his bedroom and inched down the hall to find Liza in the kitchen.

She was propped against the counter, munching on a frosted cherry Pop-Tart, the cabinet door to his stash wide open behind her. Her gaze narrowed as he entered the room. "You were ordered to rest. This isn't you resting."

"Damn difficult when you keep poking your nose in my business and kissing me."

Liza's face flamed a deep auburn. Gulping down a mouthful of his one and only luxury in life, she turned her back to him and closed the cabinet door. "I'm sorry about that. It just . . . happened."

Her defeated tone gave him a right hook to the chin. Giving his unruly hair a good rake with his fingers, he shuffled over to her. Shane gripped her elbow, tugging her around to face him. She couldn't meet his gaze.

"I'm not sorry you kissed me."

"You certainly don't act like it."

"If I didn't want to kiss you, I wouldn't have let it get as far as it did."

Her skepticism permeated the air around them.

"Fine, don't believe me. But it doesn't change what happened." He reached up and cradled her face. "Listen to me carefully. My past is something that has been a part of me for so long, it's hard to let anyone in. No one was to ever know. My parents were it, and with their deaths, my secrets remained with me alone."

She pulled his hands down, keeping a tight grip on his arms. "It must be lonely in that secret world of yours."

Weight pressed down on his shoulders. "Liza, the burden is mine to bear. Don't try to shoulder my pack."

With a sad shake of her head, she released him and backed away. "What's sad is that you think you deserve to be alone. And as one who spent a good chunk of her life alone and pissed off at the world, it freaking sucks, but not once did I think I deserved the lot life handed me. We make choices. It's how we ride out the waves of consequences that determine what kind of person we are. You're just standing in the surf taking the brutal forces and hoping like mad it doesn't knock you off your feet again."

"Why is it so important for you to know?"

She was about to answer when he brought his hands up.

"Actually, don't answer. We have different lives, and it's not like this thing between us will go any further. Once you have your proof, you'll return to your job and your family, and I'll be here." Shane turned, heading for his escape. "I shouldn't have let it go as far as it did."

"That's not fair."

"You're a foster kid. You should know nothing in life is ever fair."

She didn't give him a chance to make good on his escape, skirting around him and blocking the doorway. "This isn't a war. You don't get to retreat after firing those parting shots."

"I do if I want to get some sleep. Doctor's orders and all. I'd suggest you grab some shut-eye, too. You can have my bed. I'll rack out in my recliner since I can't seem to get out of bed easily."

"Shane."

"Liza, I hurt and I'm tired."

"Then sleep. I'm going into the department. Remember, I have a meeting with Roslin Avery."

Damn it, she was right. And he'd wanted to sit in on that conversation. "Can you reschedule so I can be there?"

"No. You're doing what the doctor ordered. I need to report to my SAC, and I'm not telling her I missed talking with Roslin, again. And I have a meeting with the school board president and school accountant." She placed a hand on his chest, next to the dangling ring. "Holding onto her ghost is only making you more miserable. What would she have told you to do if she could see you now?" She gave him a gentle pat and pulled her hand away. "Think on that."

CHAPTER TWENTY-ONE

McIntire County was growing on Liza. She grew more comfortable the longer she drove these backroads and streets. It was a nice feeling not to worry about getting lost. Driving with the windows down, she had her iPhone plugged into her system and her Eagles soundtrack was pouring through the speakers.

Over the years, she'd taken serious tongue lashings from other people of color about her choice of music. It was as if they expected her to love only R&B, rap, or soul, styles that those of her race had created. Liza ignored the pressure. She couldn't explain it in a way they'd ever understand. Something about the Eagles's songs had resonated with her. It went deep, to her bones deep. And if she had to unpack it all, maybe it was something her birth parents had instilled in her. She didn't know. What she did know was that through her years alone and bouncing from one home to the next, the music had been her one constant.

She eased her car into the gravel lot for the sheriff's department and parked in what she'd come to think of as her spot. Killing the engine, she gathered her things, shaking her head briefly when her tired eyes lost focus. She should have gotten a few zzzs before meeting with Roslin, but without knowing when the woman would arrive, Liza couldn't afford to sleep.

Composing herself, she exited the car and headed into the building. The ding of the electronic system announced her entry. As she bypassed the front counter, she halted.

"What's this?"

From behind Jennings's dispatch station, Shane's three deputies eyeballed Liza. Jolie beckoned to her.

"Agent Bartholomew, please join us."

They were all gathered in front of one computer. *This can't be good.* Circling around, Liza was greeted by two faces she hadn't expected to see on this trip.

"Liza, dear, what sort of trouble are you stirring up in my new home?" Boyce Hunt's southern drawl oozed charm.

Liza pinned the deputies with a stern stare. "Does your boss know you're tattling?"

"No, he doesn't," Cassy said over the video chat, "and we need to keep it that way for now. Where is he, by the way?"

"At home, sleeping, last I checked."

"You left him alone? He'll be out of there the moment he has the all-clear."

Liza smirked. "Not likely, since I found all of his keys and took them with me."

Boyce scoffed. "You don't know our illustrious sheriff, Liza. He'll just saddle up and ride into town."

"You can't be serious. He was shot in the side. There's no way he'd be able to lift a saddle, much less climb into it."

"Don't underestimate a determined man." Cassy gave her husband a knowing look. "That's beside the point. Jennings contacted me to update me on the situation there. And it seems we have a problem with chain of command."

Liza bent over, bracing her hands on the desktop. "Wouldn't your department defer to the police chief?"

Cassy's gaze darted to the young woman next to Liza. Jolie Murdoch shrugged.

"Not really," Cassy said. "I'm the under-sheriff, and since I'm not there, I can't take command of the office."

"Well, who would be next in line?"

"That should be me," Deacon Nash said, his hand shot up to halt anyone from speaking, "but I don't have the experience."

"Which is where you come in, Agent Bartholomew."

"You can't be serious? I'm not authorized to man a sheriff's department."

"Actually, in this case, the district judge and I can grant you the authorization. With Hamilton injured and trouble going on there, we need someone to handle this. I can't leave here, or I'm out of the K-9 program. In this case, you're the most senior officer we have."

"Cassy, this has to be cleared with my office, and I know for a fact my SAC won't allow it."

"Then tell Montrose to bring her happy ass down there to help," Boyce said. "I always thought she lost her touch as a field agent when she sat behind a desk."

"Boyce, there's no way she'd . . . scratch that. There's no way I can nail this case if she's here running things."

"Then take command."

Liza looked at each of the deputies surrounding her. "Is this what you want?"

"Ma'am, we all have our places, and being in charge isn't one of them," Jennings said. "Sheriff Hamilton has done a bang-up job of giving us enough leeway to take charge of certain things on our own, but he's not sheriff without reason. We need orders."

"He's right, Liza."

So glad they have a vote of confidence in me. How was she supposed to do this and complete her investigation and get home to Quinn? The expectant faces peering at her were no help. She didn't know the first thing about commanding people, much less how to run a sheriff's department. Damn it, she was trying to get out of law enforcement, not get sucked further in.

"Team, take five," Cassy said.

The deputies dispersed, leaving Liza as alone as one could get with a video chat over a computer.

Cassy leaned closer to the screen. "Liza, listen, if I could, I'd be there in a heartbeat. I know this is not what you're supposed to do. But I can't ask Nic to take my place."

Nic! Why hadn't Liza suggested her first? "Why not?"

Cassy sighed. "First, she's pregnant again. Second, she's supposed to leave tomorrow with her mother-in-law to go on a trip to Ireland. Con doesn't know that's where they're going, by the way, so keep this to yourself. Some kind of secret reason about going back home for something. I don't know for sure."

"Okay. Wait, didn't she just have a baby. Don't those two know how that all works?"

Boyce snorted, then gasped when his wife elbowed him in the ribs.

"Nic is running out of time and they wanted a lot of kids. I know, I know, it doesn't seem possible with her, but she's found her niche as a mother. Hence why I don't want her running things while I'm gone and Hamilton is laid up. Nic has to think about her kids, and she won't let just anyone watch over them. Besides that, her mother-in-law would never let Nic back out of their trip so she could be sheriff for the day."

"You're more than capable of handling this until Hamilton is able to resume his duties," Boyce said.

"I'm glad you both think so, but . . . " God, should she tell them? Liza glanced about, finding the deputies thoroughly engrossed in whatever it was they were doing. She hunkered down, staring at the couple on the screen. "You two must be the bearers of secrets." Liza shook her head. "After I wrap this case, I'm out. Done. No more FBI and no more law enforcement."

Boyce frowned. "Why? You're a good agent."

"Glad you think so, but I have obligations of my own that I can't keep pushing aside anymore. I have to finalize my findings here and get back to Cedar Rapids. I really can't be here much longer. What about the former sheriff? Would he come in?"

"He has too many health issues," Cassy said. "Liza, I realize . . . "

The electronic bell chimed, and Liza didn't hear the rest of what Cassy said. Peering over the top of the computer, she spotted Roslin. She ducked down. "Guys, I've got an interview to conduct. You should consider someone else."

Cassy checked her watch. "If I can find someone else."

"Hello?" came Roslin Avery's voice.

"Sorry, you two, gotta go. Later." Liza killed the video feed and popped up. "Mrs. Avery." She hustled around the counter as the deputies emerged.

Roslin frowned. "Is the sheriff here?"

"He's out of the office this morning."

"Oh, I was supposed to meet with him. I guess I can come back later." Roslin started to turn.

"Wait, you were going to meet with me. The sheriff just set up the meeting."

Roslin blinked, confusion playing havoc on her features. "You?" She squinted. "You look familiar."

"Probably. I was . . . the one who tackled you at the fire."

"Yeah. Why did you do that?"

Was this woman for real? "Because you were pointing a gun at the sheriff."

Roslin pressed her hand to her O-shaped mouth. "I didn't."

She was for real. Or pulling off the perfect clueless act. Liza couldn't get a good read on Roslin. If she got her to sit down and talk, maybe she'd figure the woman out.

Liza stuck out her hand. "Agent Bartholomew, FBI."

"FBI? Why do you need to talk to me? I'm in big enough trouble for that fire."

"I'm aware of that. However, I wanted to ask about your husband, Gene."

"Whatever for?"

Liza looked back at the milling deputies. "Deputy Murdoch, would it be okay to use the sheriff's office?"

Jolie shrugged. "Fine by us. Nash and I will be heading out to patrol. You need anything, Jennings will be here."

Shane's office felt empty without his commanding presence. His scent, however, hung heavy in the air. Liza's heart fluttered at the memory of his earthy scent surrounding her as they kissed. Banishing the sudden desire, she rounded his desk and took the chair, regretting her move when she was wrapped in more of Shane Hamilton.

Focus, Liza!

She found a pen and paper in the side drawers, along with an empty Pop-Tarts box. It appeared Shane was overdue for a restock. Liza did not touch the box of files she'd left in his office, noting that there was an extra banker's box next to it. One of the deputies, probably Jennings, had brought in the warranted school files. She would have to scour those before she met with the school board officials.

On the other side of the desk, Roslin arranged herself, crossing her legs at the knees and getting generally comfortable. When she was satisfied, she tilted her chin and looked at Liza. An air of self-importance replaced the once confused one. "What do you need to know about my Gene?"

Her Gene? Interesting.

"Well, let's start with how you met him."

Roslin wagged her right hand in an "ah posh" gesture. "We met several years ago." She sobered. "I was working in a bank in Clarinda. He walked in, and I was in love."

That Mr. Ripley slash Gene Avery walked into a bank was surprising, but Roslin's immediate attraction to him was not. He'd had a charisma that snagged women easily, which worked to his advantage.

"We were married three months later, and then he got the job here as a superintendent."

"Mrs. Avery, was he a superintendent when you met?"

Her brunette hair swung. "Naw, he was just finishing his schooling to be one."

"What was he doing in the bank?"

Roslin seemed to chew on this question. Four clicks of the second hand later, her gaze dropped to her lap. She twirled her wedding band. "He was thinking of getting a loan to finish paying for his classes."

"Did he? Get a loan?"

"I don't know. I wasn't in charge of that."

For Ripley to take out a loan was suspicious. The man hadn't made any attempt to embezzle money from banks. It wasn't as easy a score as hitting small businesses and citizens. That he'd reached a point of conning a school was a bold step for him.

How had Roslin fit into all of this? Smokescreen? A piece of arm candy to deflect any undue suspicion from him? Then there was the matter of his hep C and possible love affair with another man. Liza would get to that soon enough.

"Did he talk about his job a lot?"

"Not really." Roslin gnawed on a fingernail.

"What does 'not really' mean?"

Shrugging, she ceased her nail biting and balled her hand in her lap. "He would talk about the kids. Never naming names." A little too hurried on that part. Could be something to do with confidentiality school officials were supposed to keep. "Other than that, he didn't say much."

Liza tapped the legal pad, rereading the notes. This part was going to get real messy. "Mrs. Avery, you loved your husband, didn't you?"

She nodded. A sheen coated her eyes. Aw, crap. If she started crying, Liza wouldn't get anywhere with her. Slow and easy.

"Did he ever feel ill, or generally unwell with no explanation?"

Roslin's grief was circumvented with a frown. "Not that he mentioned, no."

"Sorry for the intrusive question, but how often did you have sex with him?"

That floored her. Roslin gaped at Liza, her mouth working like a fish's. When the initial shock wore off, red tinged the high points of her face. "I don't see how that's any business of yours or this department."

"Better the question come from me than the sheriff a bit later."

"And why would that have any bearing on my husband's death? Sex lives are a private matter."

"Not if they cross lines that prove motive."

Roslin let out a half shriek, half laugh. "Are you telling me the sheriff thinks *I* killed Gene?"

Leaning forward, Liza stared at the woman. Roslin stared back. It looked like the widow had a backbone after all. Of course, Liza was well aware of this; she was the one who had to fight the crazy stoner before she shot the sheriff.

"Please answer the question, Mrs. Avery."

"No. I believe my lawyer would tell me to not answer."

Liza sat back. "Well, when your lawyer decides she's ready to resume her duties, then we can ask again." Making a show of shuffling papers that Shane had left on his desk, Liza counted off the seconds. "You might want to be tested for some things, like say, oh, some of the hepatitis strains."

Heated silence filled the office. This was why she liked interrogating people. Everyone who sat on the other side of her assumed she was a pushover, the good cop. They were not prepared for the fastballs. And Roslin Avery would not be the exception to the rule.

"Why did you burn the house?" Liza braced for the fallout over that zinger.

"I don't remember why"—clipped words, pissy attitude—"since everything about that day is hazy."

That tended to happen when one mixed drugs and alcohol.

"What kind of FBI agent are you?"

"The kind that is looking into an embezzling case."

"You mean stealing?"

"Something like that."

Roslin's eyes widened. "Is that why Neil Lundy called me last night? He kept asking me a ton of questions I had no answers for."

"Neil Lundy, the school board president?"

"Yes. He wanted to know if Gene ever had large amounts of cash at home or brought lots of paperwork that looked like school stuff."

"Did Gene?"

Roslin shrugged again. That seemed to be her go-to answer for everything. "I don't know. I already told you, he didn't talk about his job or bring anything home. I told Neil to mind his own business and quit bothering me; didn't he realize my husband was murdered? Is that why Gene was killed? He was stealing money?"

"Mrs. Avery, I have no idea at this point."

Her hand flying to her face, Roslin gasped. "Was he caught up with the mob or something? Oh, maybe burning the house was a good thing if he left anything there they could want."

The crazy woman had returned.

"Mrs. Avery, your husband was not involved with the mob."

"How do you know?"

Patience, Liza, patience. "I just know. Back to Mr. Lundy, was there anything else he asked you?"

She shook her head. "He was just angry that I couldn't tell him where Gene took the money."

And she couldn't clue in to what was going on from that? This woman was shaping up to be as useful as a concrete parachute.

"Thank you, Mrs. Avery, that will be all for today." She stood, hoping the woman got the hint and left.

Liza had more research to do before Lundy and the rest of the school board arrived. If that man was nosing around in her investigation, he had some explaining to do. He had been overly concerned, as he should be if he was in charge of the board when money went missing under his watch, but harassing the widow for answers was her job.

God, would this case ever come to an end? The clock was ticking.

CHAPTER TWENTY-TWO

What did Liza know? She was wrong. She knew nothing about his situation and was only playing guessing games. What would Cheyenne think, indeed? He had nothing to worry about, and just because he wanted to kiss the hell out of her didn't mean a damn thing.

Crude as it sounded, he was scratching an itch. A sixteen-year itch.

God, he was such an ass.

With that piercing thought, the drugs kicked in, and he finally found sleep. Except, the hydrocodone gave him whacked-out dreams. Once their heavy effect wore off and he woke again, Shane was disorientated but a little more enlightened. Next time he would rather tough out the pain than relive a psychedelic trip down memory lane. Yet, had it not been for the drugs, he might have forgotten a vital piece of information that had slipped his mind after being shot.

The person who shot him was a woman. Thank God she was a piss-poor shot or he'd not be breathing air.

He tried to dredge up any recollection of her voice and her shape, but everything was a blur. Things happened too fast, and he was still hazy over details. He did recall he'd fired back, and may have scored a hit on the woman trying to kill him.

To be sure, he was going back to Riker's, hoping against hell that Con and his crew were long cleared out. Not a conversation Shane was willing to have with his friend, if he got caught disobeying orders and not taking it easy with his wound. Especially if word got back to Liza.

Since the narcotic-induced haze had cleared from his head, he felt comfortable enough to drive, but the breath-stealing pain needed remedied. Popping enough aspirin to choke a horse, he geared up and snuck out to his dad's beat-up Ford. Liza had been thorough in locating all of his keys, but he had secret stashes in places where no one would think to look. No human soul could claim he wasn't prepared for a *Red Dawn* scenario.

By the time he reached the opposite side of town, the aspirin had kicked in enough to take the edge off his pain. Once he reached the field where he'd parked last night, his body picked up Superman's vibes, and he was able to exit his old beater with the ease of a thirty-year-old. Scratch that, he moved more like a forty-year-old. Now he just had to remind himself to take it easy out here and not overdo it or cause his injury to bleed through the stitches.

After a check with his binoculars—not an Eider police officer in sight—he set off across the field. Following the bent grass, he returned to the tree grove, pausing long enough to catch his breath. Damn, this was more difficult than he expected.

He could hear Drummond's lecture like the man was standing right next to him. *"Sheriff, your body is using all its resources to repair the damage inflicted upon it. You'll tire easily and quickly. That's why I told you to rest."*

"Well, Doc, no one ever said I had a lick of sense in my noggin'."

Dismissing his mental physician, Shane picked his way through the grove to the point where he'd been shot. Which was easy enough to find with all the blood that had gushed from his wound. Squares of trauma gauze and ripped gloves from the EMS's attempts to staunch the flow were still laying about. Shane situated his body as it had been just as the woman had shot him. Closing his eyes, he took a few deep—as deep as his tender abdomen would allow—breaths, then opened his eyes and looked at the scene with the eyes of a seasoned investigator.

Here, in the grove, he got stronger flashes of how it went down.

Shane's gaze focused, and he watched the female phantom fade into the trees to his far right.

He scanned the ground. Too trampled here. He pushed farther out. Each step was measured, his brain calculating and categorizing between useless and potential clues. But fatigue dragged on his limbs, making it difficult to breathe normally. He leaned against a tree.

Fatigue dragged on his limbs, making it difficult to breathe normally. Resisting the urge to sit down and not get back up, he gave himself a few minutes, then pressed on, slower this time. He emerged from the tree grove and stopped.

Two distinct paths cut through the overgrown field, a few yards apart. Eenie meenie miney mo, which way did the shooter go? Probably through the field going away from the road.

He might be covered in ticks before this jaunt was over. His wound alone would prove complicated in twisting and bending over to check and rid his body of the parasitic nuisances.

Too late for preventative measures. In for an inch, in for a mile.

Halfway along he spotted a dark blotch on the faded grass. Squatting down, he pulled out his phone and prepared to photograph it. Lifting the blades up for closer inspection, he grunted. Blood.

Gotcha.

He snapped a few pictures and sent them to storage. Pulling out one of the paper bags he'd snatched out of his cabinet, he snipped the blades, letting them drop inside the bag. He was about to stand when his body finally gave out. Flopping back on his ass jarred his injury.

"Sonofabitch!"

Shane sat there, panting through the waves of pain. Sweat beaded on his forehead. Gulping, he tried to shift, stopping the instant his ravaged nerves screamed. A red haze shrouded his vision. His head felt like it would float away, the sensation turning his stomach.

Any attempt to get up would be futile. Resigning to his fate, he laid back, gasping as the pain made a path along his torso like someone stair-stepping punches up his body. Through the whoosh of blood in his ears, he made out the faint ringing sound. The noise increased as his pulse settled. His phone.

Pawing it out of his coat, he didn't bother with the caller ID. "Hamilton," he ground out.

"Where are you?"

Her voice penetrated his fogged brain. "Nic?"

"Yes, Shane. Where are you?"

Oh God, oh God! Breathe through the pain. Once the wave receded, leaving him quaking from the adrenalin dump, his brain was a bit clearer. "Where are you?"

"Oh, you're in so much trouble, mister. I'm sitting in your driveway, and your old beater is missing. Damn it, Shane Hamilton, I always knew you had a death wish."

"Shit, Nic, I didn't know you cared."

"I shouldn't. God only knows why the hell I do. Maybe it's because if Con lost you as a friend, I'd have to pull my husband back together. Now where the hell did you run off to?"

"Why are you at my house?"

She let go with a litany of off-colored words he hadn't heard her use in ages. Motherhood had tamed that tongue of hers, but it appeared it was only on a leash. "Answer me. Where are you?"

"Well," he panted, "I'm looking at a . . . " he gingerly probed his side and checked his fingers, "blood spot."

"You went back to Riker's? Ah, shit! Get your ass back home, right now."

Shane chuckled. That had been the wrong move. "Nic, that's impossible at the moment."

Her hiss of exasperation would have tickled his ear. "Don't move," she growled.

"I don't plan on it."

CHAPTER TWENTY-THREE

At the rustle of clothing against the grass, Shane peeled one eyelid open and squinted at the figure blocking the sun.

"You are in such big trouble, mister."

"So you've already said." In the time he waited for Nic to find him, the pain had subsided, but he wasn't glutton enough to make a solo attempt back to his truck. "What took you so long?"

"You didn't exactly wave a red flag so I could locate you." Nic reached down and flicked something from his coat. "Oh, how fun. You're covered in ticks." Her eyes widened. "And bleeding."

"About that." He pulled out the paper bag and held it up to her. "Would you get this to your husband? I managed to wing the woman who shot me."

"A woman?" Nic took the bag. "How do you know it was a woman?"

"She spoke. I don't think she cared to disguise it, probably thinking she'd kill me and no one would be wiser."

"Oh, you bastard, you couldn't even die. Now what's she going to do?"

"Smart ass."

Nic flashed one of her best shit-eating grins. "At your service. Let's get your ass off the ground and to my truck."

Shane struggled up onto his elbows, wheezing as pain radiated from the wound. "This might take a bit."

"Manage to get yourself into a sit; I can't lift you from the ground like that."

"What's wrong, marine? Has retirement softened you?"

"Bite me." She crouched next to his head. "If you must be an ass about it, I'm pregnant."

It took four point eight seconds for her words to penetrate his befuddled mind. "You are? Damn, O'Hanlon, do you two go at it like rabbits?"

Her bemused expression darkened. "If you weren't already trying to kill yourself, I'd sock you in the gut for that remark."

"And that's why I said it."

After a few failed attempts, he got off the ground, and then with Nic's support, he managed to get onto his feet. Shane did his best not to lean too much on Nic, but the woman was considerably shorter than he was, and it was difficult not to rely on her strength. Nic was one of the toughest women he'd met, and that was saying a lot as she was the only female to have ever passed the Marine Recon's rigorous sniper training, and still the lone female in American military history to hold the title.

"I should drive my truck home."

"You're doing no such thing."

"I'm not leaving it here."

"Let me handle it."

Her tone brokered no objections. Shane put a clamp down on his tongue and cowboyed up. It was a crying shame she'd retired from police work. He'd had aspirations of making her the next sheriff, but Nic had other plans. In the long run, it was for the best she had left law enforcement. Her PTSD could prove unpredictable when she was put in life-or-death situations. For the last few years she'd been seeking professional help, and that along with Con and her babies, Nic was finally calming the demons.

"I miss the good ole days," he said.

"Good ole days of what?" She guided him over a hump in the field.

"When things hadn't gone to hell in a handbasket. When you were still one of the best damn deputies I ever had."

"I still am, I'm just retired. And what about Cassy?"

"She's not you."

Nic chuckled. "No one can be me. I'm unique." She adjusted his arm over her shoulders and marched on.

Once they reached her vehicle, she deposited him in the passenger seat. Shane groaned as he reclined the seat. His whole body was on fire now, and it was killing him to breathe.

"Next time you'll listen to the doctor's orders," Nic said as she dug out her cell phone.

"To quote you, bite me."

Her sardonic smile brought back memories of the Nic he'd first hired after she arrived in the middle of nowhere Iowa to interview for his lowly deputy position.

"Murdoch, it's Nic. Load up that Aussie half brother of mine and haul him out to the field behind Riker's Club . . . Yes, you heard me right . . . Because I said so. Don't make me pull rank on you, squirt . . . Make it fast." She ended the call and tossed her phone back into the cup holder.

"You're enjoying this a little too much."

"Not every day you get to rip your old boss a new one for playing the dumbass card not once but twice."

"I had my reasons."

"What? To get shot and die from blood loss? I'm going to have to call Drummond to check on your stitches and make sure you didn't rip anything out. As soaked as that bandage is, I'm betting you did."

"I should have called Liza."

"Hmm, you're calling an FBI agent by her first name."

Shane rolled his head to glare at Nic. "Yeah, so what of it?"

Her eyes gleamed with some of that Irish mischief she'd gleaned from her in-laws as she wagged her dark hair back and forth. "You don't like the FBI. Not once in the all the years I've known you would you call an agent by their first name. Hell, it took you almost a year to actually say Boyce. What gives?"

"Nothing."

"Bullshit. Frankly, Bartholomew was acting strange about you, too. Is there something going on between the two of you?"

"When I say nothing, does that mean anything to you?"

"Only for me to push harder. Damn it, Shane, I've seen you at your best and now at your worst, but the one thing you've always shied away from is a relationship. What the hell for?"

"Nic—"

"Can it, cowboy, I won't hear excuses. If that FBI agent brings out the thing that has been long dead inside of you, it's time to get back up on that damn horse and ride it out. Quit lying to yourself."

Shane broke eye contact and closed his eyes. Damn her bluntness, but he wasn't about to listen to her nag. The only woman allowed to do that was his mom, and she wasn't here to do it. "I'm not arguing with you over this. While we're waiting on Murdoch and Hartmann, I'm going to rest." He peeked at her through a half-open lid. "Good with you?"

Nic saluted and then shut the truck door with a smack. The sound rattled through Shane's body, jarring his inflamed injury.

Yeah, he didn't miss her pissy attitude that much. And he wasn't going to miss Liza, either. It was time for all of them to hit the road.

• • •

"You didn't lose any stitches, but you disturbed the whole wound, which is why you started bleeding again."

And ruined another good T-shirt, along with his jacket. "But I found what I was looking for."

The good doc was not amused. "Shane, if you don't stay home, I'll admit you to the hospital and have the nurses put you in restraints."

"I swear I'll stay home. Swear it on my honor as a cowboy."

"A fat lot of good that'll do you." Drummond packed up his portable kit. "Nic, are you and Xavier going to stay here until I can find a suitable nursemaid for this big pain in the ass?"

"We can hang for a bit," she said from her perch leaning against the doorframe to Shane's bedroom.

"After the way he busted my ass, I'm going to enjoy this," Xavier called up the hall.

Nic snickered. "Don't be too hard on him, li'l brother"—which was a total oxymoron, because Xavier outweighed and stood a good four to five feet taller than Nic, though he was younger than her—"he did set you up with Jolie."

"You had to go and ruin it," the Aussie bemoaned.

"See what I get for sticking up for you?"

"Thanks, I guess," Shane groused.

Drummond sighed. "If you'll excuse me, I have an autopsy report to type."

"Wait, Doc." He shifted on the bed. "What's the verdict on Schofield?"

"He died from a gunshot wound to the heart, and that's all you get to know as it's not your case."

"What about the final results on Frost?"

"Shane, as your doctor in this situation, put a cork in it. I'll give any and all findings to Agent Bartholomew or your deputies. You're off duty." Drummond nodded to Nic. "Later."

"Ass," Shane called out.

"One of the best," Drummond answered from the hallway.

Nic's bemused expression remained as they waited for the front door to close. Once Drummond had officially exited, she pushed off the doorway and moved to Shane's bedside. "Who was the ring for?"

He grasped the troublesome thing and hid it in his fist. "There are still some sacred things in my life."

"All right, for that I won't pry." She turned her back to him, starting to leave. "Just curious, since I haven't seen that before today, and it looks like it's a part of you." She paused in the doorway to look back over her shoulder. "Does Liza know about it?"

"Return to your post, Marine."

In a childish move that was unlike Nic, she stuck her tongue out at him and then disappeared. She'd been hanging around children too long.

Shane sagged into the mattress. The narcotics had kicked in the moment Drummond arrived to poke around. Well, at least he hadn't undone all the good doc's hard work at patching him up. But that didn't stop the sizable amount of ass-kicking Shane was giving himself for pulling the stunt. He should have waited for Liza to return and gone out there together. But he never was one to wait on others. It's what got him a chest full of medals and too many fast-track promotions.

Shane had a death wish then, and it looked like it had never left.

His weighted eyelids drifted down. He tried to snap them open, but the pull of sleep was powerfully motivated by drugs.

He lost track of time, and when he came to next, there was a pair of dark eyes looking back at him.

"Next time I'm going to remove the batteries."

He smiled. "Please tell me you didn't learn how to do that boosting cars?"

Liza scowled. "My foster brother was a mechanic in the army."

"When?"

"About the same time you were." She said it more like a question than a reply, but he wasn't going to confirm it. Liza had figured out too much without his help.

She reached up and traced a crease in Shane's forehead. "Why'd you go out there alone?"

"I can't explain it."

Her gaze searched his face. "That's not good enough for me."

"Liza, I'm not used to relying on anyone for help. I give the orders, and I do what I have to."

"Quotes a stubborn man. Well, guess what, you're now confined to a bed because you couldn't follow orders. Worse, had Nic not got a hair up her ass to come check on you, you could have died out there."

"I would have called you."

Her hand stilled, and she frowned. "Why? I mean, we aren't exactly friends or partners."

His right hand unclenched—shit, had he been clutching Cheyenne's ring the whole time he was sleeping?—and he took hold of hers. "No, we're not, but there's something here. I know you feel it, too." He might deny to others there was anything going on, but for some reason—maybe it was the hydrocodone talking—there was a connection.

"I think it's just bad food. Pop-Tarts aren't a recommended part of a healthy diet."

"Are you still mad at me?"

Suspicion creased her features. "What do you think?"

Quickly, before she clued in, he lifted his head off the pillow and claimed her lips. Liza stiffened for a fraction of a second but melted as he nudged her to accept his kiss. It was as good as he thought the first time. She was both parts sweet and spicy, and he couldn't get enough of her taste.

Stilling, she sighed against his lips and pulled away, resting her forehead to his. "You're confusing."

"How so?"

Liza sat upright. "Never mind."

She pushed off the bed and walked over to the antique dresser his mother's family had passed down from generation to generation. Liza fingered the brown-checked cloth cover that protected the wood from scuffs and then picked up one of his champion belt buckles. Cradling the massive thing, she stared at it.

"Liza?"

She set the buckle down. "My meeting with Roslin went nowhere."

Okay, so they were moving on from a discussion about them. "She couldn't tell you anything you didn't already know?"

"Either she's playing dumb expertly, or she really is clueless about Ripley's motives. What bothers me is how he met her, in a bank, apparently getting a loan."

"A ruse to get close to her? Maybe he targeted her? Knew she'd be the perfect addition to his next job?"

Liza shrugged one shoulder. "It's the only explanation I can think of for why he'd want an in with a bank. She still worked in one after they moved here."

"It would have given him eyes on the school's bank accounts."

"Which was my next thought after I talked with the few members of the school board who showed up. I want to talk to her again. I've set up a private conversation with Neil Lundy this evening."

"Didn't he give you want you wanted today?"

"Some, but I learned from Roslin that he was harassing her last night. I didn't want to embarrass the man in front of his colleagues by demanding what he was interrogating her about. I had hoped to do it right after I finished with them, but . . . " Liza gave him a pointed look, "I got a message from Dr. Drummond and Nic telling me about your little escapade."

"Would you have let me go if I brought you along?"

She turned to face him, resting her elbow on the dresser top. “First off, you would have never left the house. I would have gone myself. And second, what could have been so damn important that you’d risk it?”

“Nic didn’t tell you?”

“She felt it was best that you explain yourself to me. God only knows why. And I’m not sure how to interpret whatever hidden message she was trying to give me. She was freaking me out.”

“Ignore her. She’s a trained sniper and thinks she can see it all.”

With her head propped on her fist, Liza stared at him.

“What?”

“Are you going to tell me, or do I have to threaten you?”

“You don’t have a leg to stand on.”

“I’m an FBI agent, and you want to chance that I can’t pull up some sensitive information about you that you’ve done a bang-up job of keeping from everyone in this county?”

Shane’s body seized at that. It was one thing for her to piece together the ordeal with Cheyenne and his reason for enlisting, but there was no way in hell he wanted Liza digging around in his service record.

“By the look of panic on your face, you know I’m right.”

“You don’t have to make threats. I was going to tell you.” He shifted on the bed to ease the pressure on his hips. This whole bedridden deal wasn’t going to last long. He needed to sit up. “I remembered something about the person who took a shot at me.”

“This couldn’t have waited for me to come back?”

“Would you let me finish?”

She held up her hand in surrender and then beckoned for him to continue. Impatient woman.

“It was a woman, but she wore a hood of some kind to hide her face, and her voice wasn’t familiar. ’Course, with a gun pointed at me, I wasn’t paying too much attention to that detail, just how to get out of it without getting killed.”

"It was a woman. Something to go on. But I heard multiple shots."

"I returned fire, and I winged her. I wasn't sure, but once back there, I remembered hearing her cry out after I fired. And I guessed right—she was hurt, and I found blood on the path she took to escape."

"Did you tell—?"

"Nic knows and so does Murdoch. I got a sample before my body gave out on me. Murdoch took the sample to Con. He's supposed to get Drummond to test the blood."

Liza moved back to the bed. "You do realize this means there is a woman out there who has a gunshot wound?"

"Yes, and I overheard Nic tell her husband to get on it. But I don't see this woman going to any clinics or hospitals anywhere near here."

"Maybe, if she's bad off, she'll get desperate."

"Eider police will monitor, along with the hospital staff." Shane's words were slurring. Damn this fatigue.

"You need to sleep."

"I don't want to." He grasped her hand. "You should sleep, too."

"I will, after I meet with Lundy. I'll check with Drummond on what he suggests for you, and I'll bring back some food."

"Be careful."

"I'm not the one running around getting shot." She pressed a kiss to his knuckles and placed his hand on his chest. "Sleep."

The last thing he saw as his eyes drifted shut was her walking out of the room. He could never get enough of seeing that side of her.

CHAPTER TWENTY-FOUR

A woman had shot him. Liza paced the front room floor, tapping her head. If this was the same person who waltzed into the club and shot Derek Schofield, why hang around to potentially get caught? Admiring their handiwork?

Shane said the shooter told him he shouldn't have come there. Where, the tree grove? The club?

Liza's mind whirled. She stopped mid-stride, and, tilting her face to the ceiling, she closed her eyes and relaxed. *One piece at a time.* Working backward through the chain of events that had occurred in the time since she'd arrived two days ago—was it really two days ago? God, it felt like she'd been here a week or more. Her mental flip through the incidents came to a stop on what had brought her here in the first place: Gene Avery, a.k.a. Mr. Ripley.

Her eyes flew open. The way to get to the bottom of what was going on was to find whoever killed Ripley.

Liza pulled out her iPhone and made the call.

"O'Hanlon."

"Detective, can we meet?"

"Is this meeting about our fearless sheriff?"

"In a way, but not like you think. I'm coming loaded with all the information on my guy and what I've learned so far with the school. Do you happen to have autopsy reports from Dr. Drummond?"

"Not yet, but I can get him to fast-track them. Autopsies on who?"

"All three men who've died since I arrived. I have a sinking feeling in my gut there's something connected about all of them."

"Gotcha. What time?"

"In the next thirty minutes okay with you?"

"Perfect. Meet me here at the police station."

Call ended, Liza headed into the kitchen. Her stomach was pitching the biggest tantrum, and the single Pop-Tart she'd confiscated this morning was long gone. She needed food, and that reminded her she needed to get Drummond's recommendations on food for Shane to eat.

Look at her, being all domestic and . . . attached. What was wrong with her? This was not normal. Wait, scratch that. She did have some kind of maternal instincts with Quinn, and she was beyond attached to that kid.

She lingered in the kitchen entry, staring at the closed door to Shane's room. What had he done to her? Two kisses—two very hot and bothered kisses—and she turned into Claire Huxtable. Turning from the room, she slipped into the kitchen.

"I don't want this," she whispered.

Keep lying to yourself. We both know you want what Kurt had with Stephanie, and what your adoptive parents have.

She liked Shane, as a colleague, and that's all the further it could go.

Her phone buzzed. Oops, she forgot she'd turned off the ringer. She retrieved the phone out of her pocket. A local number?

"Agent Bartholomew."

"Agent, it's Deputy Murdoch. I went back to Pamela Frost's home, checking to see if she was around."

"And you're telling me this why?"

"Since our esteemed sheriff is out of commission and Deputy Hunt still wants us deferring to you on this, I'm telling you because Pamela is home. And she doesn't look too good."

"What does 'doesn't look too good' mean?"

"It's hard to describe over the phone. Come out to her place and see for yourself."

Liza checked the time. "I can't. I have a meeting with Detective O'Hanlon in twenty-five minutes."

"Are you leaving the sheriff alone again?"

"No." Shit! She needed to get someone over here to make sure he didn't repeat his disappearing act. "I have . . . "

"Stop. I'll have Xavier go over. He's on mandatory vacation, and he's been driving me nuts because he's bored."

"Wasn't he already here?"

"He won't mind. Xavier and the sheriff have some weird thing between them ever since Hamilton threw Xavier in jail."

Wha . . . wait? That was a story Liza was going to have to hear, later. "I'm on my way. How do I get there?" *Oh God, don't get lost.*

"It's easy. I'll send you directions to your phone."

Phew! Now that Siri wasn't acting like a bitch, Liza should be able to find this place and not look like an utter failure.

"And by the way," Murdoch said, "call Detective O'Hanlon and tell him to come out. He's going to want to see and hear about this, too."

What was Deputy Murdoch sitting on?

• • •

Praise God and sing halleluiah! Liza made it to the Frost home without one bad turn. Liza parked behind Deputy Murdoch's car and was soon joined by Con's large green truck. They were nearly a block away from the house. It was a quiet area with houses sprinkled here and there in what appeared to be an urban style development. Most of the homes looked empty—everyone was off to work, except for the Frost home, where a lone gray/silver SUV sat in the driveway.

Liza stared at the vehicle in the drive. Was it the same one that had followed her yesterday to the hospital? She needed to look at the front more closely. She exited her car to congregate at Murdoch's squad vehicle.

"How long has she been in there?" Con asked right off.

"About an hour now. I have no idea if she spotted me when she arrived. She certainly didn't act like she'd noticed it. But with the way she was moving, I don't think she was paying any attention to her surroundings."

"How was she moving?" Liza asked, her gaze narrowing on the opulent house. "Must be a nice, fat salary she enjoys as a lawyer."

"You have no idea," Murdoch said. "Anyway, she moved like she was drunk. She drove that way, too. But it was kinda funky, not like a normal drunk's stagger."

"Why didn't you pull her over and check?" Con demanded.

"Because, Detective, it's Pamela Frost, and the sheriff warned me to not engage. It was to be his duty. It's why I called Agent Bartholomew."

"I'm not doing it."

"Don't fight it, Liza. Cassy isn't one to disagree with."

How in the world? "Detective, is someone talking to you that shouldn't be?"

He grinned. "Shall we?" Con held out his hand for her to precede him. "Deputy Murdoch, stand post. If there's trouble, you know what to do."

The redhead's grin was like a cocked gun. "Oh, don't I." She winked.

As Liza led Con across the street, she slowed her pace to walk alongside him. "What was that about?"

He chuckled. "Xavier is something of an MMA fighter and has been teaching Jolie his skills. Eight months or so ago, she beat the hell out of a sex trafficker. The asshole sorely misjudged that woman's intestinal fortitude."

Liza peeked back over her shoulder at the spindly sheriff's deputy. Wonders never cease.

They approached the driveway, censoring their steps. Liza peeled away from Con to inspect the front end of the SUV. It looked exactly like the one that had been tailing her, but there was nothing special to distinguish it from other SUVs like it. The longer she stared at it, the more her situational awareness jacked up. Pamela Frost would know Derek Schofield because his wife was her secretary. Liza could picture the lawyer knowing about the affairs and doing something about it. But murder? Her hand crept to her belt line and came to rest next to her gun butt.

"Careful, Agent. We don't need any misunderstandings."

"Something's off."

Con hesitated next to the car, placing his hand on the hood. "I agree."

They lingered, neither speaking. Liza's nerves were processing information at the speed of light, and her muscles were tingling with warmth. This was not good, so not good.

"I'm going around back," Con said. He turned and signaled Murdoch to stand by. "You take front."

"Con, I don't have a radio. There's no way to communicate."

He pulled out his cell and called hers. "Leave it connected."

Placing the activated phone in her front shirt pocket, she headed for the porch. Liza's body hummed. She crept over the tiled stoop, trying to peek through the windows with their lace curtains, but she couldn't see anything. The house was dark except for where the sun poked through the gloom. A solid dark blue front door, no glass, stood between her and whatever waited on the inside. The festive green wreath covered in pink, white, and blue tulips seemed out of character for the woman Liza briefly encountered yesterday.

"I'm in position," Con whispered through the phone.

She itched to draw her weapon, but she couldn't drive the woman off. She gave a heavy handed rap on the door and stepped to the side.

One Mississippi, two Mississippi ...

At six Mississippi, she knocked again. More like pounded on the door. "Mrs. Frost?"

Ten Mississippi, nine Mississippi ...

"Do you hear anything?" she said into her shoulder.

"I hear a faint screech . . . like a teakettle."

Liza pulled her weapon and leaned around the corner post to confirm Murdoch's position. The deputy had stationed herself inside her opened car door and was gripping the radio on her shoulder.

God, please don't let it be bad.

The force of her blow against the door now made the wreath tremble. "Pamela, it's Agent Bartholomew. Open the door."

"That's definitely a teakettle," Con's voice drifted through their connection.

"Should I go in?"

"Is the door locked?"

Testing it, she found give in the handle. "Not locked. Door back there?"

"Yes, but it's one of those sliding glass patio doors, curtains are covering it, and it's locked. Have Murdoch come over."

Liza waved over the younger woman. Once Murdoch was behind her, she gripped the handle again and popped the latch.

"Going in," she told Con. "Mrs. Frost, Pamela, I'm entering the house."

With the door opened, she could hear the sound Con mentioned, and it was a screaming teakettle. Wincing, Liza slipped inside, her gaze darting from one corner to the next.

"Clear," she alerted both Con and Murdoch.

Liza inched along a narrow hallway. "Pamela?" A wide, carpeted staircase to her right led upstairs. Liza hated to leave that position open, but she had to kill that kettle. Down the hall into the kitchen, she cleared the area, and then shoved the kettle off the burner, turning off the flame. As a matter of habit after being around Quinn, she checked all the other burner knobs and the stove. Everything was turned off.

She moved into the dining room next and found the sliding doors. Pushing the curtain aside, she unlocked the door. Con stepped into the doorway.

"Anything?"

She shook her head then pointed upstairs. "I'm going up."

"I'll sweep the bottom level."

Spotting Murdoch in the hallway, Liza exchanged okay signs and then made a beeline for the staircase. Step by step, she ascended, her senses on high alert. She fought the tunnel vision encroaching on her sight. All that training, and she still couldn't master this one feat.

At the top of the steps, she hesitated on the landing, assessing her surroundings. Three doors: two possible bedrooms, one bathroom, all doors open.

"Pamela, it's the FBI. Are you here?"

"Liza," Con called from somewhere below.

She ignored him. The God-awful tension in her body was screaming to go to the door directly in front of her. With her weapon leveled in front of her, she rushed to the door.

"Liza!"

Entering the room, she pulled up short. "Damn it!"

Crumpled on the floor at the end of a king-sized bed, in a puddle of vomit and foaming at the mouth, Pamela Frost convulsed as if in the throes of a seizure.

Heavy footsteps pounded up the stairs. "Liza, we need to get out."

She turned as Con blew into the room. "Why?"

"There's a fire. Can't you smell the smoke?"

At the mention of it, the acrid bite to the air hit her. "Crap!"

Con cursed in his native tongue at the sight of Pamela's twitching body. "I'll take her. Get out."

"No, I'm not leaving you alone."

Growling something, Con reached down and hoisted Pamela over his shoulder in a fireman's hold. "Lead the way."

When they hit the landing, smoke had clouded every available space. Heat crackled in the air.

"Come on!" Murdoch hollered from the bottom of the steps.

Coughing, Liza hurried down, pausing long enough to make certain Con was right behind her. She turned toward the front door, seeing flames licking at the walls near the kitchen. "That's moving way too fast."

Once outside, they headed straight for the vehicles.

"I made the call. All emergency vehicles are in route," Murdoch reported.

"Where was the fire? And why didn't we smell it when we came in?"

"Don't know about the latter. But the fire was in the basement. I think I helped it along when I opened the door." Con laid Pamela down on the pavement. "What is wrong with her?"

Pamela had stopped convulsing and was staring up at the sky with blank eyes.

Liza knelt next to Con as he checked Pamela's pulse. "She acts like she's OD'd."

"No pulse." Con scrambled to start chest compressions. "Murdoch, get your defibrillator."

Pamela was dying. Why? This was not happening.

Behind them, snaps, pops, and crackles indicated the fire gaining purchase on the home.

"Con, did you see her briefcase or something like it?"

"No," he said between compressions.

Liza hadn't either. The car. She hopped onto her feet and jogged over.

"Liza! Stay out of the house."

"I'm not going inside." She grabbed the handle. Locked. Peering inside the windows, she spotted a satchel and manila folders. In the backseat was a pile of clothing. "Does she have her keys on her?"

"No," came the answer.

No two ways about this, she was going in the hard way. Using the butt of her gun, she slammed it into the glass, shattering it. Clearing a sizable hole for her arm, she reached in and popped the door. Just in case, she checked the interior for an extra set of keys and came up empty-handed. Retreating, she waved for Murdoch.

"What?"

"I'm shifting this sucker into neutral, and we need to back it out of the drive. I don't want it damaged by the fire." The house itself was pouring off heat and the place was spewing smoke.

"Why?"

Liza pointed inside. "Evidence."

Together, they pushed the car to the curb, letting it roll to a stop as the first fire truck barreled onto the scene, followed by an ambulance. Once the EMTs took over, Con backpedaled away from the crew working on Pamela. He staggered to Liza and Murdoch.

"I don't think she's going to live." He bent at the waist and sucked air.

"Did you use a guard?" Liza demanded.

"Yes, mother."

"I had one in my kit," Murdoch said.

"Con, I don't know if she OD'd on something or was poisoned."

His head whipped up at that. "Why would it have happened at all?"

Liza watched the fire consume the front of the house. "Someone is trying to clean house." Her gaze narrowed. "And I'm going to find out who."

CHAPTER TWENTY-FIVE

Hunger gnawed at his guts. Shane tested the waters and found his body lacking. He'd really overdone it. Gingerly rolling onto his injured side, he pushed himself into a sitting position. After a few moments of rest, he got out of the bed and wandered out the door and into the bathroom.

When he emerged, he found a beefy sentinel standing in the middle of the hallway, arms crossed over a wide chest.

"Hartmann, what the hell are you doing here, again?"

"Liza had to leave."

Why? Hold it, that's right. She had a meeting with Lundy. Damn, how long had he been out this time?

"What time is it?"

"Past five. You look like shit."

"Thanks for that observation, marine."

"Don't go knocking my corps, *army*."

They stared at each other. Hartmann gave Shane a sloppy smile.

"Jarhead," Shane shot back.

"Hoorah." Hartmann gimped down the hallway. His prosthetic leg must be aggravating his stump. "You hungry?"

"Starving." Shane hobbled around and followed the Aussie into the kitchen. Weren't they a pair, a disabled marine and a wounded grunt. "Did Liza tell you?"

"Tell me what?" Hartmann picked up a note, squinting at it. "Says here I'm not supposed to let you eat that crap you call food."

"Says who?"

That surfer boy lopsided grin returned.

When she got back here, she and he were going to have a conversation about her bossiness.

Hartmann opened the fridge. "Would you look at that, the man knows how to stock a fridge."

"Kiss my ass." Shane shuffled to his table and eased onto a chair, his body giving a sigh of relief. He tracked Hartmann's movements as the Aussie pulled out a carton of eggs, milk, and a colorful array of veggies. "I like my omelets with a kick."

"And I don't." Hartmann reached in the cabinet next to the stove, pulled out the bottle of Tabasco sauce, and plopped it on the table with a thunk by Shane's elbow. "When you get heartburn, blame yourself."

Having the other man cook for him made Shane's self-worth bristle like a pissed-off dog. How did he get himself into this mess? Since leaving the army and becoming a law officer, Shane had lost all desire to see his life end and join Cheyenne. He started the anniversary binge the first year after he discharged out, as a way to process the grief he'd locked up for so long while he waited for that one bullet or IED to take his life. God had some sick sense of humor to allow Shane to make it through six years and four tours unscathed except for the usual mind rape. There were things one saw when they went to war that left scars no one could see.

And Shane's went deep.

"How do you know?" he insisted.

Hartmann didn't miss a step as he beat the eggs. "I suspected for a while. Hard as you try to act like your training is from being a cop, you carry yourself like a soldier." He peered over his shoulder. "And if I don't miss a guess, you climbed those ranks, fast."

Too fast. When you could prove you were prime fighting material and had the respect of those commanding you, it didn't take the army long to find ways to promote you. And into special ops. What's worse was that everyone around him was beginning to figure it all out. After all this time, he'd thought he'd done a better job of hiding it.

"Who else suspects?"

Hartmann hmphed. "Who do you think, mate?"

Nic, Con, and Cassy, which meant Boyce knew, too, and probably Jolie. Shit. Shane had done a piss-poor job of keeping the secret.

"Don't beat yourself up too much. We all respected your secret and haven't revealed it. Those in the know figured it out on their own." The veggies sizzled in a pool of butter in the skillet. "And not a word will be said without your consent."

"I should be thankful for that much."

Shane's stomach gave a mighty twist at the tantalizing aroma of onions, garlic, and peppers sautéing in the pan. Hartmann better hurry up with that food.

A Harley engine revving echoed in the room. Hartmann dug in his pocket and pulled out his phone, pouring the egg mixture in the skillet. "What can I do for you, love?"

"Are you still with the sheriff?" Jolie's voice came over the speaker, jolting Shane.

The man turned to Shane. "Yeah. Tell him what you need."

"Sheriff, we located Pamela Frost."

"And?" Shane asked loudly, hoping the speaker picked him up.

"Well, it's not good, sir. Agent Bartholomew doesn't know I'm calling you. But, um, you need to get over to the hospital." Good girl. She was a smart cookie to know he wasn't about to sit out the rest of this investigation.

Hartmann turned the stove off and slid the omelet onto a plate.

"I'm on my way, Murdoch." That response earned him a nasty scowl from the Aussie. Boo hoo on him.

"Hurry, sir. And, Xavier, don't fight him." With that, Jolie ended her connection.

Shane pushed onto his feet. "You heard her, let's go."

"If it weren't for that woman I love, you'd be getting a beat down so I didn't have to listen to my sister."

"Man up, marine, and pack my food to go."

• • •

Shane had a love/hate relationship with hospitals. Loved that emergency care was readily available when needed, especially during his wild and woolly days as a bronc rider. Hated it because, in the last four years, too many of his deputies had spent time in here being treated for beatings, gunshots, and hypothermia. And lest he forget, the numerous bodies he has viewed in the morgue.

Yeah, this was the last place he wanted to be.

When he and Hartmann located Jolie, she was in a small powwow with Con and Liza. The bitter sting of smoke smacked him in the face when he reached the group.

"What the hell happened?"

Liza's features twisted in anger. "What are you doing here?"

"Don't worry, I didn't drive so I couldn't kill myself. Hartmann tried to do it for the both of us."

"Wanker," Hartmann muttered.

"I reiterate, Shane, what are you doing here?" Liza snarled.

"I told him to come, ma'am," Jolie threw herself under the bus. "He needs to know what happened."

That dangerous scowl was directed at his young deputy, but Jolie didn't back down. Shane had never been more proud of her than he was in that moment.

"Deputy Murdoch, we'll discuss this later."

"There won't be any discussing anything with her later, Liza. You forget, I'm still the sheriff."

"Who was put on medical leave due to a gunshot wound. Or are you so doped up that you've forgotten that little detail?"

"Children, please. We have more troubling matters to attend to," Con butted in.

"Which is why I'm here. What is going on with Pamela Frost?" Shane asked.

The three dirty, smelly law enforcement personnel looked between each other, and then all three settled their collective somber gazes on him. His gut pitched backward into his spine.

"We did all we could, but it was too late," Con said.

God damn it! "She's dead?"

Liza's throat bobbed as she broke rank and reached out to him. "Sadly, she is. We're waiting on Drummond to tell us what he can find."

"Why do you all smell like smoke?"

She gripped his arm this time. "The Frost home was set on fire."

Again. Another house fire, in the span of two days. What the effing hell was going on?

"Where was Roslin when this all happened?"

"I told you he'd jump right to her," Con said.

Sighing, Liza tugged on Shane's arm. "Sit down before you collapse again."

He jerked his arm out of her grip. "I'm not a cripple. Quit treating me like one."

Hurt flashed through her umber eyes. The pain he'd caused her injected into his heart, poisoning him. Blame the painkillers or blame the situation blowing up in his face—either way, he was being an asshole. Liza didn't give him a chance to repent of his sins. A wall went up and the windows slammed shut. He'd officially put the foreclosure on reconciliation.

Turning, he walked away.

"Sheriff, stop."

He about-faced at Drummond's command.

"Come with me." The doctor summoned.

The entire group followed him into an empty exam room. Shane sank into one of the chairs. Breathing easier, he let his body relax into the uncomfortable seat. In no way was he ever going to tell anyone how taxed he'd become just walking into the blasted building.

"This will make my explanation quick and easy," Drummond started. "I will do the autopsy on Pamela later, but I did a thorough exam of her." He sighed. "I can't determine what actually killed her yet, but her body is showing all the signs of poisoning. Once the lab tests have been run, we'll be able to determine what it was exactly."

"If it matches anything you found in her husband or Gene Avery, tell me immediately," Con said.

"Whoa, hold your horses, O'Hanlon. Those are my cases."

Con gestured like a grand duke. "By all means, be my guest, Sheriff."

"Aren't we all testy," Drummond said.

From the corner of Shane's eyes, he caught Liza crossing her arms and passing an ugly look his way. Testy was putting it lightly.

"What you'll find most interesting, Sheriff, is that Pamela had a wound on her right arm. Until I can inspect it, my initial assessment is the wound is from a bullet. She might be the one who shot you."

A deathly hush fell over the group.

"Damn it to hell," Shane barked. "These murders are a convoluted mess."

CHAPTER TWENTY-SIX

Air, she needed air. Shane was right. He wasn't the only one who couldn't make heads or tails of any of it. Liza exited the hospital, striding across the parking lot straight for her car. Distance from the people in that hospital was her saving grace at this moment.

Stinging from Shane's rebuke—God, did he have to snap at her like that?—she braced her hands on the trunk and bent over the car. With the strength born of necessity she'd held her tongue. A miracle considering how badly she'd wanted to let loose with both barrels. That man infuriated and intrigued her, and it turned her mind into a tangled web of yarn where there was no beginning nor end in sight. Closing her eyes, she sucked air like a drowning woman.

This had to be a reality check for her. She'd been getting too comfortable with him, thinking of things that were impossible. For God's sake, she barely knew the man. There was no reason, none, to be getting crazy ideas in her head. He had more baggage than a Boeing 737. That kind of crap was the last thing she wanted in her already loaded life.

Liza lifted her head and stared at the darkened world around her. Checking the time, she stiffened. "Oh, crap."

Scrambling to the passenger side, she yanked open the door and dug through the scattered mess of reports and files until she found the card. "Damn." Like a frantic teenager, she tapped in the number and waited for the other line to pick up.

"This is Neil."

"Mr. Lundy, I apologize for missing our meeting. We had a crisis, and I'm still dealing with the fallout."

Silence met her entreaty. Oh joy, he was going to be an ass about this.

"I heard about the Frosts' home burning. I'll assume that is the crisis of which you speak."

Okay, maybe this wouldn't be so bad. "You would assume correctly." As long as that's all people knew about. "Is it too late to try this again?"

Lundy sighed. "I believe this situation we are meeting about is worth the time it takes. Would you care to meet me at my home instead of the sheriff's department?"

She screwed up her face in a grimace. Another place to find, and in the dark. *Siri, please don't fail me.* Swallowing the log in her throat, Liza said, "That would be fine."

He gave her his address, and they ended their call. She was about to tell Siri the address when the phone beeped. She'd missed a call. Ugh! From Montrose.

"Ma'am, I'm sorry I missed your call. I was on the line with a person of interest."

"I don't care. What I want to know is why I'm getting nasty phone calls from Kurt Bartholomew."

The blood drained from Liza's body. "He didn't."

"Your brother is about to find himself face to face with me if he calls here one more time demanding to know where you are and to bring you home. Bartholomew, family interference isn't tolerated under my command."

"I'm aware of that, ma'am, and I've explained that to him countless times. I'm sorry he's been—"

"Stop apologizing. When you took the oath of this office, you swore that your duties came above all else, even family. Either you put an end to this, or I will."

"Yes, ma'am."

"Since I have your undivided attention, update me on the process of this case."

"It's not good. There have been two more deaths since we last spoke."

"What the hell?"

Liza had this sudden urge to curl inside of herself and just let the world pass on by.

"Bartholomew, do these deaths have anything to do with your case?"

"I'm beginning to think so. I have yet to connect the pieces outside of some weird instances, but it's there, I can sense it."

Montrose hmphed. "I want solid proof, not weird instances. Send me a report, tonight, on everything that's happened. Give me the evidence or you're done. Copy?"

"Copy."

And that was the end of that conversation.

With a sad shake of her head, Liza shoved her mess into a pile and closed the door. Exhaustion and hunger dragged on her bones. She'd been running on adrenaline all day, and the crash was about to come. The urge to let loose with a string of nasty words tickled her tongue. No, she would not stoop to that level. She was a professional.

"Liza."

She jolted badly enough to bang her knee into the car. "Ow! Damn it, Shane. Don't sneak up on me like that."

"I wasn't sneaking . . . never mind."

Rubbing her throbbing knee, she scowled at him, not even sure he could see her face in the dark. "What?"

He stood there, his body contorted to relieve the pressure on his wounded side.

Have some compassion for the man. He was shot, and he learned that the possible shooter was a woman who just died. Yeah, not gonna happen. Liza was seconds away from a full-on brain shutdown, and her patience was being pushed to the limits. Not a good thing to have hanging over her head when she went to meet with Neil Lundy.

Shane cleared his throat. "Are you leaving?"

"Yes. I'm a few hours late for my meeting with Lundy. I need to go." She turned to leave.

"I'm coming with you."

Like a whip crack, she rounded on him. "No. You're going back home and giving that wound a break."

"Liza."

"Don't Liza me. I'm tired, I'm cranky, and I haven't had any food since that Pop-Tart this morning. I've got my SAC breathing down my neck and making threats she's capable of carrying out. And let's not forget to mention my asshat brother who is taking his asshattery to a whole new level." She jabbed a finger Shane's way. "Then there's you." She sliced the air with her hand. "I'm doing this alone." With that, she circled the car and got in, slamming the door to finalize her tirade.

To punctuate her ire, she revved the engine and then drove the car forward through the open slot in front of her. Let him stew in his pot. He started this, and like hell she was going to let him finish it.

Gripping the steering wheel, she glared out the windshield. "Siri, take me to 300 Robin Lane."

"Okay."

• • •

Liza was starting to think anyone who lived in a fancy house in this county was bound to have it burn down around their ears. She studied the monstrosity that was the Lundy home and found it lacking.

"Compensate much?" she muttered as she stalked up the walk.

Blowing at a disobedient coil, she caught a whiff of herself and grimaced. Oh, who gave two shits? Lundy was just going to have to deal. She punched the doorbell, backing up to the side. Ah, what the hell, why not? She rested her hand on her gun butt and waited.

I'm comin' atcha with a whole lotta attitude, man.

Lundy opened the door, wearing the same business casual khakis and polo he'd had on earlier today. The only change were the house slippers instead of loafers. He gave her the once over, and then stepped back to allow her entry.

"My wife has retired for the night, Agent. We'll take this into my office."

"Actually, Mr. Lundy, I'd prefer to conduct this in a less private setting. Here or your living room will do."

"If you insist." He led her into a large room that was just off the entryway. "If you would, please don't sit on the upholstery."

"Didn't plan on it." Liza hooked her hands on her hips, shifting her legs for a comfortable stance. "I refrained from embarrassing you in front of your fellow school board members today. Now I don't care. Would you care to explain to me why you were questioning Roslin Avery about her husband's supposed activities?"

Red tinged the man's features. "I would say that's my job as the school board president. If there's suspicion of wrong doing, I'm well within my rights to question who I feel might have knowledge of such activities."

"Wrong. When there is a federal or state investigation going on, you are to stay out of it. The damage you could have done to my case puts me in a serious bind, Mr. Lundy."

"I don't see how it could. Roslin had no prior knowledge of what her husband was doing. Or so she claimed."

Restraint, Liza. To keep from crossing the floor to throttle the man, she tucked her hands under her arms and screwed on the meanest glare possible.

"Let me put it this way. If I catch you meddling in my investigation again, I will have you arrested for obstruction. As of now, you get a pass, considering the fact that you were ignorant in proper procedure."

He turned pale at her warning. "Duly noted." Crossing his arms over his chest, his gaze flicking all about the room to avoid hers, he sighed. "Is there anything else you needed to discuss with me?"

"Who else have you bothered with your questioning?"

"No one, I swear."

Liza studied him, hoping her scrutiny made him hop like a flea under the scope. Actually, that was about the best description of the man she could come up with; a flea. A little bloodsucker.

The doorbell pealed.

Cocking her body about, Liza peered back at the entry. "Were you expecting someone else tonight?"

"No."

An adrenaline dump hit her like a tank dropped from a C130. When Lundy took a step, she reached out and clamped down on his arm, dragging him back. "Don't."

He scowled at her hand on his arm. "Agent, I don't see—"

She held a finger in front of his nose. "If you resist me, I'll put you on the floor and cuff you. I've seen one too many people die in this county in the last thirty-two hours."

"What are you talking about?"

The doorbell echoed through the house once more.

Propelling the man into a corner of the living room, she pushed her finger into his chest. "Stay put." She surveyed the room. Damn it, she was too freaking tired. She'd slipped and hadn't scoped her escape routes.

Large windows covering the south-facing wall were blocked by heavy darkening curtains. Good, no one would be seeing in that way. There was one other exit from the room. Liza strode over and poked her head around the corner. Hallway, one open entry, one, two, three doors, stairs, and a curve in the hall leading back to the entryway. Okay, access points noted. She returned to Lundy, finding the man had actually listened to her orders.

"Go upstairs, make sure your wife is okay, and call 911."

"Agent—"

"Boy, you question my authority again, I'll slap you."

With a wobbled nod, Lundy went through the living room and through the hallway. She followed him, making sure he went upstairs. Once he was out of sight, she hurried to the back of the house, popping into the kitchen. No exit here, but there was a door. Liza tried it and discovered the entrance to the basement. Using the flashlight app on her phone—damn, she needed the flashlight that was in her car—she crept down the carpeted steps. The weak light of her phone showed a finished basement resplendent with a man cave and a . . . tanning bed. Geesh. Explained the man's perpetual tan. Slinking through the dark, Liza spotted the exit.

She hurried over and breathed a sigh of relief when she found the door locked. After the way the Frost home went up in flames, there was no way she was going to chance another house burning.

She was about to return upstairs when a scuffing at the door made her freeze. Crouching down, she leaned against the wall. A splash of liquid against the door made her jerk back. The vapors hit her hard. Diesel fuel.

Oh no you don't.

Sliding her gun free of its holster, Liza went upright, flipped the dead bolt, and flung open the door. "FBI!"

The figure was too many yards out, drizzling the fuel on the ground. Startled, the person dropped the canister and took off at a sprint.

"Shit!" Liza bolted after. This one was not getting away.

Emulating Florence Griffith Joyner, Liza kicked on the speed and cut the distance between her and the fleeing suspect. She was close, ready to tackle.

Ka-Boom!

Liza tripped and slammed into the ground, skidding to a halt, eating grass and dirt. She managed to spot the backside of the culprit as they vanished behind another house. Spitting her vegetarian dish, she rolled, coughing and sputtering. A ball of black smoke rose into the night sky, a huge bright glow coming from the front side of the Lundy house.

Clambering to her feet, she pushed past the pain of her fall and ran to the front side of the home.

"No!"

Her car was a roiling inferno, belching black smoke. It was gone. All of that evidence, new and old, gone. Her chance for finally putting a cap on the Ripley case right along with it.

There was no coming back from this.

CHAPTER TWENTY-SEVEN

Shane was out of the truck before it came to a complete stop. As much as his agonized body would allow, he stormed over to the woman arguing with the fire chief.

"Liza!"

She whipped around. In the two seconds it took to close the distance between them, he noted the shocked look on her face. He grabbed her and planted a kiss on her the likes of which no one in this damnable county had ever seen. She stiffened. When he drew back, she blinked in confusion.

"Don't ever do that to me again," he whispered.

Liza's mouth dropped open, then she shut it with a click of her teeth. Wiggling out of his hold, she took a step away from him. "Excuse me, *Sheriff*." She put her back to him and walked off.

"Ouch," Con said next to him.

Ignoring his friend, Shane took in the smoldering remains of Liza's car. The fire department was dousing the blackened shell and the charred remains of the Lundys' garage. Neil Lundy, with his arm draped around his wife, was deep in conversation with the police chief. Just what Shane didn't need—another encounter with the chief.

"Stay here," Con said, and then he went over to his boss.

Feeling as useless as a bag of rusted nails, Shane's gaze met the fire chief's. "Jim."

"Sheriff." Jim nodded.

In the light of the fire trucks, you couldn't miss the bemused grin on the man's face. "Got something on your mind, Jim?"

He shook his head. "Nope, Sheriff, not a thing." And like that, Jim returned to barking orders at his men.

Shane found Liza sitting on the curb, far from the miles of hose and bustle of the crews. Her head was buried in her hands, and she was hunched over. The world had certainly beaten the hell out of her today.

And he hadn't made it any easier kissing her like a man possessed. It didn't help that when he heard about her car, he'd feared she was dead. It brought back all those horrid memories of the accident that took Cheyenne and Trigger. His fight with Trigger had led to his friend leaving with his fiancée. During a downpour, and drunker than a skunk, Trigger tore out of that honky-tonk parking lot, hell-bent on getting as far from Shane as he could. They didn't make it far.

Less than five miles down the road, the truck hydroplaned and flipped right into the path of an oncoming eighteen-wheeler.

All of those memories. The fight, Cheyenne's anger, her leaving with Trigger, their deaths—it all crashed over Shane. And Liza had come close to a near repeat.

Sick to his stomach, he turned his back on her. This was the reason he never got close to another woman. Death had a way of creeping up on him and stealing what he wanted. He'd sworn he wouldn't put his heart through it ever again.

And all that had gone to hell in a handbasket.

A hand on his arm startled him. Liza stood in front of him, her head bent.

"Shane, I'm sorry." She looked up at him. "Would you take me to your house, please?"

He took hold of her hands. "Yes."

She wrapped her arms around his waist, careful to not disturb his wounded side, and lay on his chest. She buried her face in his neck and stayed there. Once the shock wore off, he covered her in his own embrace and settled his chin on her springy hair.

He was too late for recrimination.

CHAPTER TWENTY-EIGHT

Shane rose at his normal time and fed his horses, spending time with them to absorb their strength and calm. Returning to the house after a stroll along the perimeter, he gave himself a sink bath and then dressed in his uniform shirt and loose fitting jeans. On his way to the kitchen, he peeked in on Liza.

Curled in a ball, hugging the extra pillow, her hair a wild mess, she slept on. Last night, she had staggered into his home, showered, put on the smallest set of shorts and a t-shirt he could find for her, and crashed in the guest room. He'd left her alone, but he hadn't missed the sobs coming from the bathroom while she showered.

Her phone had gone off twice before she turned it off and disappeared into the bedroom. If Shane had to take a guess, it was Montrose checking on her. And that was not a conversation Liza was up for.

Closing the door with a soft click, Shane continued to the kitchen. He was feeling every ache in his abdomen and the pull of the stitches, but he wasn't going to let it hinder him. Come hell or high water, he was putting an end to the deaths in his county and locking up the killer. Today, if at all possible.

He got the coffee going, and, with an unexplained urge, made French toast. Liza hadn't eaten when he got her home, either. So at this point, her stomach must be gnawing on her insides. When he had a sufficient stack, he went to wake her.

A strong knock on his front door brought him to a halt. It was much too early for visitors. And if it was one of his deputies, they would have called, not shown up here.

He made a pit stop in his room to secure his weapon and then ambled down the hall. Easing the brown-checked curtain aside with the tip of his fingers, he peeked outside.

Now that was a surprise.

Holstering his weapon, he unlocked the door.

"Madam Mayor."

The woman gave him a courteous nod. "Sheriff."

The mayor was dressed in her normal attire of sharp, pressed slacks and a blouse under a dark blue jacket with *Mayor* embroidered in white on her left shoulder. They had known each other all their lives, were in the same class through school, and came from farming families. While Shane went off to chase his dreams and then to war, she'd gone to college, got a degree, married well, held a career, and raised her family. Now they both ran in the same political circles.

And for that, Shane had always respected her.

"May I come in?"

Stepping aside, he allowed her entry. She went straight to the living room. Before closing the door, Shane double-checked the perimeter. All clear. He joined the mayor, who had taken station in the center of the floor.

"Is it safe to ask what brings you here to my humble abode?"

"Sheriff . . . Shane, you know that I trust your capabilities as the sheriff and have never known you to put the lives and well-being of our public at risk." She clasped her hands together in front of her body. "Yet, I was asked by the city council and the mayors from the villages and towns around McIntire County to approach you about a serious matter."

"Ma'am, if this is in regard to the current string of deaths and fires—"

She held up her hand. "It is my understanding that an FBI agent has been here for the past few days investigating a fraud case. One, without my knowledge, and two, under your supervision. Is this true?"

"Where is this going?"

"Please answer the questions, Sheriff."

Crossing his arms, he shifted his weight off his bad side. "True to both."

"Am I also correct in understanding that these rash of deaths and fires have started from the moment she arrived?"

"Now hold on one minute. Two of those deaths happened prior to her arrival and before I knew she was even here."

"Is not one of them connected to her?"

"Ma'am, if I may be so blunt, how the hell do you know so much about these cases?"

Mountains could not be moved easily, nor could the will of Eider's mayor. She stared at him, her features hard as stone.

"I know it would not have been my deputies or Detective O'Hanlon." Shane's gaze narrowed on the woman. "The only person bold enough to go behind my back and pull such a stunt is the only one with the ear of the city council." Eider's chief of police. *Damn prick.*

"Sheriff, I'm here as a friend, not an enemy. Please don't make this into a war zone."

"Let's stop pussyfooting around the matter and get to it. What are you demanding, Madam Mayor?"

"I was asked by the agency director to come speak with Agent Bartholomew, as she's not answering her phone, and . . . uh, you might not be so willing to comply with the agency's directive."

"Why would they think I wouldn't comply?"

"Sheriff, they want her to return to Cedar Rapids."

"Why wouldn't I comply?"

The mayor gave him a hardened stare. "Because you obviously have a personal interest in keeping her here."

"That doesn't matter. I'm on medical leave, making us shorthanded, and all of these deaths are connecting with her case. She's not leaving."

"Actually, Shane." He turned as Liza entered the room wearing her last set of unruined clothing. She nodded to the mayor and then hugged her body. "I'm leaving on my own accord. Everything that I've worked for in the last four years went up in flames in my car last night." She hung her head, defeat swallowing her whole. "My career is over. I'm resigning before the Bureau can fire me."

Taking a bullet to the side was minor compared the punch she landed with that statement. "Liza . . . "

She shook her head. Her gaze drifted to the mayor. "Ma'am, you can assure those involved that I've obeyed."

Had he not willed the iron in his spine, Shane would have crumbled under the weight of her words. She couldn't leave. Not . . . not until he . . . Until he what?

"Agent Bartholomew, I'm truly sorry for this, but it's for the best."

"Madam Mayor, I understand."

The mayor cleared her throat. "I'll show myself out." As she passed Shane, she squeezed his shoulder.

He didn't look at her, he didn't watch her leave, and he sure as hell didn't care. His gaze never left the woman standing there wearing a crown of shame.

"Why?" he whispered.

• • •

For the duration of her shower last night and before she finally surrendered to sleep, Liza had known what needed done. She didn't return Montrose's calls. She had to reset her mind, process what had happened, and sleep, though sleep had been fitful at best.

What hurt the most was that she had failed all those people who had been victims of Ripley's schemes and theft, especially the ones who had needlessly died. Even from the grave, Ripley had beaten her.

And it wasn't just her failure she'd cried over. She was leaving Shane. There was no logical reason for any part of her to weep at the thought of returning to Cedar Rapids while he remained here, but she could not pursue a relationship with a man married to his career and a memory of what could have been. There was a little boy trapped in his own world waiting for her back in Cedar Rapids. That was her family.

"Liza, don't give in like this."

"I don't have a choice. I've bombed for the last time. There's no way in hell Montrose will let me finish this now. It's time to swallow my pride, admit defeat, and quit. "

"It's not over."

She bit her lips to stem the tears building in her eyes. Drawing in a deep breath, she released it slowly. "It is for me. I'm done with being an agent. In fact, I'm so done with the whole law enforcement profession. I can't handle the stress of it anymore. It's time to get out while the getting is good." She choked out a pathetic laugh. "Kurt is going to be thrilled over this."

Looking at him pulled apart the tear in her heart more. In a few days, Shane Hamilton had done what no man had before: he'd gotten inside her and opened up the possibility of love.

Oh God, how could she even think the word? It was too new, too soon. A few shared kisses did not love make. Besides, as long as he continued to hide from his past, there would be no room for her. Liza did not play second fiddle to a ghost. Forget the agony she saw etched in his face. There was no way he could have true feelings for her. Not for an utter failure.

"I made breakfast," he said. His features smoothed out, as if he were packing up any hurt she was causing him and storing it away.

"Not Pop-Tarts, I hope."

His chuckle was halfhearted. "Naw." He ran a hand over his tight curls. "Do you need a ride somewhere?"

"Where's the nearest car rental place?"

"Not far. I'll take you there."

No, the last thing she needed was to be alone with him in a vehicle. "I'll ask Xavier or Con. Despite doctor's orders, I see you're planning to go into the department, and I won't keep you from it."

"Liza."

"Please, Shane, let me have it my way." She turned her back to him. "Let's have breakfast. Okay?"

CHAPTER TWENTY-NINE

Not too many miles later, Liza sat in Montrose's office, waiting for Thor's hammer to drop. There would be a God-awful fallout over this.

Liza distracted herself with thoughts of Shane. What was he doing? How was he holding up? Did he do something monumentally stupid again and this time do more damage to his wound?

Was he missing her?

"Bartholomew." Montrose's voice startled Liza out of her mind stroll.

Sitting up, she clasped her hands together on her lap and met the woman's strict gaze.

"I don't know what to say," Montrose said. "This whole thing turned into a fiasco. And you want to bail now?" She held up the letter of resignation Liza had long ago composed in the event she finalized the Ripley case.

"Ma'am, it's either I resign or the FBI fires me. I choose the former."

Montrose slapped the letter on her desk. "What am I supposed to tell the director?"

"That I take full responsibility for what happened, and to save the Bureau further damage, I'm gone of my own accord."

"That's not how it works, Bartholomew."

"It's how it's going to work this time, ma'am. I'm done. There's no need to embarrass yourself, the agency, or me with an internal investigation."

"By you resigning right out of the gate, there will be one. It's protocol in situations like this, to ensure there was no wrongdoing on your part that could lead to lawsuits."

Liza tilted her chin higher. "I understand, and they can do what must be done. However, I'm still gone. This fraud case has been nothing but a career ender. I think that's what he had planned all along."

"Did you ever find the money?"

She shook her head. "He never kept any bank accounts, domestic or international. He had to have kept it with him at all times. And I fear it burned in the house where he'd been living."

"Along with anything else he used," Montrose said.

Like all of Liza's case files on him that had been in her car. She should have never left them there, but where else would she have kept them? There were multiple copies here at the office, but the new stuff was gone. Nothing to report. Even the evidence she had pulled from Pamela Frost's car went up with the rest. Liza had blown it with Shane's murder investigations as well.

Montrose sighed. "Now that he's dead, we'll never know the truth. Yet the wife baffles me. Why did he deviate from his M.O. and marry?"

"I don't know. From the way the woman talked, it was love at first sight for her, and he jumped on the chance. But he wasn't satisfied with just a woman."

"Would you at least write up a report on everything that happened and that you learned? If the McIntire County sheriff's department ever solves Ripley's murder, we can add it to the file and close it out for good."

"I can do that."

"Okay, go, but don't clear out your desk yet. Let me talk with the director about all of this."

Liza stood. She wouldn't argue with Montrose, yet. Let the SAC do her job, and she would complete her own. When the time came to step up to the plate and explain to the director her reasons, she would do it. With a parting nod, she exited Montrose's office.

Not many agents were in office today; some were out doing what they were good at. What Liza had failed at. She avoided the stares of the ones here. Arriving at her desk unsolicited, she sat down and booted up her computer.

Alone with her thoughts and her electronics, Liza's mind wandered back to a tall cowboy sheriff and his penchant for Pop-Tarts, and her heart ached.

"I hope you find whoever killed all those people and set those fires," she whispered.

Maybe one day he'd tell her he did.

Maybe one day.

• • •

Shane hadn't pegged Liza for a woman to give up so easily. She'd been doggedly determined to find the bastard who'd brought her down here to McIntire County in the first place, and then to figure out why he'd been killed. Why had she given up when the screws were put to her?

The sucker punch for him was her final parting admission; she was done with law enforcement for good. For a sane man who loved his job—most of the time—that should be a reality kick to the groin. If she was done with it, she would have no call to be tied to a man who had no desire to quit it. That in and of itself should make him feel better about her leaving him.

But it didn't.

"If you keep leaving me here to figure this out on my own, I'll have to start electrocuting you."

Shane glared at his best friend. "I don't need any lip from you, Irishman." He shook a finger at the man across from him. "I'm still pissed at your boss."

"You have no proof he contacted the FBI director and told the mayor."

"Doesn't matter. What the mayor didn't say spoke loudly to me."

Con set the notes he'd been composing on Shane's desk. "Do I need to have a frank discussion with you like you did with a few people?"

Shane frowned. "What the hell are you talking about?"

"Are you in love with Liza?"

Someone shoot him. He was not having this conversation with Con. Ever.

"Aye, there's that deer in the headlights look I'm all too familiar with. You are."

"You're nuts. Then again, you're Irish, and I've been told they're all a wee bit crazy."

Con grinned. "Must be the Scottish blood. They're crazier bastards than us." He sobered. "Tell me the truth, boy, are you?"

"I barely know the woman. How can I be in love with her?"

"Jolie knew nothing about Xavier and look at them today. Planning a wedding."

"They're kids. I'm old and beyond that."

Con snorted. "You're not that old." He leaned against the desk. "Nic told me about the ring. And she's just curious enough to be a pest if you don't spill the story. I'm thinking it has a lot to do with why you never got attached to any woman until Liza."

"That's in the past, and I want it to stay there."

"Liar. Don't think we've all haven't speculated why every April at this time you disappear for a day or two and come out looking like you drove to hell and duked it out with the devil."

"You can keep your speculations to yourselves. What's mine is mine, and that's the way it stays."

"I've never known you to be so damn secretive, Shane. What gives?"

"Con, I didn't press you about your past. I expect the same regard for mine." Shane pushed to his feet and skirted around his desk to head for the door.

"Shane, sit yer arse down. We're not finished."

"Until I work these kinks out of my neck and back, we are. I need something to drink." With that, he quit the room. *A Pop-Tart, one of those chocolate fudge ones, is what I really need. Actually, the whole dang box would be nice.* And wouldn't you know it, he never restocked the drawer.

He went to pour a cup of coffee and stopped. No, not feeling it. He put the pot back on the burner and turned from the little station. He wanted something stronger, more potent. Something he hadn't drank in sixteen years. He'd already broken one vow, what the hell was another?

"Sheriff?"

His gaze clashed with Jennings's.

"Are you okay?" his dispatcher asked.

"What have you learned on that project I set you on?"

Jennings frowned but took the change in subject in stride like he was supposed to. "Still working on it. But what I do have you're not going to like."

"And?" Shane asked when his deputy didn't elaborate.

"The file Agent Bartholomew had sent was on Neil Lundy."

"So? She was covering her bases."

"Which is fine, but there was a corruption code on that file. She wasn't given the whole picture."

"What do you mean?"

Jennings picked up a piece of paper and rounded his station to hand it to Shane. "What I mean is, Neil Lundy has things to hide."

Shane released a slow breath as he read. One Neil J. Lundy, age twenty, had been arrested in 1991 on sexual assault charges. He had raped a fifteen-year-old boy.

"What the hell? Con!"

His friend hurried out of his office. "What?"

Shane thrust out the page. "Read this."

Con's face leached of color the more he read. "How the hell did he get on the school board with this on his record?"

"Jennings, call that man into this department. Now. If he gives you any shit, patch him through to me." Shane hobbled back to his office.

Con followed him in. "What are you doing?"

"What I should have done the moment Liza told me the news about Gene's extracurricular activities." He dialed Drummond's cell number.

Luck be the lady!

"Drummond."

"Doc, I hope you're not busy."

"Well, Sheriff, actually, I am. Being a doctor and all."

"Get unbusy. We've got some business to discuss."

"If you insist. Give me a moment."

For Con's benefit, Shane punched the speakerphone.

"Sheriff, are you at the department after my explicit orders for you to not be?" Drummond asked.

"Doc, the mayor, and the esteemed chief of police got Agent Bartholomew sent back to Cedar Rapids. At this point, I don't have a choice with four open murder cases."

In the background a door closed, and then Drummond grunted as if sitting down. "I'm officially *unbusy*. Now what is so damned important?"

"Have you finalized the autopsy results on Donovan and Pamela Frost?"

"Yes on Donovan, no on Pamela. The toxicology isn't back for her yet."

"And what did you learn from Donovan?" Con asked.

"Well, Sheriff, that would have been nice to know that Detective O'Hanlon was there," Drummond snarked.

"It shouldn't surprise you."

"Stubborn cuss," Drummond snarled. "Donovan's screens were clean. He didn't have hep C or any other blood-born disease. And before you ask, I can neither confirm or deny if he was sexually active with men."

Con let out a whistle. "Guess we can suspect someone else as Gene Avery's extra lover."

"What about Derek Schofield?" Shane demanded.

"Clean. The only thing that killed the kid was a good old-fashioned bullet to the heart."

"Do you think Pamela was the one who walked into the club to kill him, and then shot you when you got too snoopy?" Con asked.

"Why would Pamela kill him? He was cheating on his wife, but what did she care?" Shane leaned forward. "Did you talk to Emily?"

"Extensively. She knew about the cheating, but she swears she was at her in-laws' when he was killed. Apparently Annabeth had summoned her daughter-in-law for a little meeting with her. Emily was particularly livid about that, but wouldn't say what it was over." Con held up his hand. "Don't bother to ask. Annabeth refused to tell me what it was about, too. Claimed unless I got a judge to make her tell me, it was none of my damned business."

"If Annabeth in a roundabout way vouched for Emily, then who would have that kind of motive? Where's the blood drop I found out in the field?" Shane asked.

"I have it, actually," Drummond said. "And the news is good and bad. I tested it against Pamela's blood type, and it's a match. It's a 90 percent chance she was the one who shot you, Sheriff."

"What's the bad news?"

"Any evidence that could have further proven she was there was burned in Agent Bartholomew's car. She was going to bring me what she found in Pamela's vehicle."

And Liza never got to it. Someone knew where Liza had been storing it and wanted it gone. Someone with a taste for fire.

"How do we prove any of this?" Con asked.

"By asking the hard questions."

"Must I be on the phone for you two to discuss this?" Drummond piped in.

"One last thing, Doc, and we'll let you go. Since Gene and Donovan were killed the same way, can you determine if it was the same person who did it?"

"Short answer, no. Complicated answer, if you had more to go on, it might be possible. But as it stands, you have nothing. And DCI can't wave a magic wand and tell you exactly who did it. Now, if you'll excuse me, gentlemen, I have living patients to see."

Shane hung up after Drummond disconnected the call. He spotted Jennings hovering in the doorway. "And?"

"He put up a fight, sir, but he's coming after I threatened to have Nash drag him in."

"Good." Shane's gaze slid to Con. "You thinking what I'm thinking?"

"Yes, but I don't see him as a killer."

"We'll see."

CHAPTER THIRTY

When Liza walked in the door, Quinn went crazy with excitement. Kurt sulked in the living room, refusing to look at her. Screw him. His attitude was enough to make her keep her resignation to herself. Quinn dragged her to his room, showed her all the things that happened while she was gone. Then he demanded she show him his new rock.

Oh God, it was in the rubble of the burned out shell that had been her car. *Lie, quick.*

"Hey, buddy, I left it at home. I was so excited to come see you I totally forgot to bring it with me."

Quinn stared at her with a cocked head. What had to be going through that mind? Eventually he shrugged. His way of saying, that's cool.

Praise God. She got a reprieve. *Note to self: do not forget to find another geode for him.*

He took hold of her hand and dragged her out of his room and back to the living room where Kurt sat on the sofa. Liza was propelled around the furniture, and Quinn pointed at the seat next to his father. Liza looked between the two, and when she didn't move fast enough for Quinn, he circled around her and pushed her onto the sofa. And with that, he disappeared.

"Guess he's trying to tell us something."

"Guess," Kurt said with a sore tone.

They sat in silence, neither able to look at the other. Last stand at the OK Corral. Geesh, where was this Old West cowboy stuff coming from?

Oh, you know.

"Did you close that case?" Kurt asked.

"No," she said softly.

Kurt shifted on the sofa to face her, tucking his leg under his knee. "After all the excuses and you didn't even do that."

"I didn't come here to get into another fight with you."

"Then why are you here?"

She could hear the echoes of Shane's protests earlier, telling her to not give up. But she had walked away. After a long discussion with both the FBI director for the Iowa division and Montrose, Liza had convinced them of how serious she was with her resignation. Pretty certain Kurt's reaction would be on the opposite end of that spectrum.

"It all fell apart." She pinched her fingers together and rolled an imaginary crumb between them. That crumb of an idea that she could be somebody, do good wherever she was. Be better than her past. Just a crumb. Now nothing more than a speck of dust. "I resigned today."

Silence.

From his bedroom, Quinn banged plastic containers around. When he was happy, he rearranged and straightened up his things. Liza ached to hear that boy just say one word again. Any word. Anything to let her know what he was thinking. Let him change the world.

"I don't know what to say."

She met Kurt's troubled gaze. "I thought you'd be thrilled."

He blinked. "I thought I would be, too." He left the sofa and wandered to the old-fashioned wet bar Stephanie had found at a junk yard sale and refurbished. For Kurt, it had become a shrine to his deceased wife. He picked up the purple lanyard she'd left behind the day she died and fingered the trinkets she'd kept on it. "What will you do now?" he asked.

"I don't know yet. Right now, I just want to process everything I've been through and relax." Liza pushed to her feet. "I'll stay with Quinn, for however long it takes for that job. It'll give me time to figure out where I go next."

Kurt set down the lanyard and turned to her. "What happened to the woman who wanted to save the world?"

What happened to her? She died the day she walked onto the scene of that horrific warehouse fire and learned people had perished there.

"That woman is gone, Kurt. Long gone."

• • •

"Are you out of your mind? I had to explain to my CEO why I had to leave, because he demanded it, and it was highly embarrassing."

Shane pinned Neil Lundy with a droll look. "Not as embarrassing as telling him why I dragged your sorry ass in here." He slapped the sheet Jennings had printed from Lundy's file. "Explain yourself out of this one."

Scowling, Lundy picked up the page. As he read, his face turned a ghastly white. "Where did you get this?" His gaze flicked to Shane, and in that second, Shane saw the abject horror.

"The FBI got this."

"This was never to be released."

Shane leaned back, crossing his arms. God, that hurt, but it didn't matter. Not when he was closing in on the prey. "Why's that?"

Behind Lundy, Con prowled the floor, waiting for his chance to pounce. They had both agreed this would be Shane's show, but it didn't stop Con from chomping at the bit.

"This was a complete misunderstanding. All the charges were dropped."

"Things like this don't go away so easily." Shane itched to curl his fingers around that liar's neck and squeeze. "Never that easily."

"Whatever you think happened didn't. I was lied to about the defendant's age, and it was consenting. His mother was the only one who had a problem with it because she was some religious nutcase."

"Watch your mouth," Con snapped. "My mam is religious, and she's nowhere close to being a nutcase."

"As long as I've been in law enforcement, that's the same piss-poor excuse I've heard from every pedophile I've run into."

Lundy shrank in his seat, the page crumpled in his fist as it landed in his lap.

"So, Neil, explain to me how your situation is any better," Shane said.

Like a cornered mouse, Lundy's head swiveled back and forth between Con and Shane. Lundy's once haughty posture shriveled into hunched shoulders. This was a man whose backbone had been made of uncooked spaghetti; add boiling water and he flopped.

"What do you want?" he croaked.

"Were you and Gene Avery having an affair?"

Lundy's head snapped up. Red lines popped in the whites of his eyes. This had to be some kind of interesting information. "How? . . . It's . . . how?"

God, he loved it when they wet themselves. Shane slipped off the corner of his desk and towered over the man. "Did it all go wrong? Did you take things too far? Or did he decide it was over, time to move onto greener pastures?"

"No! It was . . . I don't want to talk to you anymore. I want a lawyer."

Shane shrugged. "That's your right. We haven't actually charged you with anything, but we can wait for a lawyer. Honestly, I don't know why you would, unless you're actually guilty. What do you think, Detective O'Hanlon? Should we let him wait for his lawyer? Maybe in a cell?"

With each threat, Lundy's panic grew until he was panting. "No. No jail."

"I'm sorry, but once we charge someone with a crime, that's where we hold them until a judge tells us otherwise."

"No, I won't go back there."

"Mr. Lundy, you're not understanding me. Yes, you would have to."

Lundy bolted onto his feet. "I won't! Ever! Again!"

Jennings appeared in the doorway, his hand settled over the butt of his weapon. Shane signaled him to leave. Con would have the crazed man tackled and on the floor cuffed in seconds if Lundy tried anything.

"Help me out, Neil. Tell me what happened with Gene."

"Nothing, nothing happened. There was nothing wrong with us. Everything was good." The once cool and collected engineer fidgeted like a teenage boy about to have his first "turn your head and cough" exam. "He . . . he was the aggressive one."

"Did you ever use a cattle prod for fun?"

"Never." Lundy's face screwed up in disgust. "That's barbaric."

"When was the last time you two were together before he died?"

The floor, the ceiling, the walls—Lundy looked anywhere Shane or Con didn't stand. "We met up at our usual spot, the day he died."

"And where's the usual spot?"

"His house. He knew when his wife was gone it was our safest place."

"Did she know about it?"

The fidgeting turned into a full-out junkie tremor. Lundy couldn't stop moving, picking at imaginary lint, rubbing his palms on his streaked khakis. Jerky movements could be mistaken for a puppet master wrenching at the strings. He mumbled.

"Come again?" Shane inclined an ear the man's way.

"I don't know," Lundy whispered.

"Agent Bartholomew mentioned that you had called Roslin Avery to ask her questions about her husband's job. Was that the only reason?"

Lundy could not look Shane in the eye.

"Answer him," Con barked.

Lundy jolted. "No." That was it. He clamped up tighter than a forty-year-old virgin.

"Waiting."

"This is badgering."

"You're willingly giving us information; there's no badgering to it," Shane said. "What did you ask Roslin?"

His body finally gave out, and Lundy collapsed into the chair. With that came the blubbering. "I alluded to his not being all she thought he was."

"And what did she say?"

Lundy looked up, his red-rimmed eyes pleading. He really thought Shane gave two shits about the man's life. The only thing he gave a damn about was if the man was his killer or not.

"She laughed. And it wasn't just some nervous twitter she's known to do. It was . . . evil."

Shane's gaze clashed with Con's. As Con opened his mouth, a horrific screech of metal on metal and shattering glass sent them bailing from the office. Rounding the corner, Shane came to an abrupt halt.

A bright blue F250 sat halfway inside and outside the front of the department building.

"Holy mother of the saints."

"It's Emily," Shane said and began scaling the carnage to get to the driver's side door.

Teetering on the crumpled front counter, Shane braced against the truck. Emily was slumped over the wheel, facedown, her body convulsing. "Shit!" He grabbed the handle.

"Sheriff, don't," Jennings hollered. "Let me." He climbed up next to Shane.

He moved aside so the younger man could haul open the door. Jennings reached in and dragged Emily out. Hoisting her over his shoulders, the deputy picked his way down the rubble, Shane following. Away from the damage, Jennings laid Emily on the floor. She continued to convulse, white bubbles forming in the corners of her mouth and spilling down her chin. Blood seeped from a gash over her eyebrow.

"Damn it, she's doing the same thing Pamela was when we found her," Con said. "There's nothing we can do for her. She'll be dead in minutes."

Shane grabbed his friend's arm and jerked him around. "Don't you dare give up on her. Jennings, med kit." Now that he could see what was going on, Shane had a strong feeling he knew what had poisoned Pamela and now Emily. "Con, I need liquor."

"What? This is no time for a drink."

"Not for me. For Emily." He looked his friend in the eye. "There's a bottle of whiskey in the bottom right-hand drawer of my desk."

"What the hell?"

"Con, get it. We've got to do what we can for her. She's been poisoned by methanol or ethylene glycol."

Con let loose with a string of nasty Gaelic as he ran into the office, slamming into Neil, who was blocking the doorway.

With less care than sense, Shane dropped to the floor next to Emily and tipped her to the side to hopefully get the fluid and vomit out of her throat. She continued to seize in his arms. Con returned with the bottle, screwing off the cap as he hit the floor on his knees.

"How do you propose we get this in her system?"

"By IV."

Con's eyes widened. "Is that even safe?"

Jennings handed over the IV bag and began prepping Emily for a line.

Shane took the bottle and a syringe from the med kit. "I've done it before."

The medics would be here faster than they had been for Pamela, but Shane wasn't taking any chances. He worked in tandem with Jennings as he got the line into Emily's wrist. Once the IV was going, Shane plunged the needle into the whiskey and filled the syringe, then jabbed it into a port and slowly injected the alcohol into the line. During this, Emily threw up again, and her body continued to convulse. She was wheezing and making desperate sounds, all signs they hadn't lost her yet.

"Her pulse is all over the place," Jennings said.

"Come on," Shane ground out, reaching for the bottle for another syringe full. "Don't you die on me, girl. Con, get on the horn with the EMTs and ask them if they have fomepizole."

"Sheriff, are you even sure that's what happened to her?" Jennings asked.

"It's the only option I've got. If I'm wrong, then she was going to die anyway."

He had suspected this angle when Murdoch told him about Pamela's actions and how the woman was found before she died. He'd kept his suspicions to himself, because he wanted the proof, needed the proof from the blood tests.

"Shane, they have it," Con called from the half-destroyed dispatch station.

"Tell them to get it ready." He brushed back the damp blonde hair from Emily's face. "Hang on, Emily. Hang on."

CHAPTER THIRTY-ONE

Shane's body was all twisted and mangled from the stress of the last few hours. When he spotted Drummond striding down the hall toward them, his muscles contorted.

Let her be alive.

Drummond entered the waiting room, fatigue dragging on his features, aging him. Hell, they all looked like they'd gained about fifteen years in the last three days.

"I don't know how you knew, Sheriff, but it was ethylene glycol poisoning. Your unorthodox method worked. Emily has a long way to go to recover, but she'll live."

Groans of relief came from Shane and Con, and Emily's mother-in-law cried out. Annabeth rushed Drummond, asking a million questions, her husband trailing, pausing next to Shane.

"Sheriff."

Waves of grief rolled off the elder Schofield. He had lost his son and almost lost a daughter-in-law, and he was about to lose his entire farming operation with no one to inherit it. Holding out his hand, he nodded to Shane. "I can't thank you enough."

"Don't thank me, sir, this isn't over."

"It doesn't matter." He took Shane's hand anyway and squeezed. "You've been nothing but a post for people to beat on these last few years, with all the troubles that have fallen on this county. But you know what, you've done a far better job than anyone else in your position. Thank you."

Blinking, Shane allowed the man to finish the handshake, and then gaped at his back as he walked down the hall to join his wife and the doctor.

"He's right, you know," Con said, clapping a hand on his shoulder. "No one could have handled it better."

"I'm also right when I said it's not over. Emily's attempted murderer is still out there."

"Of all the people involved with this whole fiasco, only two are left."

"And one," Shane turned to his friend, "is too much of a coward to pull off something like this."

Shane's radio crackled. "Sheriff, you there, copy?"

"What is it, Jennings? Over."

"You need to get back to the department, ASAP. Murdoch and I found something you need to see."

"On our way."

With Con on heel, he exited the hospital. From all the excitement in the last five hours or so, Shane had forgotten about his wound. There was protest throbbing happening, but aspirin would have to be the fix.

Once buckled into the passenger seat of his own department truck—Con's had been demolished when Emily careened into it and the building—Shane dug out his aspirin bottle and popped one pill more than the recommended dosage.

"When have you had to give aid to someone who had methanol poisoning before?" Con asked as he turned onto Eider's main street.

"War."

That straight answer made Con swivel his head to gape at Shane.

"Eyes on the road, Detective."

"When in the . . . You know what? Don't answer that. I know when. Those years you were missing from town, that's when. Right after 9/11."

"Idiots who had enough of being dry would drink some of the local swill, and it wasn't exactly liquor. I never had to do that with someone as far along as Emily was. I'm just glad it worked."

"Shane, what else are you keeping from me?"

"Nothing that you haven't already figured out on your own."

"How about your feelings for a certain FBI agent?"

"I'm okay with Cassy being married to Boyce, but he's still an ass."

Con's mouth pinched as he tried not to smile. "You know who I mean."

"That was never going to happen. Why are you even bothering to press the matter?"

"Because it's as plain as the damn ring on your chest that you love her. So admit it already and go after her."

Shane shook his head. "You're nuts. Matter closed."

"Matter not closed. If you don't get your head out of your ass and realize she's probably done more to open you up than anyone else, you're doomed for the rest of your life. A man isn't meant to be alone, Shane. And neither are women."

"Why are you pushing? I told you, it's not going to happen."

"Sure, you're great about doling out the advice and pressure on the rest of us but damn yourself to a lonely existence with no love. Whatever you're punishing yourself for, you need to stop."

"I'm not punishing myself. I already gave my heart to another. I'm not opening that wound again."

"God didn't make us to love one person for the entirety of our lives, or else He'd never have made families. Finish this case, get your suspect, and then go get her back."

If he didn't ache so bad from the wound, Shane would have punched his friend to shut him up. There was no going to get Liza. Except for a few kisses, nothing had passed between them. He'd been vulnerable and weak when she arrived, and that was all there was to it. Done. Over.

"Drive, Con. Jennings is waiting."

• • •

His deputy was indeed waiting in the back of the department, away from the bustle of the crews clearing out Emily's truck and debris.

"What is it?" Shane asked Jennings and Murdoch.

"Before anyone else touched the truck, we found Emily's phone on the floorboard." Jennings tapped the screen of a pink camouflage phone and then handed it to Shane. "Her passcode was easy to crack."

Shane held up the phone as a video of Emily began playing.

"Sheriff, if you've found this, something horrible has happened to me like it did to Pamela. I'm not feeling well, I think I've been poisoned, and I'm trying to get to you or to the hospital, whichever is closest." She paused, her face going white as she winced, the pain her body had to be going through as the wood alcohol did a number on her. When the wave had passed, she looked right into the phone recorder. Sweat glistened on her forehead.

"I never wanted it to happen like it did." She choked on a sob, gathered herself and continued. "Roslin came into Pamela's office four weeks ago, they talked about something for a long time, and when Roslin left, Pamela was furious. She went home that day, and I didn't see her for the next two days. When she came back, she told me she found out her husband was having an affair with multiple women. And that she knew for a fact, because Roslin had shown her, that Derek was, too."

A clicking sound, like a blinker, came through the audio. Emily paused long enough to make a turn, then the truck's engine roared.

"Sheriff, I know Derek was with another woman the night he was killed. But I'm telling you right now; it wasn't me. I didn't pull the trigger. I wasn't there. All I know is that Roslin and Pamela had been plotting to get back at their husbands. And they did. But now I think Roslin is trying to kill off anyone who knew about it. She came to my house last night, upset about Pamela—we talked and she left. This morning, I started feeling sick. I don't know why or what she did, but I think Roslin poisoned me."

She heaved and then started vomiting. The video ended.

"Where's Neil Lundy?" Shane asked, his voice cold even to his ears.

"Nash is sitting on him. The man is scared spitless after seeing Emily," Murdoch answered.

"As he should be." Shane cut a hard stare at his deputies. "Find that woman and bring her to me."

"Already on it, sir. Since she never gave anyone an address or a number to contact her with, we're having a hard time."

"Jennings, tell me you've got your mad computer hacking skills at work."

He smiled. "That I am, sir." He beckoned them over to his reestablished computer center. "I went through my system from the day she called into the office and was able to snag a phone number. She's had it on a few times, and the GPS has pinged on towers in the area. But she's not stupid; the phone is off."

"When was the last time it was on?"

Jennings scrolled through his computer jargon. "An hour ago."

"Where?"

Accessing a different program, Jennings typed something into the search bar, and the spinning wheel popped up. Once it finished, a map jumped onto the screen, a red flag at the last point of contact. Jennings zoomed out the map.

"Damn it to hell. She's heading for Cedar Rapids." Shane turned on his heel.

"Why would she be going there?" Con asked after him.

"She's after Liza."

"Where are you going?" Con demanded.

"To stop her before she kills Liza."

CHAPTER THIRTY-TWO

Liza finished drying the last pan, putting it away in the cabinet when Quinn came barreling into the kitchen. He grabbed her sleeve and tugged hard enough to make her waver as she lost her balance. The kid did not know his own strength.

"What is it, buddy?"

He tugged harder, trying to drag her to the doorway.

"Okay, hang on." She tossed the drying towel onto the counter and allowed Quinn to lead her into the living room.

Quinn was in the midst of his evening ritual of watching the news. He released her and jabbed a finger at the screen. Liza inched closer, watching the talking heads as they described the scene of an accident in McIntire County. She sank onto the sofa, glued to the screen.

What had happened? Was Shane okay? Her heart catapulted like it was thrown from a trebuchet right into her throat. He couldn't be hurt. Not after what he'd already gone through.

The sofa shifted next to her. Given Quinn's perplexed face, she forced a smile she damn well didn't feel.

"Is this what you wanted to show me?"

Quinn stared at her, trying to get a read on her. He struggled to understand normal emotions, but there were times where he got this uncanny sense. Hide all she wanted, he knew something was wrong. Why else would he have brought her in here to see the news report?

She cupped his cheek. He allowed it for three seconds before wiggling out of her touch and scooting over to his normal spot on the sofa. Liza glanced back at the TV, confirmed the newscast had moved onto another report, and then got up. Walking behind the sofa, she pulled out her phone.

He hadn't called her or left a message. And for some stupid reason, she wasn't getting any reception inside the house.

"What the hell?" She glanced back at Quinn. Too absorbed in his information overload, he didn't hear her. "Kurt, I'm stepping outside to check my phone."

From down the hall, he grunted a response. She frowned. That was weird. Oh, wait, he was supposed to be talking with his boss at the oil company. She shrugged off his non-committal response and went outside.

It took five minutes of walking around and finally standing in the middle of the yard with her phone out in front of her to get enough bars. Once the phone recognized the connection, she was blasted by ding after ding after ding of message alerts.

"Crap," she muttered, bringing the iPhone closer to scroll through the list.

There were a few messages from Montrose, requests for her to return to the office tomorrow to finalize her resignation and the typical processing out of a federal agent. Another message was an urgent request for her to call Montrose, right now. Well, Liza wasn't calling her right now. She was tired, and whatever her former supervisor needed to discuss with her could wait.

There was a ton of missed calls from a number in the McIntire County area. But who would have tried calling her from there besides Shane? She cleared out those missed calls . . . and found one from Shane.

Her heart squeezed. Please, oh please let this be a message from him telling her he was all right.

"Liza, Shane. Whatever you're doing, stop it and find a safe place with your weapon. We think we've figured out who the murderer is, and Roslin's heading your way."

Roslin?

Turning back to the house, Liza stared at it. This was supposed to be her safe haven. No one should find her here.

No one.

And if they did . . . Her gut twisted into a sailor's knot. If they did, they had found a way to track her. Her phone.

Damn it! How could she have been so stupid? She turned the offending object off and shoved it in her pocket, then went back inside. Quinn was still watching TV; he didn't even look at her when the door clapped shut. Halfway down the hall, she halted. She didn't have her backup weapon. It was still locked in her rental car. She never carried her weapon around Quinn.

You're being paranoid. Kurt is fine. You're fine.

Then why would Shane tell her to prepare? Something wasn't right.

Oh God, how she wanted to turn right around and run for the car to get her weapon. But how the hell was she going to explain it to Kurt when Quinn saw it and freaked out? Quinn was calm, in his world, and needed an emotional break from a meltdown. He'd had way too many in the last few days. Even she needed an emotional break.

Move it along. Ease your mind.

She stepped up to Kurt's closed bedroom door and listened. Silence. Frowning, she lifted her hand to knock but hesitated. It punched her right then. That tension she always got when danger was nearby. Her gaze flicked to the part of the hall that led to a back patio. Kurt always kept that door locked and triggered with an alarm in case Quinn tried to leave without anyone knowing. Her gaze returned to the door in front of her.

Screw it! She rapped hard. "Kurt?"

One Mississippi, two Mississippi, three Mississippi . . .

"Yeah?"

Liza's back muscle tightened; she reached for the gun. Not there. Damn it!

"Can I come in?"

The pregnant pause was enough to make her want to throw up.

"Uh, not right now. I'm . . . not dressed."

Kurt would have answered the door in his boxers. He didn't care; she was his annoying younger sister. Liza wanted to sob. Someone was in there with him. Someone was going to hurt him. She'd brought this on them.

Get your act together, and do what you've been trained to do.

First thing, secure Quinn. She turned and froze. Quinn stood in the middle of the hall, staring at her. Liza rushed him, grabbed him by the arm and dragged him toward his room. She stilled in the next second when a door latch clicked. She turned back just as Quinn let out a scream.

Liza wrapped her arms around his body and dove for the open doorway, cradling his fragile frame against her chest. They slammed into the floor as bullets ripped through the wall and wood trim.

Quinn continued to scream as she inch-wormed them farther into the room. The moment her feet passed the edge of the door, she kicked it shut. More bullets thwacked into the wood. Liza held fast as Quinn began to thrash, screaming his lungs out. If she weren't focused on their safety, she would be singing praises that he was using his voice.

But death in the form of Roslin Avery with a gun was coming down that hall.

Liza rolled on top of Quinn and pinned him to the floor.

"Quinn, stop it!"

He froze at her command. She jumped to her feet and reached the door handle in time to lock it. Whipping around, she ran for the window. She threw the latch and shoved it up, as alarms began screaming. Every possible escape route was rigged to an alarm. And right now, she didn't give a damn.

She reached back and grabbed Quinn's arm, hauling him toward the window. "Out you go."

"I wouldn't do that if I were you," Roslin called through the door.

That's when Liza smelled it. Smoke rolled past the window; less than fifteen feet away flames licked the air. A huge circle of fire surrounded the house. Quinn would never make it out; he'd have no clue how to get away. She clutched him to her body.

"That fire will soon reach this house." Hannibal Lector's cadence rolled over her, sending a fist of fear to Liza's chest.

"What the hell do you want?"

"Why, you, Agent Bartholomew. The proverbial thorn in my side."

"Liza! Go! Get Quinn out!"

"I told you to shut up." Roslin tapped on the door. "Come out, and I'll let these two boys go free."

Liza's arms tightened around Quinn. "Why don't I believe you?"

"That's your choice. But I'd say this fire is getting really close to letting loose."

Quinn squirmed, pushing against Liza's hold. If she let him go, he'd run to the door and open it. How long did she have before someone noticed the fire and called the fire department? Kurt's place was the last home on the block and surrounded by trees on one side and a huge sports complex beyond that.

"Clock is ticking, Agent Bartholomew."

"Why do you want me so bad? How was I ever a thorn in your side?"

"I always knew you were thickskulled. It's what made getting away from you so easy."

This was wrong. How could Roslin have been . . .? Two years ago. Liza looked back at the fire rising above the window divider.

The warehouse, the victims dead in a horrific fire. Her gaze swung back to the closed door. A man hell-bent on never getting caught so he changed his M.O. to fire.

Gene Avery was her quarry, not Roslin. Gene was dead.

"Who are you?"

Roslin chuckled, a sadistic kind of chuckle that made Liza's blood run cold. It wasn't right for a woman. It was almost . . .

Liza's grip relaxed on Quinn, and he took advantage of it. Breaking free, he bolted for the door, flipping the lock and yanking it open before Liza could get a hold on him. Her hand covered his mouth before he screamed again.

Kurt's chin was pointed to the ceiling with the gun barrel jammed into his throat. His eyes pleaded with Liza to do what she must to get Quinn out of this.

Behind him, Roslin's features were twisted into an ugly sneer. It was then Liza finally saw it. Saw past the surgical changes, the enhancements, and the changed voice. The boo-hoo widow who pulled off the perfect airhead personality. Despite all that, the eyes had never changed. Dead, soulless eyes. The eyes of a stone-cold killer.

"Came to your senses, I see."

"It's you." She swallowed back the bile. "All this time. It was you."

"Figured it out, did you?"

He had killed all the witnesses in the fire. It was the same time that Roslin claimed she met Gene Avery, married him and moved to McIntire County. Liza had been right about one thing: it was where Ripley had disappeared to stage his next scam. But Ripley had never been Gene Avery. That poor bastard had been one more pawn in the game.

But never had Liza imagined . . . "A woman?"

He laughed. "Oh, dear. It was the perfect disguise. You would have never figured it out."

Now she had.

"And you know what that means." He cocked his head to the side so as to get a better look at her. "You all die."

"No!" Kurt stomped down on Ripley's foot, and managed to twist himself free, punching Ripley in the face as he bent over.

Liza shoved Quinn toward his father and went for Ripley. Blood pouring from his busted nose, he straightened right as she tackled him. They slammed into the hallway wall. She'd wrestled with this asshole before and won; no way was she going to lose.

"Get out of here, Kurt! Take Quinn and run!"

Ripley freed a hand and smashed his fist into her chin. Dazed by the blow, she lost her hold and staggered to the floor, crashing down. She rolled over in time to watch Ripley aim and shoot at the fleeing Kurt.

"No!"

Kurt jerked as the bullet ripped through him. Quinn flew from his arms and landed inches from his father's prone body.

Red-hot anger pulsated through Liza. She pushed to her feet and rushed Ripley again as he aimed for her nephew.

"I'll kill you!"

He swung around, his punching arm missing her by inches. She plowed into his body and rammed him hard into the wall a second time. The clatter of metal hitting the hardwood floor bolstered her. Rearing back, she drove one hand into his throat, pressing his neck into the wall to choke him out. He clawed into her arm, ripping away the skin and drawing long, bloody trails. Liza punched him. His head jerked sideways and whipped back.

The smoke began to pour into the hallway, stinging her eyes and filling her mouth with its poison. But she refused to let up. This bastard was going to die.

Searing pain stabbed her in the side. He kneed her again, and she lurched back, releasing her grip on his throat. Like a raging bull, he charged at her. Liza wrenched to the side and managed to dodge out of his reach. She had a fleeting glimpse of Quinn bowed over his father's unmoving body. Pain like a thousands shards of glass sliced at Liza's mind.

She wheeled on Ripley. This time she waited as he came at her. When he was close, she took fistfuls of his clothing and allowed herself to fall backward. Using their momentum, she slammed into the floor and threw him over her body. He flipped, landing with a sickening thud into the old wet bar. Stephanie's pictures and mementos crashed and shattered on the floor around Ripley.

Liza rolled onto her feet slower than she had the previous times. When she straightened, Ripley was just rising himself. Behind him the flames licked at the kitchen walls. He looked like the devil incarnate.

"Guess you were a more formidable opponent than I expected." He spit a stream of blood. "Too bad it has to end this way, Agent Bartholomew."

"Who the hell are you?"

He smiled, his painted lips smeared and bloody. "An enigma. You know, I liked that you called me Mr. Ripley. But where he got it wrong, I get it right."

Liza lowered her head, building the energy to do what needed to be done. "Even if we have to both die, I'm not letting you leave here alive."

"That's where you're wrong, Agent Bartholomew." He reached behind his back and pulled out a second weapon. "I fully intend to leave here alive. You, on the other hand, can just die, bitch."

The front door crashed open. Liza had enough time to dive for cover. Multiple shots were fired at once. She rolled to her side as Ripley hit the floor on his knees, his gaze zeroed on her as he thumped down on his ass.

A darkened figure strode into her view, bending down to rip the gun from Ripley's limp hand, and then he turned to Liza.

"Shane?"

"Let's get out of here." He coughed, holding out his hand.

The smoke had thickened, and heat was pouring from the kitchen.

"Not yet." Liza scrambled onto her knees and crawled over to Ripley. She grabbed the lapels of the coat and made the dying man look at her. "Where's the money?"

He sneered. "Like I'd ever tell you."

It hit her, like a 50 caliber slug. When he burned down the Avery home, he'd been screaming, "he cheated." Gene might have died, but he'd outfoxed Ripley.

"It's gone. Isn't it?"

Ripley's gaze glazed over. "They . . . all . . . lose." His voice trailed off in a hiss. He slumped, and she let him fall.

"Liza," Shane coughed, "we've got to get out of here."

Her hand snapped back. "Kurt, Quinn." Grabbing Shane's arm, she jerked him down. He hit the floor next to her. "He shot Kurt; they're in the hall."

Together, they crawled down the hall, finding Quinn slumped over his father. The smoke had gotten to her nephew. Shane flipped Kurt over, checking for a pulse. Smoke stung Liza's eyes, clogging her airways, but there was no fire back here, yet.

"He's got a weak pulse."

Coughing, Liza pulled her shirt up over her mouth. "There's a back door this way. Take Quinn, I've got Kurt."

Hooking her arms under Kurt's, she shuffled backward, dragging his dead weight down the hall to the door. Shane carried Quinn's limp body in his arms.

"The door is too hot."

Panic and smoke inhalation were beginning to cloud Liza's mind. They had to get out. No way in hell was she dying this way. It would take longer, but they'd use the front door. She turned to peer down the clouded hallway, wishing she could just scream and wake up from this nightmare. Flames now blocked that escape route. The fire had them trapped.

Gagging on her fear and smoke, she looked up at Shane.

"It's not over," he said.

"How is it not? We can't get out the front door, and if we open the back door, there'll be a backdraft. There are no windows here."

"Can you get him into that bedroom?" He pointed at Kurt's room.

She was going to have to. "Go."

Gathering the last of her strength, Liza dragged Kurt over the plush carpet, leaving a bloody trail in his wake. Shane slammed the door, buying them a few precious minutes. Liza's hopes plummeted when she saw the towering flames outside.

Ripley was going to win after all. She would perish here, in a fire, like all the others, and he'd still get away with it. She watched Shane lay Quinn on the bed. At least she wouldn't be alone. She had the three most important men in her life, all of whom she loved. Shane turned back to her, and clarity cleared her fogged mind.

Standing, she walked over to him and grabbed hold of his coat. "I love you."

If their situation hadn't been so dire, his shocked expression would have been comical. But Liza didn't have time for humor. She kissed him, hard. Shane returned it with fervor but pushed her back too soon.

"Hold that thought, darlin'." With that, he climbed onto Kurt's bed and shoved open the window. "We're not out of this yet." He held out his hand to her. "Ladies first."

"You're not going to be able to get Kurt through the window. Your injury—"

"Is going to have to suffer. Stop coming up with excuses, Liza, and get your ass out the window."

No more arguments from her. She pushed out the screen and crawled backward through the gap, dropping the short distance to the ground. She had a few moments to check on the oxygen-hungry flames roaring behind her. Off in the distance she could hear the faint sounds of sirens. Help was coming. Now if they could get out of the ring of fire, it would make all the difference in the world.

"Incoming."

She grabbed Quinn's legs and guided his limp body to the ground, laying him off to the side. Then she turned back to the window and prepped to catch her foster brother's weight. She could make out Shane struggling to lift the man onto the bed and up through the window. Behind her the sirens were getting louder. As was the roar of the fire.

Hurry up!

First the feet, then legs, and most of Kurt's torso came through the window. Liza did her best to bear his weight as he slid out of the window into her waiting arms, but she couldn't stand up to the sudden shift and fell back with her brother on top of her. Wiggling out from under him was proving harder than she expected. The lack of sleep, the fight in the house, the smoke, and fear had zapped her. Liza lay on the ground, struggling to breathe.

This is it. I'm done for.

Suddenly the weight lifted.

"I told you this isn't over yet." Shane squatted down, and, as if he'd been doing a dead-weight lift, slung Kurt over his shoulders and hefted her brother up. "Grab the kid and follow me."

Heaving her own heavy body up, she cradled her nephew's body in her arms and turned to Shane. The sight of him with the fire as a backdrop was enough to make her whole body produce one last strong shot of adrenaline. He might never consider himself a hero, but right now, the cowboy was living up to his larger-than-life persona.

Shane led the way back to the sidewalk. Now they could see the fire trucks. Someone hollered, "I see someone!"

Next thing Liza knew water sprayed over her and Quinn, cooling her overheated body and making her sputter. A path was cleared for them to cross through the ring of fire. Liza stumbled past the flames, landing on her knees feet away from the nearest human being.

She felt Quinn being lifted from her arms. With his weight gone, she gave up. Her brain briefly registered the feel of ground meeting her face. Darkness shrouded her mind, and she embraced it.

Blessed sleep.

CHAPTER THIRTY-THREE

Three Weeks Later

Working the wire tightener like a mad man, Shane wiped the sweat from his forehead as he cranked. With the barbed wire pulled tight, he pounded the clamp deep into the wood post, wrapping the loose end around the post once, and drove another clamp into the wrapped length. Releasing the crank, he let it drop to the ground and took a moment to stretch his sore back.

His mount grazed nearby, completely ignoring the herd of mares and foals in the distance. Shane rested his arm on the top of the post and watched his herd flick at the early summer flies and graze on the deep green grass.

It was good to breathe fresh air and let the stress of the last few weeks sweat away. After rescuing Liza and her family from the fire, Shane had been whisked off for an exam that led to a few breathing treatments. Before he left the hospital in Iowa City, he checked on an unconscious Liza, who had been admitted for smoke inhalation and bruised ribs. The doctor had assured Shane she would be fine, which were the words he needed to hear.

Those moments before their escape, with the fire pressing in on them, he'd been pissed. All this time, all those years in war, trying to die, wishing he could die, and God saw fit to never grant him that damn wish. Shane finally, finally, found a reason to move on with his life, and some pyromaniac nut-job was going to wipe him out. He would never know if Liza had felt the same way. In the seconds before Liza kissed him, Shane had realized the truth. He had fallen in love with her.

And that scared the hell out of him. So, he hadn't gone back to Cedar Rapids to see her since. She needed time to recover. And he needed time to think over what she'd said, and figure out if his heart and head were in sync.

Word had reached Shane that her foster brother would live. The bullet had hit a lung, but the way he fell saved him from suffocating on his blood. His son was recovering from the shock of the attack and wouldn't leave his father's side. The Bartholomews, Liza and Kurt's adoptive parents, had stepped in to care for the boy and his father while Liza herself recovered.

Shane's body had healed, the wound nothing more than a scar and a memory. Her admission of love, however, stayed with him. Surely it was some kind of last rites confession.

It only made sense.

Break time over, Shane resumed his fence mending.

The county was putting in overtime to repair the damage done to the sheriff's department, and while they were at it, the council decided maybe it was time for an upgrade. Shane gave them no objections. For the time being, his crew was working out of a construction zone and their vehicles.

When word broke of what happened to the school district's finances, heads rolled. The county was in the throes of a new election as all seven of the school board members had resigned amid the scandals. And Gene Avery had had the last laugh. What Liza figured out as Ripley died had been true. The stolen money had been tucked away in a mysterious account at the bank where Ripley/Roslin had "worked." All that time, Gene had been stealing the school's money, probably under Ripley's commands, but hid it from him. Neil Lundy had discovered the truth when he received a letter mailed the day Gene had died. An old-fashioned "gotcha!" that wasn't about to save Lundy's seat on the school board.

Reporters and the public had badgered Shane to give his take on the news, and he gave them all the same line: "Not my job to decide what the public wants. I'm just doing my job as the sheriff."

Lundy's secret remained that. Shane had no desire to dredge up more bad news for anyone else involved with the whole Avery/Ripley embezzlement and murders. Far as Shane was concerned, he'd let sleeping dogs lie.

Seemed the longer he continued on as sheriff, the more the dirt and ugliness that had long been buried in McIntire County came to the surface. One thing was clear—he'd keep cleaning up the residue each time it came up. Because it was what he was good at, and as long as the voting public thought so, he'd keep doing it.

Maybe that was why he couldn't muster the courage to face Liza. She wanted to be done with law enforcement; he had no desire to leave. And if he was truthful with himself, she hadn't made the effort to come see him or even call. The more time that passed, the more he had to admit the God's honest truth: Liza had blurted those words of love because she thought she was going to die. She meant nothing by them.

The second wire replaced, he moved on to the next hole. With the crank in place, he was running the wire through when his horse whinnied. He stopped and looked over his shoulder at an answering whinny.

Two riders crested the hill, halting at the top. One rider pointed his way and then turned back their horse. He let got of the wire and turned as the second rider continued down the hill. As she rode closer, his heart began hammering away at his ribs.

Could it be?

The mount picked up the pace, jarring his rider as he trotted right up to his companion and skid to a halt. Liza righted herself and blew at a wayward coil.

"You, Shane Hamilton, are one difficult man to locate." She swung down, landing with a hop and skip back from his horse. Freed, the horse wandered over to his partner to nuzzle.

"What are you doing here?" Oh, that was intelligent.

She chuckled. "Looking for you." She strolled through the tall grass, examining the herd over his shoulder. "So, this is where you keep the rest of your horses?"

She was a sight. Snug-fitting jeans, a bright yellow blouse, and boots. Her hair was tucked back in a loose ponytail, the freed coils framing her face under a wide-brimmed hat. His sore eyes drank her in.

Her gaze returned to him when he didn't answer. "Earth to Shane."

"Why are you here, Liza?"

Hooking her hands on her hips, she cocked her head to the side and regarded him. "As I recall, there was a moment when we were trying to escape that fire that I told you something. And you said, and I quote: 'Hold that thought, darlin'.' Well, I'm resuming that thought."

She moved closer, the scent of warm grass and dirt mingling with her natural one of sweet and spicy. He ached to touch her, but what if she turned out to be only his imagination? Why else would she be here? This was not a place for Liza Bartholomew. He wasn't the man for her.

She touched his chest. His body went quiet and still. Her hand ran up and along his neck, cupping it as she drew flush to him, her fingers toying with the long curls at the nape of his neck.

"You smell like a hard-working man."

"That tends to happen when you sweat."

Her smile was coy and seductive, full of promise. "I could get used to it."

"Did you mean it?" he asked softly.

"Every word of it. When I say something, I never do it lightly. And telling you I love you, I meant every blessed word of it. I don't hand over my heart to just anyone." She massaged the corded muscles of his neck. "That's why I had to come. I had to know if you feel the same way."

And that's what the heart of the matter came down to. Why he had to take these last three weeks to himself. He had to know if he was ready to move on from Cheyenne, bury his past, and take the next step. The longer he was away from Liza, the more he missed her, ached for her.

Liza had been able to look past his defenses and see the man he'd hidden from the rest of the world. A man too afraid to love again for fear his heart would shatter for good, killing him. He hadn't been willing to take those chances. And what had she done? She'd taken his broken heart and mended it. He was a different man, a better man.

He loved her.

So he'd finally removed Cheyenne's ring and given it away. And then he'd waited. Blasted fool, he should have just gone to Liza and told her. But that was neither here nor there, because she was finally here. With him.

Tugging off his gloves, he tucked them in his belt and then drove his fingers into Liza's hair, knocking the hat from her head. "I should have told you then, but I wasn't sure." He studied those deep umber eyes, losing himself in them. "I had to know before I said anything. My heart has been beat up, banged up, and scarred. It never knew what it wanted until you came along." He pressed a light kiss to her lips. "All the love I have left in it is yours if you want it."

She smiled. "I wouldn't be here if I didn't." She kissed him, knocking him flat.

In the scheme of things, sixteen years sober hadn't been all that bad. Shane had something now he hadn't back then.

Perspective.

And the love of a damn good woman.

Really, that was all a man needed. It was all his for the taking.

Acknowledgments

First and forever foremost, to my Father above, who is the rock on which I stand.

This book created the most headaches, stress-induced panic attacks, and reality checks I have ever had in my short career as an author. And yet, it brought about the solid support of some utterly fantastic people in my life. This is my eighth book, and I feel like it was the best book I've written so far. All because of these teammates.

Marisa Corvisiero, a truly awesome agent who helped me get back on track with the original concept in one phone call during my lunch hour.

Rachel Smith, who is the other half of my brain. She was just as shocked at the ending as I was, and that's saying a lot for both of us, because we normally can see the other's path before it happens. There's no better writing partner.

Tara, Julie, and the whole production team at Crimson Romance. I've been with the house since it opened its doors, and it has been a fantastic ride, right up to when we became a part of Simon and Schuster. Thank ya'll!

Always a big part of why I do this, my family. In the writing of this book, I watched my two eldest graduate from high school then move on to the next phase in their lives; one son followed his dad's footsteps into the military and the other son to college to pursue a career as a tradesman. My daughter has become a young woman with goals that blow my mind. And my youngest son is beginning the journey of becoming a young man.

To the love my life, my husband. We've weathered much, and we'll weather more, but my love will never change. I love you.

Finally, to the fans. You are what keep us authors going strong. Thank you.

About the Author

Winter Austin perpetually answers the question "were you born in the winter?" with a flat "nope." Living in the middle of Nowheresville, Iowa, with her husband, four teenagers, and two crazy dogs, Winter is trying to juggle a job while writing deadly romantic thrillers.

Find Winter Austin at www.winteraustin.com, on Facebook, and on Twitter @WinterAustin_.

More Praise for Winter Austin

Don't miss the first books in the McIntire County series:

Atonement

"Austin's series opener has much to entertain readers ... it paints a picture of a strong, fearless woman with a sympathetic plight." —Library Journal

"*Atonement* is a gripping start to Austin's new romantic suspense series." —RT Book Reviews

"To have such a girl-power-driven novel, rooting for her happily ever after with Con was as natural as the changing of the seasons." —5 stars, *InD'Tale Magazine*

"Once in a while you come across a book that simply grabs your attention not letting you go. This is one of those books." —5+ stars, Romancing the Book

"Nic is just wow! ...This was a great read and I was caught up in the ride ... There were plenty of twists and turns that kept me on the edge of my seat." —4 stars, Night Owl Reviews

Born to Die

"Lots of tension and intrigue will keep readers hanging on until the very satisfying end. An excellent second offering in the series." —*Library Journal*, Starred Review

"Crisp as an Iowa winter! Winter Austin's *Born To Die* is vibrant and exciting." —*New York Times* and *USA Today* best-selling author Toni Anderson

"The book is solidly written and well-paced, the attention to detail in the procedural side is excellent, and the combination of robberies, murders, and great characters will keep readers hooked." —BTS Book Reviews

"The history of the characters is easy to gauge from their dialogue, and while the reader will want the characters to catch the bad guy, they'll also be rooting for the lovers to get together in the end." —4.5 stars, *InD'Tale Magazine*

"A stark and chilling tale that strikes all the right notes. Fans of *Atonement* will love this!" —Robin Burcell, bestselling author of *The Kill Order*.

"There were times my heart was racing due to the violence and malevolence that was tangible ... Austin incorporated a lot of emotions both in the characters and what she drew out from me." —Romancing the Book

"I LOVED this pairing … if you are looking awesome reads that involve romance with a thrilling mystery, well developed storyline and characters, I would recommend these two in a heartbeat!!" —4.5 stars, The Reading Cafe

Sins of the Father

"A searingly hot male hero fighting his inner demons and a sassy heroine who can hold her own … from the first page, the hook is embedded deep and it doesn't let go until the end." —starred review, *InD'Tale Magazine*

"OMG, I don't think I'm going to sleep tonight." —5 stars, Long and Short Reviews

For more from Winter Austin, check out the
Degrees of Darkness series:

Relentless

Retribution

Revenge

Reckoning

"Beautifully written with a plot that blew my mind away . . . I totally recommend this to all readers that love suspense with romance. Pick it up today and enjoy." —The Romance Reviews

"The romance between Cody and Remy is tender, yet teasing, and invites the reader into their budding relationship." —4 stars, *InD'Tale Magazine*

"…a taut, complex, fast-moving thriller with a twist you won't see coming while it still manages to include a little hot romance, relational drama (and silliness), and the characters who work very hard to protect each other yet somehow cause each other to end up in life or death situations. A bittersweet but satisfying conclusion to this well-done series. Winter Austin ends it with a bang." —Hope of Glory-Into the Fire

Printed in the United States
By Bookmasters